SPY

LIE

DIE

A Novel

Poss Pragoff

ISBN-10: 1530561310
ISBN 13: 9781530561315

This is a work of fiction. Names, characters, businesses, places, events and incidents are either the products of the author's imagination or used in a fictitious manner. Any resemblance to actual persons, living or dead, or actual events is purely coincidental.

For Crispie

TABLE OF CONTENTS

• • •

CHAPTER ONE

1919
Archangel Railway

Bolshie Ozerki, Russia, May 19, 1919

"Summon the prisoners. Now!"

Corporal Melev knew from Kosarov's harsh tone that he was in a foul mood. Not that the political commissar was ever in a good mood, but the corporal knew that today would be particularly ugly.

Kosarov sat at a plank desk, smoking and reading documents from a folder. He kept on reading when Melev and another guard prodded a pair of unshaven, unwashed men into the room with rifle butts. They pushed them against the rough wall, facing Kosarov, who continued to turn pages slowly.

The young commissar—political officer, in fact—stubbed out his cigarette on the tabletop after lighting a fresh one from its butt. A cloud of smoke hung over his desk against the low ceiling.

The taller prisoner turned slightly toward the other as if to speak, and was rewarded with a rifle butt to the kidneys. Doubled over, Melev hissed at him to stand up straight, and with pain washing over his face, the prisoner tried to obey, standing but still slightly bent. The sound of his labored breathing mingled with each soft slap as Kosarov finished each page, turned it, and moved on to the next. Seven pages later, Kosarov gathered the papers into a pile, put them into a folder, closed it, and put it in the desk drawer.

Without standing, he looked at the prisoners. From the interrogations, he had culled them from the other prisoners for one reason: they both spoke Russian.

"Captain Forman, Lieutenant Handy. So, now your fate is

sealed. Your miserable attempt to interfere in the affairs of the Soviet state have come to an end. You and the British scum— the so-called British-American Expedition Forces! Some expedition! The last of the pathetic pack of dogs that dared to trespass upon our soil are being removed. Your czarist-loving, spineless leaders call it a withdrawal, but the world will know you were humbled and defeated by the Red Army. The Russian people didn't want you here, but you came anyhow. And now, for you both, it's over."

The British-American Expedition had entered Russia during the post-revolution struggles between the Red and White Armies. While the military expedition—1,500 strong—was cloaked in words of peacekeeping and neutrality, it was obvious that Western leaders had committed the forces in hopes of supporting the Whites at the expense of the Communists, who were doubted by the Americans and loathed by the British. Winston Churchill had said its mission was "to strangle at birth the Bolshevik State."

The expedition had been an unmitigated disaster. The majority of the White Army was on the run and had moved rapidly into the vast eastern terrain of Russia. In time, many of them would flee the country from its eastern borders into Japan, China, and on to the U.S.

The expedition sought to aid the Whites in the north as they moved to fight the Reds with Murmansk at their backs. But the expedition was quickly hemmed in by the Reds, distrusted by the peasants it avowed to protect, and, to a man , learned what had undone Napoleon a century earlier: that there was no winter anywhere else on earth like the life-sucking Russian cold.

Red Army snipers picked off patrols. Terrified peasants informed on the expedition's redoubts. Nearly frozen troops surrendered to the Russians, desperate for warmth and an escape from the numbing grip of the cold. Their corpses were never found.

Scrambling to evacuate the expedition, and rapidly being surrounded by the 7th Red Army, weary expedition officers commandeered a train on the Archangel Railway. With the Red Army closing in from both sides, the Americans armored the train by welding ugly sheets of scavenged steel to the locomotive and freight cars. Three passenger cars found abandoned on a siding were attached to the end of the train, the last a caboose. No more armoring steel was found for the cars or the caboose.

At a crossroads town now called Bolshie Ozerki, American officers herded British troops, their own, and a few Russian civilians—women and children—onto the train. Before they could board, Forman's dwindling command was pinned down by incoming artillery fire. They waged a retreating firefight with the advancing Russian forces as the panicked American forces clambered aboard the last train to Murmansk.

Forman and Handy unbolted a Browning M19 from the roof of the tender behind the armored engine and dragged it into a narrow alley between brick buildings near the tracks. They set up the Browning with a commanding view of the town's railroad square as the last of the troops boarded the train.

The Army commander succumbed to the clamoring crowd of women and children. Soldiers leaped from the train. As stokers shoveled coal into the blazing engine furnaces, the soldiers formed a line to pass small children and infants onto the train, where their only seats were the laps of exhausted and wounded infantrymen.

A shriek from the engine whistle signaled imminent departure. The lifeline dissolved as its row of soldiers jumped for the train that was now creeping out of the station. Hundreds of remaining civilians fled the square, dragging or carrying their children, as mortar shells rained down. From his position guarding the caboose platform, an infantryman watched a horde of Russian soldiers charge into the square as Jay Handy opened fire. The last thing he saw before drifting smoke from the engine obscured his vision were the bodies of two-dozen Russians splashed across the cobblestone square. Then the next salvo of Russian artillery shells arrived, smashing the building where Forman and Handy crouched.

Abandoning their position and the Browning, Forman and Handy sprinted twenty yards through smoke to the next alley between buildings, safe for a moment. Then that building took a direct hit and virtually disintegrated. When the smoke cleared, Forman and Handy had survived. Both were found unarmed and unconscious in the rubble.

Jailed in an unheated stone cellar with thin straw mattresses, a coarse blanket each, and a bucket for a toilet, neither American had bathed for weeks. Captain Forman and Lieutenant Handy had been told "no talking," and when once overheard by guards, were both beaten with staves to unconsciousness. Thereafter, as they bled, scabbed, and tried to heal, they communicated by whisper, with Forman pressing his lips to Handy's good ear, and Handy occasionally turning to whisper back to Forman's remaining "good" ear.

They had discussed what they imagined their fate would be. Both were under no illusions; they were likely to be shot, or at least put on a public trial their captors would use for propaganda purposes, then buried in a jail no Western power would ever find. At their latest whispering session, Forman had offered his conviction that even if the Russians didn't kill them, if they wanted to trot them out to the world in a trial, they only needed one of them, not both. So whatever happened, one of them must stay alive and eventually, maybe—faint hope—get out of this mess.

Forman ran through a series of worsening scenarios, each one widening Handy's eyes, until Handy finally grabbed Forman's forearm as if to stop his catalog of terror.

"No, listen to me, Handy. I am ordering you to listen to what I have to say."

Handy heeded the command, but thereafter, he lay awake until morning, when they were roused, unfed, by the guards and summoned by Kosarov.

Seated at his desk , Kosarov motioned for the guards to move Forman and Handy out across a courtyard and into a one-story building with walls of thick stone and a dirt floor. Forman's first thought was that the building was like the icehouse back on his family's farm in Ohio. His second was that in a place this cold, there was no need for an icehouse. Looking down at the dirt floor, and smelling the iron of dried blood, his final thought was that this was a killing chamber.

Kosarov stepped in and heeled the door behind him shut. He signaled to the guards to unshoulder their weapons and pointed at Handy. Obeying, the guards swung their machine pistols and their arcs stopped when they reached Handy's chest.

Kosarov spoke: "Your punishment is decided. One of you dies, the other is released back to the West to deliver to your superior this warning: Death awaits intruders. Never again trifle with the *Rodina*. You spy, you pry, you die."

The weakened Forman croaked, "Don't shoot him. Shoot me."

Kosarov looked mildly amused. "Why not? The prisoner's last wish is granted. And so, you die. Floka-pa-KA," he said with a nod to the guards.

The machine pistols swung back in unison. Two short bursts flung Forman against the rock wall. His blood ran onto the dirt floor.

Handy stood transfixed, watching Forman's blood run and seep into cracks in the dirt, as though the floor were a parched garden desperate for moisture.

CHAPTER TWO

Solemn Ceremony

Washington, D.C., February 12, 1920

"Strangest one of these occasions I've ever seen," remarked the captain of the Color Guard. "No brass, no reporters or photographers. It's an Army show, but a Navy man is presenting. A rite always the prerogative of the president. They're breaking all the rules. Don't ask me why."

It took just three minutes. A gaunt officer was ushered into the office of the Secretary of the Army. Flag. Color Guard at halt. Salutes.

"At ease," called an Army general. He was as puzzled as the Color Guard's captain, but orders were orders. Facing the emaciated lieutenant, he read out the citation.

"For extreme bravery in the field of battle; for single-handedly dispatching two dozen of the enemy, putting the welfare of his fellow soldiers ahead of his own; for securing the evacuation and saving the lives of hundreds of innocent women and children; with the gratitude of a nation, on behalf of the commander-in-chief, I hereby award First Lieutenant Jay Handy the Medal of Honor." The general paused. "Representing the president in making the presentation today is the former Assistant Secretary of the Navy, Franklin Delano Roosevelt."

The handsome, athletic New Yorker sprang to his feet. Draping the medal around the recipient's neck, he shook his hand and beamed, automatically turning to the Color Guard and general as if posing. But on this occasion, there were no photographers.

"Well done, young man. Well done."

Handy murmured, "Thank you, sir."

CHAPTER THREE

1929
The Black Chamber

New York, August 18, 1929

McIntyre waited two days before the governor's office called back with a request that he meet the governor in his Manhattan office the following evening at six. McIntyre had barely taken a seat in the anteroom when an aide came and escorted him through double doors, down a quiet hallway, ushered him into the inner sanctum, and discreetly withdrew. His host sat beneath high ceilings, surrounded by dark paneling, warmed by a fireplace.

Franklin Roosevelt beamed. "James Hardison McIntyre! My favorite military officer outside the Navy! And in mufti, to boot!"

The tall, dark-suited McIntyre exchanged a strong handshake with the wheel-chair-bound governor. Roosevelt gestured to a nearby sofa.

"Hardy, take a pew while I concoct adult beverages. Will you have a martini, or something darker?"

"Bourbon if you have it. On the rocks, please."

As he adroitly bartended from a low drinks table, Roosevelt looked over his shoulder at the trim McIntyre. "And you, Hardy, are *you* on the rocks?"

"No, sir. I am fine, or will be fine, once the dust settles."

The ritual included a proffering of the glass, a sip, and an appreciative nod. That out of the way, Roosevelt spun his chair. "All right, bring me up to speed."

McIntyre had always been at ease with the charismatic Roosevelt. He had grown up near Hyde Park, his patrician family friendly with the Roosevelts. Of course, FDR, a former

Secretary of the Navy and true-blue, had urged him to "go Navy," but the McIntyres had a long history of Army service. A McIntyre had stood at George Washington's side in 1783 as the Continental Army disbanded at West Point, the Revolutionary War over and won. When the young McIntyre opted to continue the tradition, Roosevelt respected his decision, but gently joshed him about his choice whenever they met. It never failed.

Another sip. McIntyre began. "As you may recall, the Cipher Bureau was jointly funded by the State Department and the Army. After nine years, State pulled the plug and the Army was struggling to foot the bill. In effect, Secretary Stimson shut down the major intelligence-gathering operation in the country."

"And Henry Stimson's rationale?"

"He said, 'Gentlemen don't read other gentlemen's mail.'"

Roosevelt shook his head. "How fatuous of Henry. As a rule, I've found him a lot more astute than that."

"Well, Yardley has been instructed to close the office and disband the entire activity. I am the only staff member to stay on until the records have been destroyed."

Herbert O. Yardley, the former head of the cryptographic section of Military Intelligence (MI-8) during the World War, had assembled a team of two-dozen mathematics wizards and cipher-crackers and established them under the cover of a commercial cable company in New York, ostensibly providing codes for businesses to use in transacting business abroad. Their successes were kept under wraps and included breaking Japanese and other diplomatic and military codes. Recognizing an aptitude for intelligence and discretion, the Army had offered a young Captain McIntyre a posting to the "Cipher Bureau" in 1926.

Those in the know referred to the unit as the "Black Chamber." Before taking the post, he had sought Roosevelt's opinion of the assignment, and had been encouraged by the patrician New Yorker.

But now, it was about to be gone.

"Good time to transfer from the Army to the Navy, wouldn't you say?" Roosevelt said.

"Respectfully, sir, I think the Army is going to have to

redevelop intelligence capabilities from scratch, even if cryptography is currently in bad order. I am one of the few junior officers with the experience, and within a short time, the need will be recognized."

"I can't disagree with that," said FDR, topping off McIntyre's glass from a decanter of bourbon, then giving himself a dividend from the martini pitcher. "So, can I assume you have a question for me this fine evening?"

McIntyre paused for just a moment. "Yes. Do you think it sound to destroy the basis of the information we have accumulated—the codes of countries such as Japan, who many observers believe is moving in the direction of military conquest in the Asian theater? And the order to shut down comes on the heels of our latest success, the cracking of some Russian ciphers, both commercial and military."

"Hmm, that's quite a coup. I'm sure you've been in the thick of it, read some interesting exchanges. How's your Russian?"

"Enough to get the gist of the decoded messages."

FDR swirled his near-empty glass reflectively. "Are you prepared to buck the system? Raise a formal inquiry? That's a good way to short-circuit your Army career. Do that and even the Navy wouldn't have you."

"No, sir. But I feel strongly that destroying vital material is not in the country's best interests."

"And in effect, you're in charge of doing just that over the next few weeks?"

McIntyre nodded.

"Far be it from me to advise you to defy orders, then. You'll just have to soldier on." Roosevelt lifted his martini glass. "Cheers! Now tell me what your family's been up to. You're the only McIntyre I've seen in the last year."

"Cheers!" Hardy McIntyre raised his glass. *Mission accomplished. I've let him know.*

CHAPTER FOUR

1962
Frozen Source

October 1, Washington

In a darkened office, the handler picked up the phone and cradled it to his ear, but made no greeting. Just listened.

The phone call was unnerving. A source reported the latest: tomorrow, military forces were going to DEFCON three. Leave was cancelled for all senior officers and all travel from their assignments was suspended. Emphasis: *all travel*. Not even local movements.

One could read between the lines in the paper; see beyond the clipped presentations on the evening news.

On August 31, New York's Senator Kenneth Keating had informed fellow senators—some of whom told reporters—there was evidence that the Russians were installing missiles in Cuba. And he urged the president to take action. The Russians did some sword-rattling at the UN. Kennedy had ordered up the U-2s to overfly Cuba, but squalls and weather fronts forced a surveillance postponement for nearly a week. So, no confirmation yet. But those in the know, knew.

I know. I overheard a Keating staffer a month ago, just after the senator first brought it up. He was circumspect, but I heard. And now? You don't need much more than the phrase "DEFCON three." Military leave cancelled. Commands in lock-down. The Joint Chiefs must be prepping for the worst. Turn the office light out. Think in the dark. Think!

With everything frozen, how to get the latest defense posture—and get it to the embassy? My source can't leave his unit. He's frozen in place. We will never break the rules and trust information to the mail or telephone. The clerk! What about the clerk? I remember the conversation clearly, but want to look at the notes I took.

Turn on the lights. Open the safe. Find notes from the last meeting when Source Oppor was here in D.C. *Here they are.*

"Quite by chance in a diner near Fort Dix, I overheard two NCOs in the next booth. They didn't see me, but I recognized one of them as a clerk at the base. This clerk, who didn't sound too bright, was bitching about his job and telling the other clerk he's so pissed off at the staff sergeant, he's just about ready to take a few pages of classified material and sell it to the Russians!

This is a very dumb kid. Young. Green. Maybe twenty. Scrawny. Don't ask me how the Army lets someone like him handle classified files—even if he is just filing them. I've heard this kind of stupid talk before, and it's probably just talk. In this case, I don't want any undue attention by blowing the whistle on him, but thought to pass it along to you. If he acts and gets caught, it could be too close to home."

The handler turned the lights out. Smoked a cigarette in the dark. Another. Thought.

Christ! I've been doing this for a long time. Probably too long. Think!

An hour later, he made his decision, turned the lights back on and picked up the phone. Dialed an extension.

"I need you to address a unique situation. Come see me right away."

CHAPTER FIVE

Embassy Watch

October 5, Washington, D.C.

They were using four cameras. The first sat on a tripod two feet back from the 2nd floor window, which was slightly ajar, in an elegant apartment building across Massachusetts Avenue. The camera operators—there were three, each pulling an eight-hour shift—had a clear view of the front steps and entrance of the embassy. Close to their window was a maple tree, which masked their purpose. Through the leaves, the lens enlarged the features of everyone who entered and left.

Residents sometimes washed their cars at the curb. Kids walked in and out of the frame on their way to school and back. People walked their dogs to and from a nearby park, including one hapless embassy clerk who emerged from the embassy's front door three times a day to walk the ambassador's Borzoi—usually to the park, occasionally along leafy nearby streets.

For the past several months, Attorney General Kennedy had taken FBI Director Hoover to task, frustrated by what he saw as an overarching obsession with catching Communists, and virtually no effort in disrupting organized crime.

"There is no such thing as the Mafia," the director stated publicly.

In private, he had grudgingly agreed to transfer manpower and budgets to the arrest of crime family bosses. But that didn't mean he would suspend the surveillance program, which included three other camera positions around the embassy that filmed the license plates of parked cars.

Squeezed by the budget, the director cut back the camera crews, first cancelling the 10:00 p.m. to 6:00 a.m. shift of the license plate crews. Then, with virtually no night visitors, the shift focused on the front door during daylight hours.

The attorney general observed that filming a door locked from 8:00 p.m. to 8:00 a.m. was "expendable." He paused. "Unless, of course, they revolt inside at night, throw off the oppressive yoke of the privilege of living well in an embassy, unbolt the door, come streaming out and defect en masse to Hoover's cameraman."

"Interesting idea," opined the deputy AG. "I wonder how we could stimulate that?"

"Well, I sure as hell wouldn't ask the FBI to figure it out. That's more like a job for the wily bastards at the CIA. Too bad their charter doesn't permit them to operate on U.S. soil."

Over the years, the surveillance program hadn't dredged up much. Out-of-town license plates mostly turned out to be tourists. Occasionally, a diplomat from another embassy would surface, usually because of repeated visits, and the Bureau would pass on the times and dates to the State Department.

Occasionally, known fellow travelers, activists in the peace and disarmament movements, would be identified coming and going. But the FBI already knew them well, having flooded their ranks with undercover agents.

• • •

"Anything of interest?" the Special Agent in Charge of the Diplomatic Monitoring Group asked the Supervisor of the Embassy & Consular Section.

"Here's a new one. I ran the plate. 1954 Chevrolet sedan registered to one Alvin Root, RFD, Bordentown, New Jersey."

"Check him out."

"Will do, sir."

CHAPTER SIX

Slick Willie

Trenton, New Jersey, October 6

The noise a pistol shot makes in an underground parking garage is, to say the least, magnified, as the report bounces off hard concrete. The bullet splatted into an upright wooden beam. No one hit. On purpose. But the effect was there.

The five kids surrounding the guy in the suit froze in their tracks.

"Anybody moves, they get shot."

So nobody moved.

The shooter called out to the man, "You okay?"

"Yes."

"Everything on the ground. Knives, baseball bats. I mean everything."

Eyes wide, the teenagers complied. Immediately. The clatter of the bats hitting the concrete floor echoed through the garage.

The shooter held his stance, the pistol in a two-hand grip, aimed at the nearest kid.

"Okay, you in the green sweatshirt. Leave. Walk out of here. Now. Everyone else stays."

Wide-eyed, the kid looked at the shooter.

"Now!"

The kid sprinted. His footsteps slapped as he ran up the ramp into the night.

When they faded, the shooter released a second kid. Then a third.

When the last one was gone, the shooter dropped this arm, tucked the snub-nosed revolver back in a holster on his belt, and stepped forward.

The man with the briefcase dropped his shoulders.

The shooter stepped forward and extended his hand. "Ben

Oliver. Army CIC. We work on the same floor as the FBI in the Federal Building." He took out his credentials and flashed them.

"Thank you. I'm Special Agent Tom Bennett, FBI." In a chagrined tone he added, "You got here just in time." He reached for his credentials.

Oliver held up his hand, palms out. "Don't show me your ID. Let's just forget this all happened. No report. No mention. No nothing."

Relieved, the FBI agent nodded, reached out, and shook Ben Oliver's hand. He then got into his car and drove up the ramp. A half minute later, Oliver followed.

At the top of the garage ramp, the elderly garage attendant came out of his booth. Everyone in the CIC office called him Charley. Oliver slowed to a stop.

"I hear a backfire down there?" Charley asked.

"Probably."

"Well, good luck with Slick Willie. You're bound to get him one of these days."

Slick Willie was Charley's name for Willie Sutton, and he assumed anyone from the Federal Building driving cars from garage space leased by the Federal government were focused on catching the infamous bank robber . Of course, Willie Sutton had been caught and convicted for a robbery in 1952 and was eating three square meals a day at Attica State Prison in New York, but that fact seemed to have eluded the garage attendant. He invoked Sutton's name daily, every time Oliver drove in and every time he drove out.

"I'm on the case, Charley. I'm on the case. Day and night."

CHAPTER SEVEN

Movie Reel

October 6 , 1962
The Federal Building, Trenton

The Trenton Field Office of the U.S. Army Counter-intelligence Corps was without an ounce of charm. It was a one-room, monochromatic collection of seven scarred desks, Underwoods with clotted ribbons, and spring-backed chairs with wobbly rollers. It was dusty. No cleaning service entered the room and the seven enlisted men and one officer who commanded it ignored the grime. So much for Army spic-and-span.

They didn't look like soldiers. No uniforms; slacks, half-mast ties, rumpled suit jackets. No one would confuse them with the FBI agents in the mammoth, spotless offices down the hall; or with the agents striding by who were dressed neatly, creased, hatted, and polished, never acknowledging a nod, not even in the shared garage, a block from the building. The government contracted for space for the Bureau's fleet of pristine new sedans and for the Army's modest collection of four-year-old Valiants. At least they weren't olive drab.

Ben Oliver, hunched over a desk, was pounding out a report on one of the Underwoods, using most but not all of his fingers on the keys. He was average in height, average in weight, with light-brown hair and light-brown eyes. His features were pleasant but plain. It was the intelligence in his eyes that one remembered. His kept looks. Stillness. Calm. He possessed an innate ability to not only listen intently, but to *hear* intently. Those who worked with him marveled at his remarkable affinity, uncanny really, for recall. Was it a photographic memory, or something less definable?

Ben Oliver often made connections, deductions, and sense

out of a jumble of facts. He could solve a puzzle in record time. Completed the *New York Times* Sunday crossword in minutes. In ink.

Every agent had to write reports, reports, and more reports. The Army had taught him how to type at Counterintelligence School at Fort Holabird in Dundalk, a sooty industrial suburb of Baltimore. Ben Oliver was no different. He entered the Army with machine-gun-speed skill. He could really type, and had earned more than pocket money typing papers for classmates in college. So, it was ironic that he'd been subjected to a typing class along with his fellow enlistees as a part of the counter-intelligence corps training program.

His speed and accuracy awed his fellow soldiers—and his typing instructor. They called her Clara Clicka. The real name of the schoolmarm-looking lady with her hair in a bun was Miss Groff, but the wits in the olive-drab classroom filled with a machine-gun cacophony of hundreds of keys being struck by twenty enlisted men to her cadence sounded like a herd of castanets. So, somehow it became known as Clara Clicka's Clicker Class. "Mister Oliver, it's touch typing. No looking at the keyboard, please."

There came a knock on the door. In itself, unusual. The door was unmarked. Locked, so there would be no walk-ins. Each field agent in the unit had a key. No one else.

Sal Di Giuseppe , the office clerk, went to answer it. Without admitting the knocker, he called over his shoulder, "Oliver. A visitor."

Five heads looked up and saw the visitor in the hallway, framed by the door. Watched as Ben got his feet. Watched as Ben walked out into the hallway. Watched as DiGiuseppe closed the door behind him.

FBI agent Tom Bennett put out his hand. He and Oliver shook.

"I have an unusual case that just landed in my lap. It's more Army than FBI. Would you join me down the hall?"

They walked in silence. Ben knew the rules. No fraternizing with the Feebies, who were told not to fraternize with anyone unnecessarily; the police, sheriff, the military—no one.

Once ushered into the FBI offices—light years more modern, operating-room clean—Oliver sat with Tom Bennett in a small conference room. One folder sat on the desk, and an eight-millimeter movie projector was set up on a side table, aimed at a rickety screen against the far wall.

"I'm assigned to headquarters in Washington. Only been up here on business once before," he said sheepishly. "The incident when I met you. Now this." He pointed to the projector and pull-down screen. "Movie time. This was taken by the Bureau in Washington two Sundays ago. One-twenty in the afternoon." He killed the overhead lights.

The projector on, Bennett rolled the soundless black-and-white footage. The camera was fixed on the façade of an impressive-looking building. It swung to a close-up of a polished brass plaque that read "Embassy of the Union of Soviet Socialist Republics," then back to its vigil at the entrance. A young man exited the revolving door of the embassy. Zooming in, the camera operator stopped to frame the man's shoulders and head as he stood still, looking around as if planning to meet someone. Then the shot tightened and held on the man's face. The man then moved off, out of frame. The next scene was a close-up of a New Jersey license plate, X3L456. Widening, the shot revealed a dirty-white 1957 Chevrolet two-door with a few scrapes in the rear panel behind the driver's door. For extra measure, the camera operator zoomed back in to re-frame the license plate, then panned down to the bumper and moved in even closer. The sticker read "Fort Dix, NJ 13578."

Bennett shut off the projector. "Base parking sticker. Authorized personnel."

"One of ours or a civilian?"

"One of yours. Corporal Alvin Root. Clerk, G-2, 2nd Army Headquarters. I believe G-2 is Intelligence."

"It is."

Bennett set the projector on rewind and they sat silently for the few seconds it took until the tail end of the film began to slap, then nestled into its spool. Bennett detached the spool and laid it on the desk next to the file, which he then opened and extracted from within a single sheet.

Ben read the proffered document—a single sheet headed with the FBI masthead. It indicated that the undersigned had, on behalf of the U.S. Army Counterintelligence Corps, received one eight-millimeter film and one classified FBI agent's report, both covering the subject, one Alvin Root, U.S. Army corporal.

Taking out a pen, Oliver paused before signing.

"Why me? Aren't you operating out of normal protocol here? Why not have the Bureau in D.C. transfer it to the appropriate Army unit at the Pentagon?"

"Orders from the top. Director Hoover feels in matters of espionage, time is of the essence; that the Army authorities closest to the alleged traitor should be informed as quickly as possible so they can act on the information the Bureau has provided."

"It is premature for the Army or my office to conclude that this is a case of either espionage or treason."

Oliver signed the transfer letter.

Pushing the file and film reel across the table to Oliver, Bennett smiled thinly. "Well, now it's up to you to find out."

"You could have given this to any one of the agents in our office."

Bennett smiled. "Well, you did me a favor not too long ago, which I greatly appreciate. This is my way of thanking you. This is the kind of case that might make you a star."

Rising from the table, file and reel in hand, Oliver said, "We'll see about that."

"No, not *we*. You."

I can't believe this is happening now, Oliver thought as he walked away. *Enlistment up in less than a month, getting out. Back to civilian life, whatever that means. This could be one of those cases that takes months. I can get it started, but it's unlikely I'll ever see the end of it. A treason case! Every special agent wants to work on one. Maybe if I'm lucky, I'll get half of it before I take my final leave. Who knows?*

CHAPTER EIGHT

White House Interest

October 7, 1962
Trenton Field Office, US Army Counterintelligence Corps

The morning courier delivery brought a fat envelope daily, filled with new investigative requests. In some instances, the subject may have grown up in or lived in or around Central New Jersey for a considerable period of time. In others, he or she may have attended a college, been enrolled in ROTC, held a job, or, in the case of military personnel, been posted to Fort Dix, twenty minutes east of Trenton.

When the investigative request involved a significant amount of interviews—neighbors, schools, employers—it was considered a Domiciled Case, with the bulk of the investigations centered in the area assigned to the field office. Agents stayed connected to the Trenton Field Office by public telephones, carrying belt-mounted changemakers like those worn by vendors roaming the ballpark aisles. Click a thumb and drop coins into your other hand. The agent who forgot to keep his changemaker loaded spent a lot of extra time breaking bills at coffee shops and gas stations.

The Trenton office worked north to New Brunswick, east to the Jersey Shore, south to Camden, and west to the Delaware River. From Washington's Crossing to the West of Trenton to the rolling hills of Bedminster and other expensive suburban towns, the area was dotted with small villages, Revolutionary War battle sites, and several colleges, Princeton being the most prestigious.

Around Princeton, a number of corporations had settled in, many with military contracts working on classified projects. Princeton's Forrestal Research Center operated a centrifuge and linear accelerator, continuing particle research. In Princeton, the

Institute for Defense Analysis mathematicians conducted war games scenarios, and visiting fellows conferenced at the Institute for Advanced Studies. This concentration of security-centric organizations provided a steady stream of contacts and filled up the workload for the special agents of the Trenton Field Office.

Ben Oliver was no exception. One of six agents, he was, in the final year of his three-year Army enlistment, the second most experienced agent in the office. Only Mac McKinley, an Army "lifer" with twenty-seven years in, had more investigations under his ever-widening belt. Others in the office thought McKinley was "mailing it in," busy as he was on the weekends selling real estate in the Trenton suburbs. Ben knew otherwise. Mac was savvy in the ways of the military, knew the bureaucracy, and had managed the nearly impossible.

Pleading that he was about to retire, Mac convinced the Army not to give him a final transfer for a few months elsewhere, then somehow managed to not put in his retirement papers. Playing this game, he'd been in Trenton for eight years.

Mac knew everyone in law enforcement worth knowing, and had introduced Ben to a number of "movers and shakers," including the head of the "Red Squad," the Subversives Records & Surveillance unit of the New Jersey State Police. From then on, Ben was the field office's designated special agent to make inquiries to this discreet office operating well below the public radar.

On a sunny Tuesday morning, two bulky overnight envelopes were delivered to the field office instead of the usual one. Lieutenant William Ferguson, Special Agent in Charge, opened them both. He then gave the contents of the latest one to the field office clerk, Corporal Salvatore Di Giuseppe —a.k.a. "Sal Dee" to his office mates—to be logged in as an active case.

Ferguson summoned Ben Oliver out into the hallway, away from the clatter of the single office and out of earshot of Di Giuseppe and two other agents rhythmically pounding out reports on two staccato Underwoods.

"Ben, your time has come. I'm giving you this particular investigation because of your experience and success in handling potentially tricky cases in the field. Given you have just a couple of weeks left before you become a civilian again, I want you to make sure that this case is completed, even if it means delaying others or handing off workload to other agents. If that looks like it could happen, come to me and I will lighten your load so you can handle this one and get it done, all tied up nicely in a bow. No fuss, no muss."

"I'm the lead agent on the Root investigation. I have scheduled an interview with Alvin Root at Fort Dix tomorrow."

"Right. So two key cases. I think you should hand in all your other cases to DiGiuseppe and let him reassign them. Stick with these two. They're our top two priorities in the field office.

I know you're out of here soon, and you have to use up your remaining leave before you muster out, so try to get as much done as you can before your leave starts."

"Why is the Krentz background investigation so important?"

"See these initials on the bottom left-hand corner of the investigation cover sheet?"

They read: W.H.I.

"The 'H' doesn't stand for Hyannisport, but it could. This is a clearance investigation that has the Oval Office's attention. In other words, it has a political component."

Ben knew what the initials meant: White House Interest. He'd been waiting to work on a case like this. And now, with the clock ticking down the days until his enlistment ended, it had happened.

Lieutenant Ferguson handed him the file.

On the first line of the cover sheet, Ben saw the name of the subject: Lieutenant Colonel John (NMI) Krentz, US Army Signals Corps. The second was the requesting organization. It stood out in bold relief: *National Security Council.*

CHAPTER NINE

Root Interview

Fort Dix, New Jersey, October 9, 1962

Oliver arrived at Fort Dix, and after confirming the availability of an interview room in the MP complex, went to find Corporal Root in his barracks.

Root was listlessly polishing a pair of Army boots, slouched on a bunk, socks on his feet, uniform rumpled. Comic books were strewn on the blanket.

Nice-looking kid, but sloppy. And probably not the sharpest knife in the drawer.

As Oliver approached the bunk, he held up his open credentials and badge case. "Corporal Root, I'm Agent Oliver of the CIC. We're going to walk over to another building for our interview."

"I can't do that, sir. I'm confined to quarters."

Oliver handed Root a form, directing him to report to the MP complex for an 1100 hours meeting, accompanied by Agent Oliver of the CIC.

Root stood, dropped his boots on the floor, and shoved his feet into them, saying nothing as he bent to lace them. He straightened, looked down at his feet, and said, "I'm ready."

They walked about two hundred yards without speaking. Outside the MP building, Oliver said, "Hold up a minute," wanting to establish some kind of rapport with Root before the formal interview began. "I'm here to ask you some questions, and to see if we can get a clear understanding of what happened to you in Washington."

"Thank you, sir."

"We do this whenever a member of the military has any contact with diplomats representing a foreign nation."

"I didn't know that, sir."

"Most personnel aren't aware of the regulation. It happens from time to time. That's why we have these follow-up interviews."

Inside, they settled into a small room and sat at a table scarred with cigarette burns.

"Would you like a smoke?"

"Yes, sir. Thank you, sir." Root took the offered cigarette and lit up.

"Tell you what. Since I'm not in uniform, you don't have to call me 'sir.'"

"Okay."

Oliver had read the FBI report again the previous night. It was his third reading. *An unidentified male SUBJECT was observed entering and leaving the main entrance of the embassy of the USSR on Massachusetts Avenue, Washington, D.C., on Sunday, September 12 at 1:30 p.m. and 3:22 p.m. respectively. On his departure, he walked less than two blocks, unlocked a parked 1957 Chevrolet sedan, license plate 857NPD, and drove away. The vehicle is registered to Alvin W. Root who resides at RFD Harbeson-Trenton Road, in Harbeson, NJ, a rural area eight miles west of Princeton, NJ.*

"Let's get started. I'm going to jot down some notes as we go along to help me write my report. Okay?"

Root nodded.

"Okay, confirming you are Corporal Alvin Root, company clerk, assigned to Second Army Headquarters Advanced Information Command, Fort Dix."

"Yes, sir."

"Corporal, please describe for me how you spent your time on Sunday, September 12, 1962."

"Well, we decided to go sightseeing in Washington."

"We?"

"My girlfriend Nadine and I, we just sort of decided the day before to drive down there. See the sights."

Oliver made a note. *Just Root exiting the embassy in the FBI film footage. Where was the girlfriend while Root was in the embassy?*

"So, where did you leave from?"

"Nadine's place. She was staying in a Trenton motel."

Root gave Oliver the name of the motel.

"What time did you leave?"

"After breakfast."

"Which was at about what time?"

"Oh, I guess 10:00."

"And you got to Washington about when?"

"We stopped to get some Cokes. I guess maybe 1:00."

Note: Arrived half hour before seen going into the embassy; 30 minutes for sightseeing?

"So, what sights did you go see?"

"Well, we saw the White House, Lincoln, Jefferson, the senate, the Potomac."

"And after that?"

"Well, you know..."

"Know what?"

"I went into the Russian embassy."

"About what time was that?"

"After lunch, I guess."

"You had lunch where?"

"A burger place. We were driving by and stopped."

"And then you went to the embassy?"

Root nodded, head down.

"Why?"

"Well, Nadine and me, we thought maybe after I got out of the Army next year, we'd go see Europe, drive around in a van, visit a bunch of countries."

No eye contact.

"So, why wouldn't you talk with a travel agent?"

"Well, the embassy was right there and I thought they could give me maps, and suggest places to go."

"So, did you look up the address or were you just driving by and saw the embassy?"

"Oh, I see what you mean. No, I saw it and we thought, go in and ask them."

We? Which means the girlfriend and he "thought"?

"So, isn't it kind of hard to find a parking place around there? That whole area is embassies, right?"

"If you say so. We found a place on the street."

"So, you went in. Who did you talk with?"

"Well, the receptionist. A woman."

"Did she have a name tag or a desk sign with her name on it?"

"I didn't see one."

"And what did you ask her?"

"I asked for a map of Russia and anything that could help us plan a trip."

"And what happened then?"

"She asked me if I was alone, and I told her Nadine was outside, waiting in the park. She said to take a seat, and called to get someone to help me."

"So, you sat in the lobby?"

"Yes."

"For how long?"

"About three minutes."

"Then what happened?"

"They came to get me."

"They?"

"Two men."

"What happened then?"

"One man went over to the receptionist, then outside. I went into an office with the other guy."

"Did he introduce himself?"

"Dimitri, I think. Dimitri something."

"Did he tell you what his job was?"

"Cultural something."

"So, what did he do for you?"

"Well, we went and sat down in his office and he asked me where we wanted to go in Russia."

"And?"

"I told him Moscow and Leningrad."

"Did you tell him you wanted to drive there from other European countries?"

"Yeah."

"And did he explain that you need a Russian driver's license?"

"No. He just showed us the routes."

"Through France to the Russian border?"

"Yes, France."

"What about sights to see? What did he suggest?"

Root looked at his hands. "Stuff in Leningrad. Museums."

"Any particular ones? Like the Hermitage and the Prado?"

"Yes, both of them."

"Did he give you any maps or booklets?"

"No, he showed me a map and a book, but said they didn't have another copy to give out, but they could send me one as soon as they got a new supply."

"Did he take your address and telephone number?"

"Not really."

"What does that mean?"

"Well, he asked for it, but I thought maybe it wasn't a good idea to tell him I was in the Army."

"Why couldn't you just give him your girlfriend's address and number?"

Sheepishly, Root replied, "Well, that's what I did. Me, care of Nadine's address. The motel."

"Did Dimitri ask you what you did for a living?"

"Yes, but I didn't tell him I was a soldier. I said I worked on a farm."

"So, how would you describe Dimitri?"

"Describe? He was a Russian."

"No, I mean, how old, how tall, color of hair..."

"Oh. Let's see. He is maybe forty, maybe five foot ten, I guess. Maybe shorter."

"Hair? Eyes? Complexion?"

"Brown hair. I don't know the eyes."

"Stocky or thin?"

"Normal."

"Did Dimitri ask you to subscribe to the magazine *Soviet Life?*"

"No."

"Did he show you copies of *Soviet Life?*"

"Maybe one of the booklets."

"Was it a small magazine or a big one?"

"I think it was small."

"Did Dimitri invite you to return to the embassy or to any other Russian function?"

"No."

"Did he tell you where he was from, or talk about his experiences in either Leningrad or Moscow?"

"He said he'd gone to school in Leningrad."

"And did he tell you any details about places to see there?"

"Just the museums."

"Did you meet anybody else in the embassy besides the receptionist and Dimitri?"

"Not really."

"Corporal! What does 'not really' mean?"

"Well, there was this girl who I met in the lobby before I left."

"Like a secretary or assistant?"

"Yes."

"Did she introduce herself?"

"I don't remember her name."

"You mean she did introduce herself but you don't remember her name? Would her name possibly be Vera?"

"Yeah, that's it."

"Can you describe her?"

"Uh...she is twenty-five, long black hair, good-looking, good figure."

"You noticed that?"

Smile.

"What was she wearing?"

"A skirt and sweater."

"Tight?"

Another small smile. "Pretty much."

"Heels?"

"Oh, yes."

"Well, did she say anything to you?"

"She shook my hand and said she hoped to see me again if I ever came back to visit the embassy. Said she helped a lot of people plan their trips to Russia and she'd love to help me."

"So, you left. About how long were you there?"

"Maybe twenty minutes, twenty-five."

"And you went to meet Nadine?"

"I looked in the park but she wasn't there. So I went back to the car, and she was there."

"In the car?"

"Yes, she had the keys. She had driven down to D.C. I drove back."

"And did you then go see some more sights in Washington?"

"Naw. She wanted to go home."

"Did she ask you about the maps and booklets?"

"Naw, she was pissed off and tired, so we went home."

Oliver looked over his notes. "Anything else you can think of that took place on that Sunday that might help throw some light on your embassy visit, throw some light on the situation?"

"No. It was a long, dumb day. I wish it never happened. I didn't get back to Dix till almost 10:00."

Oliver walked Root back to his barracks.

"Sir, when do I get off 'confined to quarters'? I want to get back to my job."

"Corporal, I'll get my report in pronto, and then the Army will absorb it and get you squared away."

"Thank you, sir." Root turned and walked back into the barracks.

Interviews were neutral, supposedly nonthreatening. Oliver had followed procedure, asked Root soft questions, challenged nothing he said. By his count, Root had lied through his teeth. Oliver had made up names, Root confirmed them. He obviously knew nothing about European geography. You can't enter Russia from France. In the film footage, it was obvious he'd carried nothing physical away from the embassy. In standard procedure, they'd separated Root and Nadine. Did someone speak with her? In the park?

CHAPTER TEN

Root Interrogation

Trenton and Fort Dix, New Jersey
October 10-11, 1962

Oliver wrote up his agent report of the interview, indicating Root's evasions and discrepancies. He didn't have to recommend an interrogation. It would be automatic, it would be adversarial, and it wouldn't involve Oliver, who had preserved the fiction that he was interested in helping Root. It was highly unlikely Ben would ever have to deal with him again, but if it came about, he would be the only person involved who had spoken pleasantly with him.

The interrogators, freshly arrived from Washington, explained the procedure. Oliver would brief them before they started, and be available during all the sessions but not in the room. A technician would run a line with a headset to Oliver next door so he could hear everything asked and answered, and one of the interrogators could step out for a moment to ask him a question or for a comment. Oliver had a buzzer that notified one of them if he heard something false or wanted to include a follow-up question.

The lead interrogator summed it up for Oliver. "We don't use any coercion, nothing physical, but we may run long sessions to wear Root down, make him less resistant to evasion or lying. So be ready for long days, probably twelve to fourteen hours."

By the third day, everyone was getting a little punchy. Frank, the lead interrogator, was plodding, patient, asking Root to go over the embassy visit again and again. "What color was the wall painted? How high were the ceilings? Did you give them any military information? How much did they pay you?"

By now, an agent from the field office had visited Root's

bank for a look at his accounts. The Monday after his visit to the embassy, he had deposited $75 into his savings account, bringing the balance to $274.60. Prior savings deposits were $15, $20, $17. The $75 deposit was also the Monday after his most recent Army paycheck, which he had cashed on the base at the PX.

Oliver gave a question to Frank.

Frank: "What were you saving up for, with the $75 going into your savings account?"
Root: "Like I told Agent Oliver, for a trip to Europe."
Frank: "Private Root, where did the $75 you deposited in your savings account come from?"
Root: "What?"
Frank: "Seventy-five dollars in your account on September 18."
Root: "Money I saved up."
Frank: "Saved up how?"
Root: "Just saved. Part of my pay."
Frank: "Half of your monthly pay?"
Root: "Yes."
Frank: "So how can you save most of your pay and still pay for tolls and gas to drive to Washington?"
Root: "I just did."
Frank: "What did the trip to Washington cost you?"
Root: "Not much."
Frank: "How much for gas?"
Root: "Probably ten bucks."
Frank: "And tolls, how much, counting down and back?"
Root: "Maybe six dollars."
Frank: "And for lunch, I think you said a burger place. How much for lunch?"
Root: Burgers, $2."
Frank: "Did you have Cokes? Fries?"
Root: "I think so."
Frank: "So how much?"
Root: "I don't know. Maybe another dollar."

Frank:	"So I make it $19 for the trip, total. Would that be right?"
Root:	"I guess so."
Frank:	"So if you cashed your paycheck Friday for $62 and spent $19 on the trip, that would leave you with $49, is that right?"
Root:	"I guess."
Frank:	"So how could you deposit $75 in savings the following Monday, if the most you had was $49?"
Root:	"I don't know."
Frank:	"Where did the $75 come from?"
Root:	"I don't remember."
Frank:	"We're talking 10 days ago, Private Root. And you don't remember?"
Root:	"Wait, I remember, Nadine paid for the burgers and the gas and the tolls. And I had some money left over from my last paycheck. In my wallet."
Frank:	"Does she usually pay for gas?"
Root:	"She did this time."
Frank:	"And for tolls? She usually pays for them when you're on the road?"
Root:	"I'm saving for repairs."
Frank:	"To your car, Corporal?"
Root:	"Yes."
Frank:	"So why go to Washington in it?"
Root:	"Nadine said her car was in the shop."
Frank:	"So, why did you put $75 in savings instead of paying to get your car repaired?"
Root:	"My car needs a new carburetor, too."
Frank:	"It need anything else?"
Root:	"A clutch."
Frank:	"So how much all told?"
Root:	"About $300."
Frank:	"So why haven't you repaired it?"
Root:	"Well, it's waiting to go in the shop. When I have the money."
Frank:	"I asked you the name of the shop."
Root:	"Colmery's Auto Repair, in Trenton."

Frank:	"So where are you going to get the money for the repairs?"
Root:	"I don't know."
Frank:	"From Nadine? Your girlfriend?"
Root:	"No."
Frank:	"Sometimes she lends you a car, she's buying you gas, paying your tolls, buying you burgers. Why not?"
Root:	"I asked her. She said no."
Frank:	"So, what else does she pay for?"
Root:	"Nothing."
Frank:	"Is she going to pay for your trip to Europe?"
Root;	"Half. Her half."
Frank:	"Does she have more money in her savings account than you do?"
Root:	"I think so. I don't know for sure."
Frank:	"You're planning a trip to Europe but you don't know how much money you've got saved between you? How much do you think it costs to fly to Europe and back?"
Root:	"I don't know. She looked into it."
Frank:	"And she didn't tell you?"
Root:	"No."
Frank:	"Let's take a break. Do you need to go the john?"
Root:	"Yes."

Frank and Tom and Ben stretched their legs and strolled outside in the fresh air. Ben suggested they focus on the visit to the embassy.

"Look, Frank. It's obvious they weren't going to Europe. They didn't have time for sightseeing. They went in, he made a deal to sell them codes, they agreed. I don't know how $75 buys anything, but maybe he's so dumb they offered him a down payment and he took it."

Frank looked at Ben. "I'm going to listen for a while, let Tom take the lead, see what I hear. We're doing okay. He's giving us plenty of short answers. Let's get him to talk a bit more and see how it goes."

The interrogation continued after their short break.

Tom: "Corporal Root, what did your Russian friend Dimitri give you?"

Root: "Nothing."

Tom: "Nothing? You told Agent Oliver he gave you maps and books."

Root: "Well, maps and books. For travel."

Tom: "To take home and read?"

Root: "Yes."

Tom: "But you said Dimitri told you he would have to mail them to you. So which is it? Did he give them to you or did he mail them?"

Root: "That's right, he mailed them."

Tom: "To you at Fort Dix?"

Root: "No, to my house."

Tom: "That can't be. You told Agent Oliver you gave Dimitri Nadine's address. So which is it?"

Root: "Nadine's address. The motel."

Tom: "So, when did she receive the maps and books?"

Root: "I don't remember. A couple of days."

Tom: "Which? You don't remember, or a couple of days?"

Root: "A couple of days."

Tom: "So what did they send?"

Root: "What do you mean?"

Tom: "What did you receive in the mail from the Russian embassy?"

Root: "Maps and books."

Tom: "How many maps?"

Root: "I don't know. Two."

Tom: "And what language were they printed in, Russian or English?"

Root: "I don't remember."

Tom: "Wouldn't you remember if you looked at a map and found you couldn't read it because it was written in a foreign language?"

Root: "I guess English."

Tom: "So, what countries did the map show?"

Root: "Russia."

Tom: "So when it came, how much time did you spend looking at the map of Russia?"

Root: "A few minutes."

Tom: "You drove all the way to Washington, went to the embassy, told them you were planning a trip to Russia, they sent you a map to help plan your trip, and you look at it for just a few minutes?"

Root: "I was in a hurry. Late for work."

Tom: "You read your mail in the morning? I thought mail comes during the day and you read it at night."

Root: "I guess I saw it in the morning."

Tom: "Where is the map now? At your house?"

Root: "No. Nadine has it."

Tom: "We checked at Nadine's motel. She's checked out. No forwarding address. Do you know where she went?"

Root: "I don't know."

Tom: "What about the books they sent? Were they in Russian or English?"

Root: "The books? Oh…English."

Tom: "And what were they about?"

Root: "Travel. Travel in Russia."

Tom: "And what did you learn by reading them?"

Root: "I haven't read them yet."

Tom: "Why not?"

Root: "I told you, I was late for work."

Tom: "How long has it been since the books arrived in the mail?"

Root: "About a week."

Tom: "How many times have you looked at the maps or the books since they arrived?"

Root: "Uh, just the once."

Tom: "What else was in the package the maps and books came in?"

Root: "Nothing."

Tom: "Not even a note, a letter?"

Root: "A letter."

Tom: "What did it say?"

Root: "Something like, *Let us know if we can be of further help with your trip.*"

Tom: "Who signed it?"

Root: "Dimitri."

Tom: "Is it still with the books and maps?"

Root: "I guess. Nadine has them."

Tom: "Where is Nadine?"

Root: "What do you mean?"

Tom: "Where do I find her?"

Root: "She's away."

Tom: "Away where?"

Root: "On vacation."

Tom: "How can she afford that? I thought you were saving to go to Europe."

Root: "I mean taking vacation days this week."

Tom: "So again, away where?"

Root: "She went to visit friends in Virginia."

Tom: "You know their names and addresses?"

Root: "No. I don't know them."

Tom: "When is she coming back?"

Root: "Saturday."

Tom: "Does she know you're confined to quarters?"

Root: "No."

Tom: "What is Nadine's last name?"

Root: "Tortellata."

Tom: "Italian?"

Root: "I guess."

Ben immediately called Tom Bennett at the FBI and asked him to conduct a records search for Nadine Tortellata. Bennett called back an hour later.

"We found nothing. No one of that name. We checked with a Tortellata family in San Francisco but they say they have no relatives east of the Mississippi. None."

CHAPTER ELEVEN

The Code Book

When the FBI handed over the report on Root's visit to the embassy, the first step the field office took was to find out the private's unit and assignment at Fort Dix.

The news wasn't good.

The Second Army HQ at Dix maintained military codes with which it communicated with other Army commands and the brass in Washington. And codes, being changed with regularity as a routine security precaution, required code clerks to change them. In the G-2 office (Intelligence), Private Root, Command Code Clerk, had the specific task of maintaining the Master Code Log, a bulky binder held under lock and key.

The investigation by an agent from the field office completed within two hours of the FBI revelation detailed Private Root's responsibilities for maintaining the binder's voluminous sheets of coded phrases. The binder sat, available to the G-2 senior staff, on a desk manned from 6:00 a.m. to 6:00 p.m. by a code clerk. At 6:00 p.m., it was locked in the command's safe until 6:00 a.m. If needed between 6:00 p.m. and 6:00 a.m., the duty officer would call the code clerk on nightshift standby (sleeping on base) to open the code binder to provide access to the officer who needed to use it.

On the 15th and 30th of each month, a portion of the code would be revised, requiring the code clerk to unlock the binder with its twelve-pin spine, remove and shred the obsolete pages of code, and replace them with the newly arrived upgrades. Each new page had been prepunched to accommodate the twelve-pin binder pattern. New pages were slipped onto the pins in the place where the old page had been, then the binder spine was locked up to protect against unauthorized removal of any code pages.

This cumbersome operation usually took the better part of a

day, as the code clerk never knew how many new pages he would be receiving, and there were unforeseen interruptions in the replacement process when the G-2 staff needed to use the binder to either create a coded message or decode an incoming message.

The G-2 maintained a replacement log detailing every occasion on which a page was removed and replaced, with every one of those replacements being dated the 15th, 16th, 30th, 31st or 1st of the month.

Private First Class Alvin Root rotated his duty with two other code clerks. On some occasions, he had supervised the replacement of codes, but names of other clerks appeared on the replacement log for the past two months. A review of the duty rosters showed Root was either off duty or on leave for those occasions.

During a break in the interrogation, Ben Oliver read through the report several times. Then, as an MP returned Root from a bathroom break and he was led into the interrogation room, Ben signaled Frank and Tom.

Looking through the one-way mirror, observing a stoic Alvin Root sitting at the table awaiting his further questioning, Ben handed each a copy of the report. Once they'd finished reading and looked up, Ben began.

"He's around classified material every day. He helps keep it updated. But lately, he's had nothing to do with updates. For the codes to have any meaning for the Russians, they'd have to be current. Two weeks and they're obsolete. In the grand scheme of things, the material could only be of value to the Russians if it were a complete book of codes, not just a few pages that turn obsolete in a few weeks."

Tom tapped the page of the report. "And if Root is delivering it regularly, why hasn't the FBI picked him up in their surveillance more than the one time?"

Frank added, "And how can he deliver it? How could he photograph the pages? At night? There's got to be a duty log."

"Look, it's a half mile from here. I'm going over there to take another look." Ben turned to the technician working the tape recorders. "Can you make me a copy of the next session?

I'll listen to it during the breaks when I get back."

Ben badged the clerk in the office and asked to see the G-2, then took a seat. Moments later, the door opened and a clerk ushered Ben into the G-2's office.

Masterson sat behind his desk, no nonsense. "So, what's up?

"Sir, I'd like to look at the Master Code binder, specifically at those pages replaced between August 15th and September 1st or 2nd. Then the replacement log for the same period."

"Follow me."

They walked down the corridor and into the code room. The binder sat open on a stand, like a large dictionary.

"Be my guest," Masterson gestured.

Ben leafed through the binder, then the log.

"Colonel, do any of your people ever make copies of these pages?"

"It's against procedure. And to make sure, there are no copiers in this section."

Ben turned the log around so it sat alongside a page of the open code binder.

"So, if this logbook says this page has never been replaced or removed from the binder, sir, how could someone fold the page in half horizontally?"

Masterson bent down to see the faint crease that ran across the page and under the 12-pin binder cuff.

"Son of a bitch!"

• • •

Back in the interrogation suite, Ben called into the field office and briefed Ferguson. "We now have a strong indication that pages from the code book have been removed without authorization and possibly copied. Fingerprinting the code pages wouldn't reveal much, as all code clerks could, at any time, leaf through the pages to get to the ones they needed. Doesn't shine a light on Root. But now that we know the codes have been compromised, I think it likely that Root found some way to do it when others weren't present."

Ferguson said, "What about an accomplice?"

"That means two Army types with clearances are selling secrets. Longer odds. And we reviewed the files on all the other clerks. They look pretty clean."

"What's the place staffed like on the weekends?"

"One duty officer, one civilian clerk typist, one code clerk on call. So, mostly one or two people there at all times."

"So...what do we do next?"

"I've talked with Masterson. We're calling in everyone who is in the code book shop, and we will interview them individually. We'll need three agents to get it done fast."

"Can we interview the civilians who work there?"

"Yes. If they have security clearances from the Army—and they do—we have the right."

"This stuff always happen on a Friday night?"

• • •

The interrogation continued.

Tom: "Alvin, there are no maps. There are no books. There never were any. You made it up. What's the real story?"

Root: "I don't know where she put them."

Tom: "They aren't in your house. They're not in your car. So they don't exist. Why did you make it up?"

Root: "They said they would send them. I don't know."

Tom: "Wait…you told me you looked at them."

Root: "Not really."

Tom: "So, they didn't come in the mail."

Root: "No."

Tom: "So...no maps. No books. So, this is your chance to tell the truth. Why did you go to the embassy?"

Root: "On a dare."

Tom: "On a dare?"

Root: "On a dare. A dare."

Tom: "Who dared you to do what?"

Root: "Nadine dared me."

Tom: "Because?"

Root: "We thought it would be cool to fool them."

Tom: "Fool them how?"

Root: "Well, we would be sitting there and they would be talking with us and they would have no idea that I had all the secrets they wanted."

Tom: "What secrets?"

Root: "The code books at G-2. They thought I was a student and I knew all this stuff they would really want if they knew."

Tom: "So how did it go? Did they believe you were a student?"

Root: "Yes. I told them I was at Rider College in Trenton."

Tom: "What about Nadine?"

Root: "She didn't tell them anything."

Tom: "Not even that she was also a student?"

Root: "Well, that…yes."

Tom: "She told them?"

Root: "No, I did."

Tom: "So, if you were a student and you weren't there for maps and books for a supposed trip to Europe, what did you say was the reason you went to the embassy?"

Root: "Oh, we asked about Europe. Like we were students. We just didn't ask about maps."

Tom: "If you didn't ask for maps or books, why did you give them your address?"

Root: "Dimitri asked for it."

Tom: "And you gave it to him?"

Root: "Yes. Was that wrong?"

Tom: "What do you think?"

Root: "I guess so."

Tom: "So, when you were in the embassy, did you fill out any forms?"

Root: "No."

Tom: "Give them anything?"

Root: "No, not really."

Tom: "What does 'not really' mean?"

Root: "Well, I traded."

Tom: "Traded what?"

Root: "I gave them a Yankee cap and Dmitri gave me a Russian fur hat."

Tom: "Who else was present when you exchanged these gifts?"

Root: "Well...besides Dmitri, there was Vera and the guy Dimitri called to bring the hat."

Tom: "Remember his name?"

Root: "He called him 'Counselor'...I think like a camp counselor."

Tom: "Was he Dimitri's boss?"

Root: "I guess so."

● ● ●

Early for an interview he had scheduled on the Krentz background investigation, Ben stopped at a phone booth and called to check in at the field office.

DiGiuseppe gave him the news: on the strength of the interrogation, the Army has determined to convene a court-martial for Corporal Alvin Root, charged with treason.

CHAPTER TWELVE

High School Drama

October 12, 1962

On his way to the office for a morning of report writing, Ben Oliver's car radio went suddenly blank. Screamin' Jay Hawkins "I Put A Spell on You" was cut off in mid-shriek.

"BREAKING NEWS FROM WASHINGTON. NEW YORK SENATOR KENNETH KEATING, IN A PRESS CONFERENCE YESTERDAY AFTERNOON, CHARGED THAT THE SOVIET UNION IS CONSTRUCTING LAUNCH SITES FOR RUSSIAN MEDIUM-RANGE BALLISTIC MISSILES IN CUBA, NINETY MILES FROM THE U.S. MAINLAND. THE SENATOR CHARGED THAT THE SITES WERE ALMOST COMPLETE AND LACKED ONLY MISSILES TO BE INSTALLED. KEATING IS A MEMBER OF THE SENATE INTELLIGENCE COMMITTEE, AND WHILE HE DID NOT CITE THE SOURCE OF HIS INFORMATION, TOLD REPORTERS HE HAD SENT A LETTER OF GRAVE CONCERN TO THE WHITE HOUSE AND JOINT CHIEFS OF STAFF AT THE PENTAGON. MORE ON THE HOUR."

As Ben absorbed the news, the station returned to its music programming, and Hawkins ranted, "I put a spell on you..."

And Keating just put a spell on JFK. Can this be accurate? Would the Russians dare? Don't we have overflights that would spot a missile construction site? It can't be anything but huge. Then again, we're approaching the midterm elections. Maybe Keating is getting his licks in on the president. Stay tuned.

Once in the office, Ben Oliver shucked his jacket and rolled up his sleeves. Referring to his interview notebook, he began to type his first agent report of the day. He had several to type.

Agent Report
U.S. Army Counterintelligence Corps
2nd Army, Trenton Field Office
Agent: S/Sgt Benjamin R. Oliver
10/12/62 New Brunswick, New Jersey

DCR for SUBJECT Lt. Col. John (NMI) Krentz, US Army

Robert Landy, English teacher and advisor to the drama club, Raritan High School, Raritan, New Jersey, taught SUBJECT English literature for two years, 1938 & 1939, and directed SUBJECT in two plays produced by the drama club. SUBJECT graduated in June, 1939 and was accepted at Rutgers University. Landy does not know if SUBJECT pursued his interest in acting throughout his four years at Rutgers, but recalls reading in the *Newark Star Ledger* that SUBJECT was a cast member in a college play, name unknown, in his senior year (1943).

Landy remembers SUBJECT as highly intelligent, a disciplined honor student.

SUBJECT performed as the lead in "The Grass Harp" (1942) and as a supporting actor in (1943). In both instances, Landy reports SUBJECT was a polished performer who immersed himself well in his roles with skills beyond the high school level.

SUBJECT attended the Raritan High School reunions in October 1943 in an Army uniform where Landy reports he was sought out by attending classmates who congratulated him on the completion of Officers Candidate School (OCS). Landy and SUBJECT discussed the war, with SUBJECT indicating he was expecting a posting to London following a course at the Army Language School in Monterey, California. Landy recalls that SUBJECT was an exceptional language student in high school, earning high marks in Latin, French, and German, and believed SUBJECT spoke Russian and one other Slavic language learned from an emigrant housekeeper, name unknown, who was employed by SUBJECT'S parents, both college professors, disciplines unknown.

Landy recalled SUBJECT was athletic, participating in individual sports of tennis and track events. Landy described SUBJECT as "quite the man about campus," which this interviewer took to mean popular with the opposite sex.

Landy suggested that **Frances McDaniels** of Raritan, now retired as a high school French teacher, taught SUBJECT and may have kept in touch with him.

Developed Character References:

Landy recalled two fellow students, **Martha Anne Storchek** and **Sally Lambert**, were SUBJECT's classmates. Both participated in the drama club, and Storchek also went to Rutgers where she continued her acting. Storchek now acts in the Trenton Repertory, and lives in Hopewell, NJ.

Landy has no reason to question SUBJECT's loyalty, integrity, discretion, morals, and character, and recommends he be considered favorably for a position of trust within the U.S. Army.

End

This background investigation is graded: W.H.I.

CHAPTER THIRTEEN

Female Lead

Ben Oliver reviewed the 25th report he'd written for the case. He had been certain to be thorough, as this would likely be his last case before his enlistment was up.

Agent Report
U.S. Army Counterintelligence Corps
2nd Army, Trenton Field Office
Agent: S/Sgt Benjamin R. Oliver
10/12/62 Hopewell, New Jersey

<u>DCR for SUBJECT Lt. Col. John (NMI) Krentz, US Army</u>

Martha Storchek Honey was a fellow student at Rutgers University with SUBJECT from 1939-1943, but only had exposure to SUBJECT during 1942 and 1943 in classes and as co-members of the drama club where both acted in several plays together.

Honey remembers SUBJECT as a serious, quiet, but charismatic "near introvert" who possessed great discipline as an actor. Honey recalls SUBJECT weathering typical play production crises with aplomb and was lauded for his natural acting skills.

Honey has had no contact with SUBJECT other than their joint appearance at a 1943 high school reunion when SUBJECT, as a recent OCS graduate, was poised to be posted to his first Army assignment following a class at the Army Language School. Honey saw SUBJECT on several occasions subsequent to the reunion in the fall of 1943 prior to his posting to London as a member of an Army Signal Corps unit.

Honey corresponded sporadically with SUBJECT in England in 1943 and 1944 but lost contact after that time.

Honey could not recall the names of any prospective character references for SUBJECT during the period when she knew him as a fellow student and actor.

Honey has no reason to question SUBJECT's loyalty, integrity, discretion, morals and character, and recommends he be considered favorably for a position of trust within the U.S. Army.

End

This background investigation graded: W.H.I.

Ben Oliver summoned up an image of the AR he'd written after interviewing Martha Honey. *Sometimes, it's what's not in the AR that can mean everything. She was mildly embarrassed, as if I had been told that she and Krentz were close, intimately involved with the make-believe of the theater. But was there more? When I asked her about other actors, she professed to have no recollection of other cast members, an assertion that seems strange for an actor trained to remember lines and details. Is she covering up her relationship with Krentz? Or with Krentz and someone else? Martha Honey damn near blushed, but she recovered nicely. Actors can do that.*

CHAPTER FOURTEEN

Teacher's Pet

Agent Report
U.S. Army Counterintelligence Corps
2nd Army, Trenton Field Office
Agent: S/Sgt Benjamin R. Oliver
10/12/62 Hopewell, New Jersey

<u>DCR for SUBJECT Lt. Col. John (NMI) Krentz, US Army</u>

Frances McDaniels, a retired high school foreign language teacher in Raritan Ridge, New Jersey, taught SUBJECT French and German during the period 1936 to 1938. McDaniels stated SUBJECT was "far and away" the best language student she had ever taught. SUBJECT possessed a "remarkable ability" to absorb not just the basics of French and German, but "the complex nuances and idioms" common to both languages.

McDaniels described SUBJECT as an attractive, highly intelligent young man who was "far more mature" than his fellow students and theater group participants. SUBJECT maintained occasional but regular correspondence with McDaniels during his college years at Rutgers University (1939-1943) and from a variety of Army postings from 1943 until 1955. McDaniels recalls receiving letters from SUBJECT postmarked Berlin, Moscow, Brussels, and Mexico City, but is unsure of the dates and no longer has the letters.

McDaniels cited Martha Storchek, Sarah Lambert, Hope Telford, Fiona Gaitskell, and Lawrence Finnan as fellow students who were also involved in student theater performances. McDaniels did not know the current whereabouts of any of the five former students.

McDaniels has no reason to question SUBJECT's loyalty, integrity, discretion, morals and character, and recommends he be considered favorably for a position of trust within the U.S. Army.

CHAPTER FIFTEEN

In the Chopper

October 12, 1962
McGuire Air Force Base, New Jersey

"Mind the blades. Don't want a haircut!" yelled the ground crewman.

Swathed in a borrowed flying coat, Ben Oliver trundled across the tarmac to the waiting Bell Ranger, its blades swishing overhead.

Everyone ducks. Thinks they're going to get scalped. Me too. It must happen but it never makes the news.

Ben opened the door. Before clambering up the steel steps protruding from the airframe, he slung his briefcase up into the body of the chopper, then scrambled in after it. The pilot reached across and secured the flimsy door.

"Good to go!" he shouted. "Talk this way." He handed Ben a set of headphones.

When Ben had put them on, the pilot plugged them into a dashboard with over three dozen illuminated instruments. Over the headphones came the instruction "push to talk" with the pilot pointing to a button on the line running from Ben's headphones to the instrument panel.

"The U.S. Air Force calls it the 'push-to-talk' button. I'm Captain Reavis. Ready to fly?"

Ben pushed to talk. "Ben Oliver. I'm buckled in. How long to Governor's Island?"

"Forty-two minutes, sir."

"Just Ben, please."

"Roger."

They lifted and spun upwards and immediately northeast on a line for New York City. With altitude, the temperature dropped and the wind pummeled the light helicopter. It was apparent Reavis was flying fifteen degrees into it and letting the wind push the chopper back on line. Below them, Jersey cows by the hundreds ate Jersey grass. At first, the chopper flew solely over farmland. Then the farms and woodlots began to be invaded by housing developments. Then they were over Red Bank, New Jersey, and the southern, marshy end of Staten Island appeared below.

"Want to see the new bridge?" squawked Reavis.

Ahead, Ben could see the spires under construction, rising above the skyline. Reavis increased altitude as he approached the span that would connect Staten Island and New Jersey with Lower Manhattan. Scudding along, being blown on a slight angle by the westerly wind, the full span came into view, and now there was only water below.

"Want a close-up view?"

Before Ben could push to talk, Reavis flipped a switch on the instrument panel, the engine died, and the chopper began to drop rapidly toward the bay. A lifetime later, but really three seconds, Reavis flipped the switch, the rotors came back on, and the helicopter shot between the towers and under the crew stringing the massive suspension cables that would support the roadway.

Why didn't I have a heart attack? I felt my stomach float up against my rib cage. This has to be the Air Force equivalent of the dude ranch hands putting the visiting Easterner on an untamed bronco.

"You do this for all the first-time chopper passengers, Captain?"

"Every chance I get."

Still, the uncompleted bridge was already a magnificent piece of engineering and architecture. *And few people will ever see it the way I just did,* Ben mused.

Reavis gained altitude again and set his sights on Governor's Island, the headquarters of the U.S. Second Army. As they approached and descended, Ben could see the helo landing pad marked with a large white "X" and an Army jeep parked some 100 yards away, exhaust curling from its tailpipe.

The moment the chopper touched down and Reavis began

the shutdown procedures, the jeep came to life and quickly arrived at the pad.

"Stand by, Captain. I should be back within the hour."

Ben climbed down the steps, glad to be on solid ground.

"Special Agent Oliver?"

Ben held up his open credentials.

"This way, sir."

The jeep seemed as airy and rattley as the helicopter, but at least it was on the ground. The driver was a corporal in a Class-A uniform. Two minutes later, Ben was in front of Headquarters, Second U.S. Army, and was escorted by the driver directly to the CO's office.

A civilian secretary outside a pair of closed double doors with the Second Army insignia painted on them immediately buzzed the general on the intercom. "Go right in."

Major General Kent Gordon England rose from a military-neat desk that was large enough to have landed the chopper on it. "Kent England. A pleasure. I've been expecting you."

"Special Agent Benjamin Oliver."

They shook hands.

"Have a seat. Let's look at your goods."

Ben handed the file to England—the background investigation of Lieutenant Colonel John NMI Krentz, U.S. Army Signal Corps—and sat for ten minutes while England read through it.

"I see you conducted the bulk of the interviews, wrote most of the agent reports."

"Yes, sir."

"Know what W.H.I. means on the cover request for the investigation?"

"Yes, sir."

"Know why Krentz is the subject of this investigation?"

"I believe so, sir."

"What do you believe?"

"That he has been assigned as Pentagon liaison to the National Security Council, and that is why the background check is marked 'White House Interest.'"

"Truth is, the brass uses W.H.I. to make everyone jump

through hoops backwards and work twice as fast in the belief they are pleasing the commander-in-chief."

"Yes, sir."

"However, I have not seen such speed coming from the Trenton Field Office on this particular investigation. Why is that?"

"It is a function of the way I work, sir. I tend to try to develop additional character references from interviews with listed references in a focused way. If I get three teachers or two Army colleagues who served with the subject, I try to determine which knows him better."

"I applaud your approach, Agent Oliver. So, have you formed an opinion on whether Krentz should be granted the highest level security clearance?"

"I report, but I don't recommend. That's the job description."

"I know. I'm asking off the record. What do you think of the man?"

"I have a unique perspective on this particular case. I audit several classes at the Woodrow Wilson School at Princeton where, as you know, Colonel Krentz is currently seeking a master's degree. A number of senior officers have graduated from the Woody."

England grinned. "I'm one of them." He paused. "So, what's your take?"

"Krentz is very smart. Very disciplined. Not unfriendly, but reserved. He has had some extraordinary assignments in his career. He attended the Yalta Conference as an interpreter. Speaks Russian and several other languages. Been present at some other important events. To my mind, it's not surprising that he's headed to the NSC."

England slapped the folder containing the agent reports on his desk. "So, how long before you expect to wrap up the rest of the interviews?"

"About a week."

"Suits me. The president is not pacing the Oval Office waiting for them. He has other fish to fry."

The interview and hand-off was over.

England stood. "Thanks for your efforts." He walked Oliver to the door and shook his hand. "How was the flight up?"

"Routine, sir. I did get a close look at the Verrazano Narrows Bridge construction."

"Ahh, the old turn-off-the-engine trick. That's flybys for you. A bunch of cards!"

CHAPTER SIXTEEN

Advanced L.I.D.M.A.C.

October 13, 1962
Princeton, New Jersey

The first time Ben Oliver interviewed Robert Oppenheimer, a year earlier at the Institute for Advanced Studies, he felt embarrassed in front of the most famous American to ever lose a security clearance. The moment he flashed his credentials, he had apologized.

Oppenheimer laughed. "You'd be surprised how many people put me down as a reference. Half of them don't have any idea about the hearings and my provocative and threatening past." Beckoning Ben to a chair by his desk, he continued, "I would estimate that your predecessor agents have called upon me some ten or eleven times, asking me, dangerous fellow that I am painted, to vouch for the loyalty of others." He went on, "It is ironic. I was denied a clearance because of my so-called questionable connections after managing a menagerie of left-leaning and out-and-out Communists from Europe who came here and helped us build the A-bomb and defeat the Japanese." He smiled. "I lost my clearance, and then gained what is arguably one of the ten best jobs in the United States. So, who's today's victim of your unrelenting scrutiny?"

Loathing the required language, Ben proceeded, "Lieutenant Colonel John Krentz is being considered for a sensitive position in the US government."

"But he must already have one. What you are implying is that he is being promoted or his next assignment following his time at the Woody will likely be where they handle secrets every day."

"True."

"I hope he doesn't have to handle as many secrets as I had to for three years in New Mexico."

Chagrined, Ben pressed on. "So, can you describe your relationship with John Krentz? How do you happen to know him?"

Oppenheimer responded that a year ago, he had remarked to a professor at the Woody who was fluent in Czech that he was stymied, looking for an interpreter to handle a one-day conference at the Institute involving participants speaking four foreign languages: German, French, Russian, and Czech. Given the sensitive nature of the conference, he preferred to reduce the number of interpreters to two, each handling a pair of languages. The professor, whom Ben had interviewed on other background investigations, recommended Oppenheimer use his graduate student, John Krentz. Oppenheimer had talked with Krentz and liked what he saw. And, speaking a little of three of the languages himself (no Russian), had asked Krentz to interpret. After clearing it with the Army, Krentz did, and later returned to the Institute several times to interpret for other foreign visitors.

"Then there was the monkey business with the visiting Russian Orthodox patriarch and his retinue, six months ago."

"What do you mean by 'monkey business'?"

"The State Department invited the patriarch, expecting him to travel with a modest group of clerical aides and assistants. When they landed at Idlewild, twenty-seven of them were greeted by an assistant secretary of state who had the good sense to delay them long enough to warrant a spur-of-the-moment stay overnight in New York. I suppose the size of the delegation sent up an alert signal. By the next morning, we had several FBI agents hastily installed as staff aides here at the Institute, before the delegation's delayed arrival. All Russian speakers."

Ben nodded. He was quite familiar with the recent visit of the Russian clerics. No one in the State Department, FBI, or Army Counterintelligence was the least bit puzzled by the size or make-up of the group. Clerics practiced their religious rites at the pleasure of the Praesidium, and the KGB could, at any time, find a service abruptly cancelled or a church or cathedral closed for repairs. Indefinitely.

The day the delegation arrived on the Princeton campus to visit the Institute, Ben—being in the know but having no role—assumed the role of a casually interested spectator. What he'd seen was a group of six clerics, cassocked and garbed in elaborate headdresses, assisted by a few cultural attaché types—two men and a woman, relatively polished and well dressed—and a cordon of KGB types—eighteen physically imposing men in comedic-looking, baggy, cheap suits, described as a security detail.

Ben and others watched as the patriarch continually looked to one of the baggy suits for his next stage direction as they went from one brief campus location to another: Whig-Clio Hall, the university president's office, lunch at the Nassau Inn.

As they headed to the Institute meeting, Ben had gone to an appointment with an English professor to discuss a recent Princeton graduate, the subject of one of the many background investigations he was working on.

"What interest would a Russian church official have in the Institute for Advanced Studies?" Ben asked.

"That's what I asked the State Department. They told me it was to foster international understanding," Oppenheimer replied.

"And did it?"

"We didn't give them a chance. Gave them the twenty-five-cent tour, said our university fellows were unfortunately unavailable for their questions, and politely showed them the door. Oh, and Colonel Krentz was on hand. I asked him to interpret, primarily to keep the delegation away from the two Russian speakers who are current fellows."

"And did Krentz have to interpret?"

"As it turned out, largely no." He flashed an ironic smile. "Imagine the odds of every one of the troglodytes in the Russian detail speaking English. It was only the wallpaper that needed an interpreter."

"The wallpaper?"

"The Orthodox clergy."

"What interaction did Krentz have with the delegation?"

"He spent most of his time with the three Russian cultural

attachés. Do you know that even when we have an interpreter translate the Russian, they are there to double-check that no Russian phrase is misinterpreted, or that an interpreter fails to toe the Bolshevik line in making the translation? National paranoia."

Ben moved back to the interview, asking Oppenheimer to assess Krentz's character.

"I find him an impressive fellow. Very intelligent. A refreshing asset for the Army. I would also say for a layman, an above-average grasp of physics. I have invited him to several social events held here, and we've attended the same dinners a few times."

Ben started through the litany. "Do you have any reason to question his loyalty, integrity, discretion…"

Oppenheimer cut in. "…morals and character? No, I don't. Amen."

"Who else might I talk with who knows Colonel Krentz?"

"Here? Really, well, just me. Besides Professor Carnes who recommended him to me, perhaps a social connection Krentz and I share is Bonnie Ellison, who lives here in Princeton. I believe he rents her garage. They met here at a gathering. Her former husband taught at Princeton. He left. She stayed on."

Ben rose. "Thank you, Doctor Oppenheimer. I appreciate your time."

"For the U.S. government, anything." Another cat-like smile.

Oppenheimer walked Ben to the foyer.

"Agent Oliver, you know what they call an abortion in Czechoslovakia?"

Puzzled, Oliver replied, "No."

"A cancelled Czech."

"A Krentz joke?"

"Professor Carnes."

CHAPTER SEVENTEEN

Wash & Shine

October 14, 1962
Princeton, New Jersey

John Krentz had vacuumed the interior of his Porsche Super 90 that morning before driving it six miles to the event on Route 1 outside Princeton. A portion of the mall's parking lot had been cordoned off. The contestants were admitted to a corner of the vast macadam landscape, and two hours before the opening of the Concours d'Elegance, they had begun to rub, buff, fluff, tweak and otherwise remove miniscule elements of lint, dust, and dirt from their vehicles.

Despite the Porsche Club's description of the event as a "Wash & Shine" (meaning the obsessive removal of wheels to be scoured, polished, and remounted was eliminated—after all, this was just a fun event, nothing serious), zealous contestants hovered over their chargers, a few even with magnifying glasses, searching for impediments to be flushed from nooks and crannies.

The sixty-odd entrants were grouped according to year of manufacture, so it was not surprising that Ben Oliver, persuaded to enter by a friend on the Princeton campus, found himself assigned to a parking spot two cars away from Krentz. After a few moments of removing his polishing equipment from the front trunk of the Speedster and setting to work removing a film of road dust from the wheels, he stood, stretched, and noticed Krentz next to his own car, standing still and looking in his direction.

Ben strode over to Krentz, extending his arm for a handshake.

"Hello, John. No surprise seeing you here. Undoubtedly ready to pick up a trophy." Ben inclined his head toward

Krentz's Porsche.

Krentz smiled briefly. "Hello, Ben. First in class at the Woody. Now here. Are you stalking me?"

"You bet. My Speedster has a crush on your Super 90. It's lust at first sight. Every Speedster wants to be a Super 90 when it grows up."

"Every Super 90 would like to go on a diet and lose enough weight to be as nimble as a Speedster."

They talked cars for a moment, then were interrupted by other contestants wanting to examine Krentz's car closely and pepper him with questions.

Ben listened, and learned that Krentz had taken delivery at the Porsche factory in Zuffenhausen a year ago and had ordered the rare, Rudge knock-off wheels. No one asked, but Ben knew they were an option at $600. A fortune. Others inquired about the hood, trunk lid, and doors. Yes, admitted Krentz. Aluminum. Fitted for customers who wanted less weight for racing.

The best-in-show winner was a foregone conclusion, as even some of the judges appeared to swoon over Krentz's rare example long before the official judging commenced. Another Woody auditing classmate, Bonnie Ellison, showed up. She smiled and said hello to Ben without breaking stride on her way to Krentz and his car.

The judges awarded a third in class to Ben's Speedster to mild applause. First in class went to Krentz. And, to no one's surprise, so did the best in show awarded by the judges, and the people's choice, voted by the enthusiasts attending the concours.

After congratulating Ben, Bonnie asked if he would like to join her and a few others at her home in Princeton for a drink after the concours wrapped up. He accepted. She gave him the address and he agreed to be there within the hour. It took no time at all to pack up his cleaning and polishing gear, but when Ben looked around for Krentz, he saw that he was already pulling out of the mall parking lot and onto Route 1. Ben listened and drank in the rising exhaust notes as Krentz accelerated through the gears and was quickly gone.

As he pulled to the curb in front of Bonnie Ellison's home, Ben observed the garage door closing on Krentz's Porsche.

He lives here? No. Are they an item? Maybe. She's his age. Single? Divorced? Attractive. Pleasant. Sometimes saw her walking out with Krentz after class at the Woody. I wonder what gives?

After a half hour of socializing on the patio with Bonnie's guests, Ben found John Krentz and asked if he might go in the garage and look at the Super 90 in more detail.

"I'll come with you."

With the overhead lights flicked on, the shape of the Super 90 was obvious under the snug car cover. Ben helped Krentz carefully remove it. The rich burgundy finish gleamed in the fluorescent light. Ben knelt to examine the knock-off wheels with three-sided spinners. On the raised center hub were small dents where the knock-off hammer had made contact.

"The hammer does this? I've never seen one for wheels like these."

Krentz turned to a well-organized workbench, a pegboard above it covering the wall. He removed a sturdy brass hammer and handed it to Ben, who hefted it, then handed it back. He watched while Krentz reattached it to a hook on the pegboard, his gaze sweeping across the neatly arranged tools: A set of graduated-size wrenches. Jumper cables hanging from the highest peg. A short stack of three keytainers. Pliers. A set of Phillips screwdrivers. A case of oil. A carton of fresh spark plugs.

Ben gestured toward the workbench in admiration."No wonder you win trophies, John. You're well prepared."

"From my days as a Boy Scout. Shall we rejoin Bonnie and her guests?"

They put the cover back on the Porsche and returned to the patio.

Interesting. Among all the people I interviewed, not one mentioned you were a Boy Scout.

CHAPTER EIGHTEEN

The Fourth Ford

Chadds Ford, Pennsylvania
October 18, 1962

Ben Oliver always savored driving on Delaware Route 100. The mostly flat, well-paved road snaked through Delaware's "Chateau Country," passing the verdant acres surrounding the Winterthur Museum, DuPont family mansions set back on commanding ridge lines, and weaving along the banks of the Brandywine River.

Route 100 keeps its number as it crosses into Pennsylvania, bisecting the only arced state line of any state. Ben Franklin had drawn the line in an arc from the courthouse in New Castle, Delaware, back when Delaware was known as Pennsylvania's "Lower Counties" before its three counties became their own state, just in time to lead the other colonies into declaring independence.

The Brandywine flowed under U.S. Route 1 just west of the village of Chadds Ford, which sat right on the intersection of U.S. Route 1 and Pennsylvania Route 100. And standing there since the days of the Revolution was the Chadds Ford Inn, a stately two-storied stone structure, now a quaint watering hole for local farmers and a more elegant restaurant for suburban matrons and visitors to the nearby Brandywine Battlefield, from which Lord Cornwallis pressed George Washington into a further retreat toward Philadelphia.

After he zipped into the inn's parking lot, Ben Oliver braked his Porsche Speedster to a stop and turned off the engine. Often after buzzing along a country route like Route 100, he sat still for a moment at the finish, his hands resting lightly on the top of the steering wheel, reliving the last few minutes of shifting, downshifting, accelerating, and braking, in his mind;

remembering the feel of the road, the bite of the tires, the snarl of the air-cooled engine as he wound it up after exiting each turn.

As it was in the 80s at noon, Oliver reached back and flipped up the soft top until its front latches lay against the top of the small, raked windshield. He didn't fasten the top, just let it rest there to keep the interior and seats cool until he came back to the car.

Ben found James Hardison McIntyre at a table in the dining room, who rose to greet him warmly and clapped him on the shoulder. Oliver sat and they made small talk for a moment. In his late 60s, the patrician McIntyre ran a personal Washington fiefdom, the Forge Foundation, a think tank and policy incubator that professed no preference for left or right, but endorsed pragmatism as the constant tool of government.

"Hardy" McIntyre was considered a legend. Just old enough to serve in World War I, then a business career, then back in the Army after Pearl Harbor. Confidant of FDR. After the war, founder of the Forge Foundation. Kitchen-cabinet advisor to Truman, then Eisenhower.

On the drive up Route 100, Ben had reviewed what he knew about Hardison McIntyre. For years, rumors had swirled about the charismatic, connected McIntyre. He'd served for several years on the National Intelligence Board, appointed successively by Truman and Eisenhower.

Examining press coverage of successive wartime conferences at Malta, Tehran, and Yalta, one could occasionally find a fleeting image of a younger McIntyre in the background or absent from the official proceedings altogether. Unconfirmed stories circulated about how he'd spirited the transfer of Wernher von Braun and his team of rocket scientists from a defeated Germany to the U.S. research facility in Huntsville, Alabama. Mr. Von Braun dismissed the claims as unfounded. With a wry smile, McIntyre also scoffed at the suggestion.

His service in World War II was mundane, he said. But some speculated he was being circumspect, citing brief postings to U.S. embassies in Moscow and Bern, fueling suppositions he'd been involved in unspecific intelligence operations, to which McIntyre responded with amusement. He'd had an unremarkable career, primarily engaged in routine logistics and simple matters of diplomacy among the Allies.

As debates and speculation about wartime activities receded over time, the rumors were starved for fuel and thus died down. No longer did reporters rehash World War II; the Korean War, the Suez Crisis, and the Cold War had dominated current events.

In his 60s, James Hardison McIntyre was a less visible force, exerting quiet influence on national policy from his position as founder and head of the Forge Foundation. A player, yes; but he was far from being among the whiz kids—the best and the brightest from business and academia drawn to serve in the Kennedy Administration.

"Thanks for agreeing to meet me today, Hardy. I wanted to thank you for the advice and the help you gave me three years ago," Ben said.

"It's a pleasure to see you, Ben. Worked out well with my schedule, me being here. Just returned two Andrew Wyeths to the Brandywine Conservancy. We had them on loan for six months at the Foundation. Came up to make sure they hung them correctly. You just drive down from Trenton?"

"I did. I'm on my way to D.C. to look for a place to live. I'm on terminal leave, using up the twenty-five days of accumulated leave I have. Then, it's back to Fort Dix for a few days to be separated from this man's Army, and I'm a civilian again."

They ordered, then talked as they ate at a casual pace. Oliver owed a debt of gratitude to Hardison McIntyre. A friend of his parents, Hardy had materialized at their funeral a little over three years ago, as shocked as Ben by their death in a freak accident on the Pennsylvania Turnpike. After the funeral, Hardy had asked Ben about his plans, and was surprised to learn that Ben was contemplating enlistment in the Army.

"After a good education in journalism school? What on earth for?"

"I'm not sure what kind of journalist I want to be, and I think I need to take a deep breath before plunging into a lifetime of chasing stories and deadlines. I think the Army is noble and that we ought to have universal service, like the Israelis do. As we don't, I'm going to practice what I preach by enlisting."

Hardy had asked a few questions, then steered Ben away from the regular Army recruiter and to a special recruiter for the Army's Counterintelligence Corps.

"You'll like this outfit, and they'll utilize your journalism skills. Give you a chance to serve, and at the same time, you'll hone your interviewing skills as an agent conducting background investigations for those working on classified projects, both Army personnel and civilians."

Ben had thrived. After basic training and a four-month school at Fort Holabird in Baltimore, he had been assigned to the Trenton Field Office of the Counterintelligence Corps. Wearing civilian clothes, he had functioned as many an FBI agent does; conducting investigations, writing too many reports, employing an innate ability to get past generalities, bear down on the right questions, and get the details on each security clearance investigation to which he was assigned.

Ben had unearthed some flaws in candidates that should never get near classified information, and his reports were far more detailed than the others in his office. In short, he stood out. So, his superiors soon gave him the more sensitive cases, including a few designated W.H.I.— White House Interest.

Hardy sat back, sipping his post-lunch coffee. "So, with only a few weeks left as a special agent, are you wrapping things up? Breaking in a replacement?"

Ben shook his head. "No replacement. Just a push to finish up a couple of major background investigations. One on a light colonel slated to work as Army liaison to the National Security Council. And another doozy: a Fort Dix corporal suspected of passing low-grade Army codes to the Russian embassy. The case is close to being resolved, but there are a few loose ends that bug me on a personal level. I want to run them down."

"You should be busy right up to the end of your enlistment, then."

"It's worse than that. I have twenty-six days of leave as yet untaken, and I want to use some of that time to get settled in D.C. If I can't land a staff job on the *Post* or another paper right away, I'll freelance. Either way, it has to be Washington, where the action is. And in between, I can work on chasing down some leads on the espionage case. The main player is a dumb kid and the Army is ready to throw the book at him. If I can get some answers, maybe there's a novel in it." Then wryly he added, "You know, names changed to protect the guilty. And even though I'm technically on leave, I'm going to work on some Washington leads on a background investigation. I'm vetting a lieutenant colonel who's been tapped to be the Army's liaison to the NSC."

"Sounds as if you're going to have a busy transition." McIntyre took another sip of his coffee. "Let me offer you a proposition."

Ben looked at Hardison McIntyre and nodded.

"Do you know that the Forge Foundation offers occasional grants to writers, provides them, short-term, an office, clerical support, and assistance while they research and draft their hoped-for?"

"I didn't."

"We have space and the means to assist you for a month to six weeks. An office, a room in the Foundation's apartment for visiting scholars, and someone to help you with occasional research. And, of course, typing your end product. I'd be happy to offer this to you, starting right away. Solve some of your short-term tasks and give you a chance to focus on your follow-up and maybe a book. What do you say?"

Impressed, Ben didn't hesitate. He knew better than to gush his thanks.

"That would be terrific. I accept." He liked the fact that McIntyre hadn't tried to talk him out of his intentions or to steer him toward a particular path.

McIntyre signaled for the bill.

"No, Hardy. My treat."

"I believe we just conducted some Forge Foundation business." McIntyre held out his hand and the waiter handed him the bill on a small tray.

When they walked out, McIntyre turned to Ben. "Do you have a few minutes for a small tour?"

"Of course." Ben assumed McIntyre intended to take him a half mile up Route 1 to the Brandywine Museum to view his loaned paintings. Instead, McIntyre pointed to Ben's Speedster.

"You drive. We're just going a few miles up Route 100."

Ben dropped the top, they climbed in, and were soon cruising slowly along a windy section of Route 100, paralleling the Brandywine, maples shading much of it with leaves beginning to produce their fall palette.

The road turned left over a small stone bridge.

"Ford number two," said McIntyre.

In response to the comment, Ben turned his head, his forehead creased.

"The second ford at the Brandywine. The locals told Washington's aides it must be defended against a flanking movement by the British, on their way to Chadds Ford from Havre de Grace and the Head of the Elk."

Thirty seconds later, the road switched back over the Brandywine over a similar small bridge.

McIntyre held up three fingers. "Ford number three."

A minute later, they were in almost complete shade as the Speedster burbled along a straightaway.

"Up ahead, lane in the trees on the left. Turn in there."

With the Porsche parked in the shade of massive oaks, McIntyre exited the vehicle. "Let's take a short walk."

Ben followed him, and together they walked a hundred yards down the cool, dark, one-lane path that then opened upon a shallow stretch of the Brandywine.

"This is ford number four. I always thought this particular place was important. As someone in the intelligence business, you'll appreciate the story. The locals the Americans talked with weren't one hundred percent for the Revolution. John Chadd, the tavern owner—we ate in his dining room today—was all for the Revolution and instructed his family and employees to lend every assistance to Washington, Lafayette, and their troops. The problem arose because John Chadd, their chief source of local intelligence, had gone to Lancaster on business. Talking with others in the village, their advice was to defend the three fords against the oncoming British. Those others just happened to have Tory sympathies or thought the Revolution would fail, and wanted to curry favor with the British. In any case, when Cornwallis's scouts arrived on the scene, they learned that three fords were being defended, but a fourth ford existed another mile up the Brandywine. Using it, the British damn near routed Washington and Lafayette and they retreated in their socks from the battlefield when the British came at them from behind." McIntyre paused. "Had they been a little more stealthy, the American Revolution could have ended here, with history treating it as nothing more than an uprising. I find it ironic, but two object lessons: You can never have too much intelligence; and always assume a fourth ford, even when you think there are only three."

CHAPTER NINETEEN

Root Out

October 23, 1962
Washington, D.C.

The radio alarm went off exactly at 7:00 a.m. with the onset of the news.

> "TENSIONS REMAIN HIGH AS THE WHITE HOUSE ANNOUNCES THAT THE NAVY HAS DEPLOYED A LINE OF BATTLE-READY WARSHIPS IN THE ATLANTIC TO INTERDICT ALL SHIPS STEAMING TOWARD CUBA. ALREADY ESCALATING THE NATION'S MILITARY ALERT LEVEL TO DEFCON TWO, THE PENTAGON HAS DIRECTED THAT ALL NATIONS' SURFACE VESSELS WITHIN A 100-MILE CIRCUMFERENCE OF THE ISLAND OF CUBA WILL BE SUBJECT TO INSPECTION OF CARGO. THESE STEPS COME AS SIX CRUSADER JETS ARE SET TO FLY LOW-LEVEL RECONNAISSANCE MISSIONS OVER THE CUBAN MAINLAND. THE MOVE APPEARS TO BE THE ADMINISTRATION'S RESPONSE TO SOVIET AMBASSADOR DOBRINYIN'S STATEMENT THAT THERE ARE NO OFFENSIVE WEAPONS IN CUBA. STAY TUNED FOR BREAKING NEWS ON THE MISSILE CRISIS."

In the shower, Ben wondered if a military conflict was inevitable. Hardy would know, but he'd barely been seen at the Forge. Not surprising, though. As a past member of the National Intelligence Board, his input on the crisis was likely being sought.

At 8:30, Ben called into the field office. Di Giuseppe answered rapidly, his greeting just the telephone number. "Four-seven-seven-seven-three-seven-eight."

"Ben, checking in. Anything happening?"

"I'll say. The interrogators finally broke Root. He confessed. Too many contradictions he couldn't explain. Admitted he went to the embassy with the intent to sell the code sheets he copied. Said his girlfriend encouraged him. But he doesn't know where she is. Got a postcard from D.C. inviting him to come a second time. Couldn't produce it. We looked at the farm and in his billet. Couldn't find it. Anyway, from reading the transcript, the girlfriend sounds a lot smarter than he is. It wouldn't take much. The guy is pretty dumb."

"So what's the next step?"

"There is none. It gets worse. JAG put in paperwork for a court-martial for you-know-who, and they bounced it, despite the admissions he made. Held past seventy-two hours before being charged. He's been DD'd and out of the Army, as of 2:00 p.m. today. In his car, off the base, and back to the family farm."

A dishonorable discharge for a dumb kid who committed treason?

"And get this. The postscript? He admits to not one, but two visits to his D.C. friends. Consecutive weekends. Seems the FBI missed the second visit completely. That would be the day before they gave us the info on the first visit. Same drill as the first trip, but says the second time he went down and back solo."

Ben thought for a moment. "No formal separation interview? No penalties?"

"None. He skates."

Dishonorably discharged? Caught selling low-level secrets for chicken feed. Not too smart is an overstatement. Where's the mystery girlfriend? Does he keep the money? Seventy-five dollars? Or maybe $150? What's the price of treason? This is nuts. I'm glad I'm getting out. What am I missing here? The whole deal stinks to high heaven.

CHAPTER TWENTY

Enter the Forge

October 23, 1962
Washington, D.C.

"Welcome to the Forge Foundation, Mr. Oliver."

Smiling, hand extended, Stuart Endicott greeted Ben in the imposing lobby of granite floors, paneled walls, and paintings depicting scenes from the American Revolution. Ben recognized the polished Endicott from seeing him on television as the Foundation's spokesman.

A tour followed. Endicott walked him through the floors, briefly introduced him to staff members, and assured him in an aside that "I'll give you a roster sheet so you can match faces with names and jobs."

They arrived at the library. Endicott found the head librarian, explained Ben was to have "the run of the place," and then ushered him into a private office.

The librarian shook hands with a bear grip; the hand of a huge, affable man in his forties. "Walt Storek. Nice to meet you."

"What's a legendary NFL linebacker doing here?"

"Legends fade, Ben. I'm putting my history major to good use. I was a scholar athlete at Notre Dame. Loved history then, love it now."

Endicott explained that Ben could call on Walt to research information at any time.

What research? Ben wondered.

Leaving the library, Endicott led Ben down the hall to a small, empty office containing a desk, typewriter, desk chair, and visitor's chair.

"All yours. Pick some artwork from the on-loan list from the library and the custodian will hang it for you."

Endicott tossed Ben a set of keys.

"The lobby has a receptionist here from 8:00-6:00, and a guard from 6:00-8:00 , so you can come in as early and you like, stay as late as you want, work at night."

He handed Ben a small box of 500 business cards.

Benjamin L. Oliver
Visiting Fellow 1962-1963
The Forge Foundation
2100 Massachusetts Avenue NW
Washington, D.C. 20008

Endicott sat in the visitor's chair. "When you want to get information in a hurry, or need a contact with a Federal or State agency, Walt Storek is your guy. He'll get what you want and get it fast. One more item: Hardy wants you to meet Laura Prentiss. She was a Visiting Fellow here last year, then did a short stint on the staff of the NSC, and now she's back with us. Laura knows a lot of people and a lot of shortcuts, ways around the bureaucracy. Can you have lunch with her today?"

"I don't have to check my calendar, Stuart. My primary task is to find a place to stay when I'm here in D.C."

"Problem solved. The Foundation has an apartment suite around the corner, less than two blocks away, for visiting dignitaries and our people from the field. We've given you Bedroom B. The keys I gave you? One is for your office here, one for the front door of the apartment, one for Bedroom B."

"I didn't expect everything to be so easy."

"Ben, the Foundation wants to make it easy for its people so they can focus on their work. So, how about 12:30 at the Palm with Miss Prentiss?"

• • •

A photographer dropped by and took a picture for Ben's ID card. Ben was introduced to the secretarial pool, received the number of an assigned parking space in the Foundation's underground garage, and placed an order to stock his office with supplies. In the library, he selected a reproduction of Emanuel Leutze's "Washington Crossing the Delaware," then browsed in the library for a while.

At noon, Ben returned to his office to find the painting already hung, supplies delivered and stowed, and a hand-addressed envelope on his desk.

Dear Ben:

Sorry I couldn't be there to welcome you to the Foundation today. Here's hoping you find your stay rewarding, and that you can find the answers you seek. Know that I am here to help.

H.

P.S. Talk with Endicott re: Root's limbo status. He has examined the legal aspects. Looks as if you're in the clear to investigate, write about him once you're demobilized from the Army October 30.

On his way to lunch, Ben stuck his head into Stuart Endicott's office.

"Ahh, the sleuthing journalist himself," the affable Endicott smiled.

Yes, he'd checked with the Forge's attorneys. A written opinion was on the way, stating that the FBI had waived its jurisdiction in the case of Alvin Root, as they had never arrested him and had summarily passed on their filming of him to the Counterintelligence Corps. In turn, the corps and then the Army had dealt with Root, and though they had not been able to prosecute him, the matter was now outside military jurisdiction and had become so when Root had been dishonorably discharged.

Endicott gave Ben a thumbs-up. "So investigate away, soon-to-be civilian Oliver."

Ben thanked Endicott for the quick response and headed out for lunch.

I'm not waiting for my Army discharge. As soon as I can get back to New Jersey, I'm going to buy Alvin Root lunch at the McDonald's closest to the Root family farm. As dumb as he is, he has to know he's beyond prosecution. I'll get more than the Army or the FBI did. And I'll get some answers.

As Ben passed the receptionist's area, the receptionist turned up the radio on her desk. Ben slowed his stride, then stopped to listen.

"NAVY CRUISERS HAVE TAKEN UP POSITION IN A LINE 800 MILES FROM CUBA. THE QUARANTINE HAS JUST BEEN ENDORSED IN A UNANIMOUS RESOLUTION BY THE ORGANIZATION OF AMERICAN STATES. MOSCOW SEEMS UNDAUNTED. IN A LETTER FROM PREMIER KHRUSHCHEV OBJECTING TO THE QUARANTINE AND US OVERFLIGHTS OF CUBA, KHRUSHCHEV SAID THAT ACTIONS BY THE U.S. 'CONSTITUTE A SERIOUS THREAT TO PEACE AND SECURITY OF PEOPLES.' STAY TUNED FOR..."

The Palm was The Palm, be it New York or Washington. Sawdust. Bustle. Noise. Framed cartoons. A clubhouse for carnivores.

To the maître d', Ben said, "I'm Ben Oliver. Meeting Miss Prentiss at 12:30."

Before he could answer, a female voice said, "Right behind you."

Reflecting later, Ben ordered it in his mind. They both smiled. Shook hands.

Immediately, "Right this way!" from the maître d', who followed them both through the tables.

Tall. Slim, but not too. Hair touching her shoulders. Dark blue suit.

Seated, she laughed lightly. "Where else but the Forge Foundation would the next Fellow be asked to have lunch with the last Fellow! Who is not a Fellow."

Ben replied, "Hardy's idea. I appreciate you taking the time."

"When Hardison McIntyre has an idea, I tend to treat it as a command performance. But a nice idea, nonetheless."

"Hardy's a sweetheart."

"Now that's debatable! Charismatic, yes. Warm and cuddly, nope."

"Wait till you get to know him. You'll be surprised."

They fell naturally to comparing notes. Ben learned Laura had grown up in the Upper Peninsula of Michigan, had gone to Michigan State, then to Georgetown for a master's in governmental affairs. After her Foundation fellowship, she had gone to a temporary assignment on the staff of the National Security Council.

"Impressive."

Laura made a wry face and shook her head from side to side. "Not exactly. They said they might like to have me join the NSC full time, but then they dragged their feet, not quite getting around to making me permanent. Said they were waiting for the completion of my security clearance, so I get left out of a lot of meetings. Oh-so-secret! Then they announced that my assignment was temporary. Frankly, the real reason was they didn't like my parentage."

"How so?"

Laura pulled a long face. "My late father worked at the State Department until he was dismissed. It was implied but never confirmed that he was a fellow traveler, too close to an employee who was dismissed for his left-wing political past. Guilt by association."

"That's lousy."

Laura suddenly brightened. "But it was Hardy to the rescue. He asked me to come back to the Forge and here I am. I work on intriguing projects and there's no politics. Still, I look forward to the time when I won't be judged by some trumped-up accusations by frightened bureaucrats."

She took a sip of her drink and continued. "Perhaps part of the problem at NSC was that I was too young for them. In my so-called exit interview, the personnel manager told me that I lacked 'gravitas.' I told her she lacked courage."

She took another sip of water. "Let's change the subject."

Ben cooperated. "You call it 'the Forge'?"

"Most of Washington does. A lot of alumni go to State and some to the White House." She laughed. "So far, just as staff.

And the occasional cabinet member."

"So, does that mean you can't talk about what you did at the NSC?"

"Not specifically. I did research to help the Council form its positions on issues."

"Sounds bland, but I'm sure it wasn't."

"Being near the center of things, even as a worker bee, is always very exhilarating."

Worker bee? A drone she isn't. Closer to a future queen.

An attentive waiter arrived, pencil at the ready, briefly working in a rapid glance at the front of Laura's open-necked blouse. As she ordered, Ben formed impressions.

Poised. Determined. Defiant. Has to be smart. What color are her eyes? Damn!

Laura leaned in to look more closely at the large menu sheet held in one hand in front of her.

Gray?

"I'll start with a cup of Vichyssoise, and then the steak sandwich. Hold the horseradish." She handed her menu to the waiter.

Blue-gray? Blue!

"The same, but with the horseradish."

"You're a big condiment man?"

"Always. I started putting everything on burgers, and now I'm hooked. I like lots of spices with my food."

Laura reported that she shared an apartment with a friend from Smith who worked at the State Department, spent some weekends sailing with friends on the Chesapeake, sometimes working. "The Forge is not always nine to five. And to get ahead in this town, you've got to be willing to outwork the competition. That is, everyone who will do almost anything to get your job."

As they worked through their lunch, Laura asked Ben how she could help him. "Hardy told me briefly about your recent investigation. Just enough for me to understand why you think there might be more to it than meets the eye."

"Well, for one thing, I would like to get a look at the staff of the Russian embassy. For another, I need to look at a couple of

201 personnel files from the Pentagon."

"What about the FBI? They're notorious for not sharing information."

"Oh, I have no problem dealing with them."

"You don't? That's amazing. You could sell your secret to hundreds of people in Washington who would give a small fortune to get cooperation from those snobs."

"I have a pipeline to get what I want from them."

"Well, then, I'm very anxious to do you a favor. Maybe you can help me out sometime in return."

"Did The FBI withholds information from the National Security Council?"

"Every chance it got."

"So, changing topics, do you know a Lieutenant Colonel John Krentz?"

She looked at Ben sharply. "You know Colonel Krentz?"

"He and I are in a class together at Princeton. At the Woodrow Wilson School of International Affairs."

"You're a grad student, too?"

"No, I just pulled some strings with the university while I was in the CIC, and they let me audit them. Then, later, his CO at Dix told me Krentz was headed for an assignment at the NSC."

"It's not announced yet. That's why I was surprised when you brought his name up. I almost went there, to the Woody, but Georgetown offered me a fellowship and the price was right." She looked puzzled. "So, you're using the present tense. 'He and I are in class together at Princeton.' Still?"

"I plan to track down former Private First Class Root and he lives near Princeton, so I'll try to set my schedule to finish the classes I'm auditing."

When they finished, Ben asked the waiter for the check, he was told the bill was "taken care of."

"The Forge at work," smiled Laura.

As they walked out, Laura said, "I think I might be able to help you with the Russians. Will you be at the Forge this afternoon? I'll let you know."

She raised her hand while still smiling at Ben, and, as they do for all good-looking women, a cab swerved to the curb in front of her.

CHAPTER TWENTY-ONE

Cozy at the Embassy

"Ah, yes. Miss Prentiss and guest Oliver." The front desk was commanded by three middle-aged women in severe black dresses.

As expected, there were high ceilings, waiters circulating with trays, a rising noise level, heavy drapes, huge portraits of the Russian landscape, hosts in badly cut double-breasted suits with clusters of ribbons and medals on wide lapels, and fleshy men in their 60s who not-so-subtly ogled the Western women.

"I keep waiting for an appearance by Boris and Natasha," Ben said.

Laura laughed. "They've got the accent down. Television is America's gift to Soviet diplomacy."

As they moved through the large reception room toward a buffet, Ben reflected on the pace of events. Within an hour after his lunch with Laura, the phone had rung as he sat organizing his desk. Laura had secured an invitation to a reception the embassy was holding for their astronaut Yuri Gagarin.

"When is it?"

"Six thirty p.m."

"I mean, the date."

"That would be today. Three and a half hours from now."

"How did you…"

"Tell you later. What say I meet you at the Forge apartment at 6:30. We can walk from there. Three blocks."

As they approached the embassy bar, Ben saw several Americans in military uniform in the crowd. Laura introduced him to a tall, trim man in his late 40s.

"Colonel Sam Armstrong, this is Ben Oliver from the Forge Foundation."

"Good evening, Laura." For Ben, another iron grip. "Mike Armstrong. A past colleague of Laura's at the think tank?"

"It turns out I am the Forge's latest Visiting Fellow" Ben nodded to Armstrong's near-empty glass. "May I get you a drink?"

"I'll wade in with you. That way you'll get faster service. As you might suspect, Russians are in awe of uniforms."

Armstrong was right. The Russian bartender looked right past the front row of guests pressing forward.

"General, you prefer…?"

"Laura, Ben?"

They ordered gin and tonics.

"Club soda, thank you," Armstrong instructed.

As the barman assembled the drinks, Armstrong turned slightly away from him and spoke quietly to Ben. "Before you have any conversations, assume all waiters and bartenders speak fluent English and report what they overhear to the intelligence officers."

"Excuse me," said Laura. "I need to work the room. Catch up with you later." Carrying her drink, she moved toward a nearby group of guests.

Ben and Armstrong worked their way toward the buffet.

"You don't drink alcohol?"

"Not when I'm on duty." A pause. "See the rather thin gentleman who looks like the Mission Impossible actor Martin Landau? He is Dimitri Kosarov, declared to the State Department as the embassy's legal intelligence *rezident*. Then again, it would be hard not to, as we had already ID'd him in Paris as KGB when he served there in the same capacity. 'Cozy' as we call him. He's anything but."

"So, he got a promotion, What do you suppose he did in France to earn it?"

Armstrong gestured with his glass to the side of the room. They walked out of the scrum to the relative quiet of the perimeter.

"We don't suppose. He blackmailed a member of the French senate to provide a look at closed-door deliberations on France's nuclear security policy."

With this observation, Ben confirmed what he'd suspected. Armstrong was involved in military intelligence, although his shoulder insignia indicated an engineering battalion.

As if reading his mind, Armstrong turned to Ben. "You've been out of the CIC how long?"

"A month."

"And now you're becoming a journalist?"

"Resuming. Was before I went in the Army." After sipping his drink, he continued, "Tell me, Colonel, if you can, what's your current tour of duty?"

"I'm in transition. Just winding up my assignment at the NSC."

"Would your replacement be Lieutenant Colonel Krentz?"

"You know John Krentz?"

"He and I are in some grad school classes together at Princeton."

"Good man, Krentz. Among the Army's best."

"I note you didn't answer my question."

Armstrong grinned. "I note you really don't seem to require an answer." After a minute, he added, "Let's take a walk."

They began to circumnavigate the room, Armstrong providing a narration.

"Okay, a little personalities tour. You recognize Anatoly Dobrinyin, the ambassador, next to the woman in the red dress. The thug to his right is Mikael Sustov, supposedly a personal aide, but in reality he works for Cozy Kosarov, reporting back any unusual conversations non-Russians have with the ambassador. Standing near the ambassador, to his rear, another spook, Grigory Postin, also one of Cozy's. Behind the bar ahead of us, the three women serving are clerical staff in the embassy, except the one in the middle is Kosarov's new secretary, recently arrived from Moscow, Natalia Pedrova."

The two women on either side of Pedrova were short, squat, and in their forties. Pedrova was tall, young, and slim. Alvin Root's description of Vera came back to Ben. *Uh, she is twenty-five, long black hair, good-looking, good figure.*

"Colonel, is there any way I can get at photographs of all the Russians here at the embassy?"

"Sure. I may have them. Or you can request it through the Forge. Walt Storek."

"Okay. Actually, I'm looking for a specific guy, maybe a counselor. Don't know his name. About five foot ten, forty to fifty, brown hair, average build. It's logical he would be here tonight."

"Not much to go on. Let's keep walking."

They skirted a crowd gathered five-deep around Yuri Gagarin and his translator.

"You want to meet Gagarin?"

Ben looked over at the young Hero of the Soviet Union, engulfed by guests wanting to touch him. "No, thanks. I've actually seen him before, at Princeton last week. It was a circus, right in the middle of the main campus. Students pressing in on him, translators struggling with questions." Ben stopped. Gagarin was signing autographs. Next to him stood a man Ben had seen before. He had been in the crowd surrounding Gagarin in Princeton. "See the Russian with Gagarin, to his right? Know who he is?"

"Cultural attaché. Kolb. Vladimir Kolb."

"So, if he's a member of the embassy staff, aren't his movements restricted? How does he get to Princeton in the crowd around Gagarin?"

"Probably the Exception Rule."

"Which is?"

"Embassies can petition the State Department to get a waiver for employees they claim are essential to support a traveling VIP. Someone like Gagarin."

Only one problem. Kolb had been at the back of the crowd, striding around the perimeter, not at the center, holding people back from Gagarin.

Briefly, Laura rejoined Ben and Armstrong as they circulated.

"See the two Russians talking? Or, actually, one talking, one listening." Armstrong directed them with a nod of his head across a crowd of guests to a burly, dark-complected man in a baggy suit talking to a tall, thin, fair-haired man in his late thirties.

"Mutt and Jeff. Yin and Yang," murmured Laura. "Who are they, Sam?"

"The caricature Russian is the charming Cozy Dimitri Kosarov—sometimes Oleg Sustin, depending upon where he is posted, but for a while now, just bad old Dimitri Kosarov. And a bad Ivan he is. KGB all the way. Cover is as a cultural affairs officer."

Ben nodded toward an unusually well-dressed Russian. "And Fred Astaire?"

"That's a real cultural affairs officer. At least, we think so. Evgeny Nolikin. 'Clean Gene,' we call him, as all the rest of the cultural affairs gang is dirty. Nolikin is forty-four, called on as a high-level interpreter. He came up that way. Speaks four or five languages. Was some kind of language whiz kid out of the Language School in Moscow. Connections got him a plum wartime assignment as an interpreter at Tehran, Yalta. Probably the only guy in the room who's translated Roosevelt and Churchill into Russian, and Stalin into English."

"Looks like Kosarov's reading him the riot act."

"Kosarov addresses everyone that way. He's a sledge-hammer."

"Talking to a nail."

"Nolikin's a survivor. At one point married to the daughter of a politburo member. Has Kremlin connections. The NKVD has to handle his kind with kid gloves lest they rile a Kremlin big shot. Nolikin has clout. One of the few Russians here who can travel around without a nanny. Even has his teenage daughter visit several times a year. That takes some juice. She's here now, over there, behind the samovar."

"Got to mingle, fellas. Catch up with you later." Laura peeled off.

Through the crowd, Ben watched an awkward young woman, a girl really, trying to act the grown-up, pouring tea and coffee for guests who stopped at her table. She was neither fair like her father nor dark, but mid-complected. Ben's first thought was she must favor her mother, for he saw nothing of Nolikin in her features or posture.

Brunette. About fifteen or sixteen. Graceful, slight but definitely on her way to becoming an attractive young woman.

He wandered over, first placing his half-empty gin and tonic on the tray of a passing waiter.

"Hello, do you speak English?"

"Yes, sir. May I offer you tea or coffee?"

"Coffee, please."

She handed him a cup and saucer.

As Ben added cream and sugar, he smiled at her. "I'm Ben Oliver. What's your name?"

"I am Natasha. But I am not permitted to speak with strangers."

"Well, I am not a stranger, or I would not have been invited to this party, would I?"

"Yes, I see. Well, not strangers on the streets of Washington, the District of Columbia."

Ben smiled. "I don't either."

That elicited a brief smile from Natasha.

"Do you go to the embassy school?"

"Oh, no. I am a student at the language academy in Moscow. I am just visiting my father here at the embassy."

"Isn't there a Language Institute in Moscow as well?"

"Yes, it is where I will study once I graduate from the academy. Both my parents are graduates." She spoke proudly.

"Have you met Cosmonaut Gagarin?"

"Just to shake hands with him. He is very small. He has to be to fit into the Soyuz capsule."

"What did he say to you?"

"Nothing really. Just hello. He shook hands with everyone in the embassy before the reception started. I think it is so everyone can say they met the first man in space."

"Have you seen many of the sights in Washington on your visit?"

"This is my third visit. While I have been to the Lincoln Memorial and the Washington Monument once each, my father has taken me to the Washington Zoo three times. George Washington was a great revolutionary." She looked up . "Here is my father."

"Good evening, I am Evgeny Nolikin, a cultural attaché here at the embassy."

"Benjamin Oliver. Pleased to meet you. I am impressed with

your daughter's command of English."

"She is quite accomplished. Much of her skill in languages come from her mother."

"Well, I don't know any Americans her age who can speak Russian as fluently as she speaks English."

"A kind compliment. Tell me, Mister Oliver, what do you do in Washington?"

"I just moved here to look for a job."

"What type of job?"

"Well, not an interpreter or translator. I only speak one language. Probably on the Hill. I studied political science in college. I hope to land in one of the congressional offices. Right now, I have a temporary spot at the Forge Foundation."

"I've heard of it. What you Americans call a 'think tank,' yes?"

"Yes."

"I'd like to hear more about it, but I believe the reception is winding up." He shook hands with Ben, and summoned Natasha from behind the samovar. "Come, Natasha. The party is over."

Natasha curtsied to Ben, then turned and walked away, her father's arm around her shoulders.

CHAPTER TWENTY-TWO

Apartment Living

After ninety minutes at the party, Ben was about ready to go and was starting to look around for Laura, when he had an idea. He located "Vera," still standing behind one of the buffet tables, but the crowds were thinned out, most of the food was gone, and so were the two other Russian women. Natalia was alone.

"Hello. Perhaps you can help me?"

She smiled and answered in English, "I am here to try."

"I'm thinking about traveling to Russia next summer during my vacation from college. Leningrad and Moscow. Is there someone here at the embassy who can help me plan my trip?"

"I can do that. If you will make an appointment, you can come to me and I will sit down with you. Is that convenient?"

"It is. Could we do it in the next few days? Maybe even tomorrow?"

She reached behind her back, untied her apron, and placed it on the table. "Come. We will check the calendar."

Ben followed her to the lobby, and then down a corridor to a small office.

"Please sit."

"Vera" leafed through an appointment book. "Eleven tomorrow morning?"

"That would be fine. My name is Ben Oliver."

"I am Natalia Pedrova."

They shook hands, then Ben rejoined the guests leaving the embassy.

Back in the reception hall, Laura was easy to find. She beamed a smile at Ben. "Ready to vamoose?"

"I am. Enough to drink, enough to eat, enough conversation for one evening."

As they walked back toward the apartment, Laura asked Ben what he thought of Colonel Armstrong.

"Impressive. And obviously a spook."

"Just about everyone in Washington is one kind of spy or another. Here, information is currency. And the best information is gold. Mine the gold, rise to the top."

"So, what gold did you glean tonight?"

They were at the steps to the apartment. "Offer me a nightcap and I'll tell you."

"There's booze here?"

"You obviously haven't cased the joint yet. The place is well stocked."

In the living room, Laura opened a double set of wall cabinet doors to reveal a closet-turned-bar, with glasses, bottles, a mini-fridge, and a sink.

"Pour me a bourbon on the rocks, please. I'll be back in a minute," she said.

Ben rocked up two heavy, old-fashioned glasses and poured bourbon over the ice. Took a sip from one. *Ahhhh.* Carried the glasses to a coffee table surrounded by a couch and two easy chairs. Settled on the couch.

Laura spoke from behind him. "Don't turn around. I don't want to startle you, but I'm wearing a bathrobe." There was a long pause. "Okay, turn around. I meant to tell you before, I have the key to Bedroom A. I'm staying here tonight. My roommate is entertaining her boyfriend."

The Forge apartment bathrobes were big, thick, white terry cloth. Ben had seen one hanging in the closet in his room. Laura crossed to the table, gathered up her drink and curled up in the chair across from the table. She took a sip.

"Mmmmmm. So, how did you like your embassy visit?"

"Enough that I'm going back for more. Tomorrow."

Ben explained about the appointment with Natalia.

"Very clever, assuming they don't wonder what a grad student was doing at a diplomatic reception."

"They check. I'm simply 'guest Oliver' on the books."

"You're going to make the same pitch as Root did and see where they take it? Did the FBI ever tell you what the Russians sent to Root? Maps? Books?"

"No, for the simple reason that once they handed Root over

to us, they were done. No further action."

"You're kidding! Even though Root's girlfriend could be involved? She's a civilian. Within their jurisdiction."

"The FBI is out. It is the Army's case." Ben took a sip of bourbon. "Correction: it *was* the Army's case. They blew it."

"So, now it's your case."

"Thanks to Hardy and the Forge Foundation."

"To both, I'm very grateful," Laura said.

She rose, put down her drink, walked around the coffee table, sat down next to Ben and kissed him.

"Would you like to hear what I learned tonight at the embassy?"

"I would, but not right now."

• • •

Ben woke at sunrise. He hadn't managed to close the drapes completely, so the sun slanted a spear of light into the room. Lay still, listening to Laura breathing. Rewound to six hours before.

Calm on the couch, followed by less calm, followed by a retreat to the bedroom.

Laura, impishly, hands on hips. "You have me at a disadvantage. I want you in a bathrobe, too."

Ben retreated to the bathroom. When he returned, he stood at the foot of the bed, could see Laura had gone back into the living room, and was pouring out their drinks.

She turned out the lights, came back into the bedroom and closed the door. She flicked off the overhead light.

"Now I can't see you," Ben said.

Not quite accurate. Moonlight spilled in the windows.

"Then use the Braille system," Laura teased.

They could see each other well enough when their robes had come off.

Now, he stretched slowly, trying not to disturb the bed. In slow motion, he slid out and stood back from the window to look through the gap in the curtains at the morning sun. Padded to the bathroom.

When he came back, she appeared not to have moved, but within seconds of him sliding back into bed, she rose silently and walked to the bathroom.

In a moment, he turned over so he could see the bathroom door. She came through it as if on cue, backlit. *Memorize this,* he thought. *You may never see another woman this amazing.*

He lifted the sheet and she slid in. Wrapped herself around him.

"Sardines," she said into his shoulder.

"Where are the others?"

"Two are enough. Let me show you."

After they'd showered, Ben suggested they get some breakfast. "We never got around to what you learned at the embassy last night. You can tell me over coffee."

She had her hand on the door. "I need to go home for a change of clothes. Meet you at Mort's Coffee in thirty minutes."

CHAPTER TWENTY-THREE

I Like Ike

October 24, 1962

Over coffee, Laura described the people she'd met at the embassy party. "Ambassador Dobrinyin, very suave for a Russian. Knows a lot more English than he lets on. I noticed a couple of times that, as he waited for his so-called translator to relay a comment or question from a guest, he was impatient. I thought he was ready to answer and was using the delay in translation to weigh his response."

"Did you meet Yuri Gagarin?"

"Oh, yes. He's essentially a poster boy for their space program. His translator practically answered the questions rather than ask him."

"How do you know that?"

"Well, I asked him a question directly, in Russian."

"How many languages do you speak?"

"Counting English, four. French, Spanish, Russian."

"Impressive. And Yuri's response?"

"He was flustered. He turned to the translator to see if he should answer. I think he's intimidated by the fame and attention."

"So, how was it resolved?"

"The translator said Gagarin had to make a call to his family in Moscow, and they whisked him away."

"The time difference would make it about 4:00 a.m. in Moscow."

"Obviously, there's a tight rein on even a space hero."

"Walk with me as far as the embassy?"

"You're going to meet the beautiful Natalia?"

"I am. But I want to get the lay of the land, too."

They strolled toward the embassy along the leafy streets,

which had cars parked on both sides. Brownstones soared beyond the maples and flowering gum trees, their second- and third-story windows catching the sun.

"On your right is roughly where the FBI filmed Root's license plate. Somehow, on a Sunday, he found a place to park just three blocks away from the embassy."

They crossed an intersection and continued on, Ben gazing up at the houses on the left.

"Stop a moment. Without staring right at it, take a look at the second-floor window at 447. The one directly over the door."

"The one with the red 'I Like Ike' poster in it? A little outdated, I'd say."

"That's it. See any sign of life in the apartment? Lights? Window open? Movement?"

Laura seemed startled. "You think someone is watching us?"

"Unlikely. But what do you see?"

"Someone moving around. I can't see more. The window is open, up about six inches. Maybe to create a draft, move the air."

"Let's keep walking." He took a notebook and pen from his jacket pocket, wrote a name and number, and handed it to Laura. "Call Tom Bennett, he's an FBI agent. This number. Tell him you're calling for me, and that I think that 447 may be a Russian safe house."

Looking alarmed, Laura protested. "But how could you know that? It's just a typical apartment with an old campaign poster in the window."

"It may be. But the Russians have a history of locating safe houses within a few blocks of the embassy so they can get to them in a hurry when they are meeting agents."

"But really, Ben…"

"There is always a recognition signal in the window to tell an agent that it's either safe to enter or that the place is compromised. Unsafe."

"I didn't see any signal."

"The poster. The last time I saw it, it was on film, in the

background of the footage they shot of license plates on the street. The film that revealed, among others, Root's license plate."

"I still don't understand how..."

"In the film, that same window has a poster in the same position, but it's markedly different. Not in red, but in blue. It read 'Madly for Adlai.'"

"Maybe the owner just changes it around."

"Maybe. Maybe not. I've got to get to the embassy. Call Tom Bennett and tell him to check it out pronto."

Laura nodded. Two cross streets later, they stood across from the Russian embassy.

"Here's some change. Find a pay phone. Probably one in the park, over by that pavilion." Ben pointed out a green structure in the distance. "After you call Bennett, wait for me in the park. I'll be out of the embassy in about fifteen minutes."

"I need more change. Need to call the Forge to cancel a meeting."

Ben held out a handful of change and Laura plucked an extra dime from his palm.

"Tell Bennett to get a team to 447 Magnolia Avenue as fast as possible."

"Okay."

Her response sounded dubious, as if Ben were hallucinating and she was humoring him. She gave him a peck on the cheek and headed off. Ben turned and walked up the steps of the embassy.

CHAPTER TWENTY-FOUR

Safe House

Ben had kept it short, reaching his goal of meeting and identifying two of the Russians Alvin Root had met when he went to sell them code book pages. Ben gave them a story about wanting to visit Russia, and they exhibited little interest and less help. Upon exiting the embassy, Ben walked into the park toward the gazebo. No Laura in sight.

Rounding the far side of the gazebo, he spotted her on a pay phone next to the public restrooms, a hundred yards away. She looked up, waved, and continued talking. As he approached, she wound up the call.

"I'll tell him. Thanks." Cheeks flushed, she turned to Ben.

"Who are you talking to?"

"Agent Bennett., Just calling back. He looked at the film footage and confirms there was a blue Adlai Stevenson campaign poster in the window. He's on his way with a squad of agents and will meet us there. ETA, 11:50. He said to meet him there."

"Let's go."

She put her hand on Ben's arm. "Stop. Wait a second. Fill me in. How did your visit with Natalia Petrova go?"

"I'll tell you later."

She put her hand on Ben's arm again. "Not a good idea for us to be standing around on the street in front of 447 in view of the windows before the FBI arrives. Sit down a minute and tell me about Petrova."

Acknowledging her logic, Ben sat next to her on the bench. Her eyes were sparkling.

"Tell all."

Natalia had been summoned by the receptionist, came to the lobby, and walked Ben back to a small conference room. She was very cordial and expressed enthusiasm that he would want to visit the Soviet Union. "You will love it," she said, putting her hand briefly on Ben's arm.

As they looked over a map, Ben asked about driving routes and license requirements. Her answers were interrupted by a knock on the door, and she excused herself, then disappeared out into the hall. She was back within a minute, smiling and apologizing for the interruption.

Ben asked about places to exit Russia. Could he drive from Moscow down to the Black Sea, the Crimean Peninsula? Or exit through Yugoslavia? She said it could be arranged. Would he be able to visit the Russian cosmonauts' site? As an engineer who had worked on the American space program, he would find it fascinating to compare the Russian and American approaches to space exploration. Was there anyone in the embassy who might be able to help him make that side trip, once in Russia?

"She simply did not take the bait," Ben sighed. "I guessed wrong on that one."

They pounced on Root but passed on me. Why? Could they know who I was? Highly unlikely. I need to get back to New Jersey and talk with Root again.

He rose, offered his hand to Laura, and they headed for 447 Magnolia.

The street was blocked off with sawhorses and patrolled by a pair of district policemen. Looking past them, Ben and Laura could see vehicles clogging the road midblock in front of 447.

Ben flashed his credentials. "Agent Oliver and Miss Prentiss, meeting FBI Agent Bennett at 447."

"He just went upstairs. Told us to expect you."

One of the policemen pulled a sawhorse aside to let them through.

Neighbors on both sides of the street were out on their porches, trying to learn what was going on, but to no avail. An agent met Ben and Laura, escorted them into the building, and led them upstairs to the second-floor apartment.

"Ben, come on in." Bennett offered a hand.

Ben introduced Laura. "So, what do you have?" he then asked.

"An empty apartment. But only recently. Maybe someone

heard us coming. Teapot hot on the stove; two cups on the kitchen table half-filled with hot tea. Radio on low. Windows opened for air circulation. Kitchen door ajar. A set of steps down to the alley. At least two people left in their socks."

"The alley wasn't covered by your agents?"

"I sent a pair around the back before we hit the front door. Whoever left must have beat them by seconds."

"Any evidence connecting the occupants to the embassy?"

"Yes and no, and I doubt we'll know for sure. Smell of cigarettes, unlike any American brand's aroma. Very Balkan. But nothing in the ashtray. Probably because butts went down the disposal. Here."

Bennett handed an empty ashtray to Ben, who sniffed it, then offered it to Laura.

"I get your point. Anything else?"

"Ash residue on the bathroom toilet. Something got burned and flushed."

Ben asked, "Tom, suppose they saw the FBI arrive from the window. Could they have had time to dump cigarettes down the disposal, burn papers over the toilet?"

"Maybe they saw you out the window thirty minutes ago and panicked."

"We'll never know. Maybe they were run-of-the-mill criminals, not Russians. We're checking with the landlord and the phone company for anything we can get."

Bennett walked over to the bookcase and pulled out a book. "And maybe there's no Santa Claus."

He handed the volume to Ben, who looked at the cover and leafed through it. *Das Kapital,* with page after page in Cyrillic. A slip of paper fluttered to the table. Bookmark? Reminder note? On it were a few words, also written in Cyrillic.

Ben handed the note to Laura. "Can you translate this for us?"

She looked at the slip for a few moments, and shook her head. "First it's about Sunday. Then there's something in slang. I think it means 'going to the bathroom.'"

Tom called out to the agents scouring the room. "Anyone here speak or read Russian?"

"Sure." Bennett called out, "Agent Iverson, over here. Translation, please."

An agent materialized from the kitchen and took up the note. With a puzzled look, he spoke. "Agent Bennett, this is sort of a loose translation. It says 'Sunday morning patrol. Ambassador's four-legged excrement machine.'"

CHAPTER TWENTY-FIVE

Intimate Apparel

Ben and Laura waited while Bennett's team went through the rest of the library, the closets, kitchen cabinets, and the dresser drawers in two well-kept bedrooms.

"Nothing more from a cursory search," reported Bennett. "The thorough search team will be here shortly and will spend four or five hours. No sense you waiting around. Please take a few minutes to give your statements to Agent Iverson."

Laura went first, and Ben wandered around the apartment.

Why so close to the embassy? They had to know it was in the area regularly filmed by the FBI. What makes it worth the risk of exposure by surveillance, or even nosy neighbors? Downstairs apartment only used twice a month by the landlord who lives three hours out in Virginia. Maybe comes to collect the rent? Maybe just for crash meetings? A place the Russians could get to in a hurry. A place where they were unlikely to be overheard? Paranoid types, maybe a getaway from an embassy they fear is bugged. Maybe this, maybe that.

Laura interrupted his reverie. "I have to go. Got a meeting. Busy tonight. I'll call you tomorrow."

"Make it early or late. I'm driving up to New Jersey for the day."

"Will do."

Bennett watched her go. "Nice-looking lady. Dating anyone I know?"

"Beats me. What's next?"

"You have a few minutes? I think I have an idea what the message slip refers to. If I'm right, we'll get an idea who wrote it."

"So tell."

"Not tell; it's show. Back at the Bureau."

"Give me an hour."

Back at the Forge, Ben dug through his interview notebooks—he'd brought a box of them, containing all the interviews from his recent cases—and found a packet of eight, bound together with a thick rubber band. Within seconds, he found Root's home phone number at the Root family farm.

After six rings, Root picked up. "Hello?" he said anxiously.

"Alvin, it's Ben Oliver, from the Army. I'm calling from D.C. How are you doing?"

"Oh, hi. Okay, I guess."

"I tried to reach you earlier today."

"I've been cleaning the silo. Getting ready to repaint it."

"Well, I hope everything will work out for you."

"Maybe."

"Listen, I'd like to drive up from Washington tomorrow and talk with you a little more about Nadine."

"That bitch!"

"Why do you say that?"

"She called me two days ago and wanted to get together. Asked me to meet her."

"Where?"

"Right there. Where you are. Washington. Yesterday."

"And what did you say?"

"I agreed. I drove down. Instead of working on the silo, I went to meet her."

Right here? Under my nose? Damn, I should have thought to tell Alvin to let me know if he heard from her. Things are moving too fast. Slow it down. Think!

"Where did you meet?"

"Well, we never got together. It was really stupid. I mean, I was. All that way, and nothing."

"What happened?"

"Nothing. I mean, she never showed."

"Never showed where?"

"She asked me to meet her at a place I knew—the park near the embassy."

The Russian Embassy? Is she crazy? Is he?

"And you went there?"

"Drove down yesterday in my Chevy. I waited two hours,

from 2:00 to 4:00. The bitch stood me up."

Why? Why? What a risk! It makes no sense. None!

"You had no way to get in touch with her?"

The offer had to be sex. Why else would he have gone all that way?

"She said she would get a hotel. We'd meet and then go there."

What an idiot! But what's her motivation? He's burned. Doesn't she know that?

"So then what?"

"I drove back home. Got here last night." He sighed. "She never called back."

"Listen, Alvin. Did she tell you why she wanted to see you?"

"Well, you know."

"I don't. Help me out here."

"She said she missed me. Wanted to get together."

Think for a minute. Be clear.

"So, what were the arrangements?"

"Nadine said park near the embassy like we did before and walk to the park. I found a spot to park about a block away and walked past the embassy down into the park. I sat on a bench near the entrance so I would see her when she showed up. Only she never did."

Think. Take a deep breath. Think!

"Well, I'm sorry you missed her. Something must have come up to keep her from meeting you, and she had no way to call you. I'm sure she'll get in touch soon."

"I doubt it."

"Why do you say that?"

"Well, Nadine was all talk and no action, that's why. Just a big cock tease."

Looks like it worked on you! Nadine is the answer to at least some of this. Not my fault the interrogators failed to probe deeper on her, find out who she is and where she is. But I can.

"Tell you what, Alvin. I think I can help you connect with her. How about I come see you at the farm tomorrow and we can figure out how to get in touch with Nadine. In fact, I have something she left here for you. I'll bring it."

"Sure, if you want to. I'll be here, painting the silo."

"I'll see you a little before noon. Okay?"

"Okay," he replied listlessly.

Ben broke the connection. Still holding the phone, he called Tom Bennett at the FBI. He was connected immediately.

"Tom, Ben Oliver. How quickly can you look at yesterday's surveillance footage on the Russian embassy and the streets around it?"

"It was processed this afternoon and just reviewed. Nothing new on it."

"Look at it again. Pull up the park entrance and streets around the embassy between 1:30 and 4:30 yesterday afternoon."

"Why?"

"Believe it or not, Alvin Root was released from the Army a few days ago and returned to the scene of the crime."

"He must be insane!"

"No, just a dumb, lonely kid. A really dumb, horny kid. I'm on my way to you now. Rack up the footage and see if you ID Root or his car."

Ben hung up on Bennett and held the phone for a moment, thinking about Root and the missing Nadine. *Okay, what do I put in a package from a woman I don't know, who remains a mystery? Something to soften Alvin up?*

He called Laura's extension. "Can you meet me on the street in front of the Forge for a minute?"

She could and did, a few minutes later.

"What's so important? I'm jammed. Wall-to-wall meet-ings."

"I didn't want to ask you on the phone. I need a pair of your panties."

She stared at him. "Can't this wait until some evening?"

"I need a pair of panties to take to Alvin Root. I told him I had a package from his girlfriend. Not exactly true. But that's how I got him to see me tomorrow. With a little bit of luck, I may get him to tell me enough so that I can actually identify her. Track her down."

Laura looked at him, wide-eyed. "You are insane."

Ben grinned. "That too."

She frowned and shook her head in disbelief. "Follow me."

Inside the Forge, she requested a manila envelope from the receptionist. "Wait here." She entered the ladies' room. Seconds later, she emerged and handed Ben the envelope with a mock glare. Looking exasperated, she said, "The things I do for you."

"Look at it this way. It's for your country."

CHAPTER TWENTY-SIX

Dobrinyin's Borzoi

October 26, 1962
FBI Headquarters, Washington, D.C.

"Okay, here we are. Sunday, October 15th. Note the time stamp in the lower right corner."

The room was darkened as Tom Bennett and Ben Oliver watched the footage. Close-up of leafy Magnolia Street. The four hundred block. Pedestrians walking up and down both sidewalks. The occasional porch occupied by a resident reading the paper. A little unreal due to the absence of sound.

"Comparing with the film from the prior Sunday, this certainly looks like Root's car. Can't see the front license plate because of the foliage and the camera angle, but the model's the same, the color's the same."

Ben spoke. "It's his. See the dent on the fender?"

The footage held on the car, then widened to show the whole street. A tall man with a dog on a long leash crossed diagonally. Slowing, he squeezed between the rear of the car in front of Root's and Root's hood, the dog leading. He appeared to get stuck for a moment, dipped sideways as if his clothes had snagged on a bumper, then moved on, pulled again by the straining dog, the leash taut. He put one hand in his pocket, then switched hands on the leash, and the cameraman lost interest in him. The footage continued its briefly interrupted pan of the row of cars opposite 447 Magnolia.

Why cross the street at that spot? Why cross at all? Why squeeze between two closely parked cars? There were plenty of other wider spaces between cars parked before and after Root's.

"Let's call this animal lover Dog Walker. Can I see it again, Tom?"

"Sure, but we're going to run out of time. You shouldn't be here and I shouldn't be showing this to you."

"What happened to professional courtesy?"

"You're a civilian now."

"Not yet. Just on terminal leave. I'm still in the Army for another two weeks." He held up his credentials. "Here's your cover, Tom. I asked. You obliged."

"Well, I'm obliged to you for the call on the 447 Magnolia nest. I'll get some brownie points with the director. He gets his jollies thwarting the communist menace."

Ben watched the film again, then asked to see it one more time. "Can you freeze the projector and hold a particular frame?"

"Yes, but the resolution is not as clear as when the reel is running. Say when..."

The whir of the projector was the only sound. Down the street came Dog Walker, one arm stretched out, attached to the leash. He pulled at it to check the dog, who moved back toward the man.

He is picking the exact spot to cross. In checking the dog, he turned slightly toward the camera that was shooting the scene, following his progress over his right shoulder.

A gaunt-cheeked face emerged from under a snap-brim hat.

"Freeze it."

By the time Bennett stopped the projector, Dog Walker had turned away, looking across the narrow street to the row of cars on the opposite curb.

Bennett observed, "Watch. Dog Walker is picking his spot to cut between the cars. Pulling on the leash to rein in the dog, rather than letting the dog pick the opening."

"Can you rewind about five seconds and roll again? I'll want to stop it again, but a little further along, just when he gets snagged between the cars."

Bennett obliged. Rewound. Watched.

Ben called out, "Stop!"

Dog Walker seemed to stagger as he rounded the left front corner of Root's car. Being pulled by the leash attached to his left hand, he bent, put his right hand out to steady himself on the car—below the hood on the grill or bumper. In either case, at a place unseen by the camera or the two agents screening the footage. He straightened up, stepped onto the sidewalk, and yanked back on the dog. When the leash was momentarily slack, he quickly shuffled hands, switching the leash to his right hand, and placed his left hand in his jacket pocket.

One more rewind, and this time a freeze on Handler's hand. For unknown reasons and in no discernible pattern, the agents filming the license plates—perhaps out of boredom, perhaps for something to do—would alter the shot, zooming in on a detail, or a plate, once on a plastic Jesus affixed to a dashboard, once to a plastic hula girl affixed to a dashboard. Jesus was robed. The hula girl wore only a grass skirt.

This time, the camera operator zoomed in on the walker's left hand, just as he was putting it in his pocket. Extending from it was a small, metal, rectangular shape.

A harmonica? No.

About four inches long, two inches wide, one-inch high. On the end of the surface, not covered by Handler's enclosing palm, there were four slightly fuzzy yet still readable letters: k-e-y-t.

A Russian word? Part of one? Like Nyet? No. A place? A piece off the car? On the ground in front of the car? It fell off the car? It was attached to the car? Keyt? What is a Keyt? K-e-y-t is the beginning of what? Go through the vowels. Keytah. Keyteh. Keyti. Keyto. Keytu. Keyety. No. Again: Keyt-ay. Keyt-ey. Keyt...Wait. Oh. holy cow! Ben turned to Bennett. "I know what it is."

"What?"

"It is a keytainer. A magnetized box people use to attach spare keys to their cars. Also known as a hide-a-key."

"I know what a hide-a-key is. I use one on my car. Under the left front fender. One must have fallen off a parked car and when Dog Walker slipped, he saw it and picked it up."

Ben scratched behind his ear. "That's probably it. Tell you what, though. If you look through the Bureau's surveillance photographs of Russian embassy personnel, you should ID Dog Walker. I'll buy you dinner at Duke Zeibert's if he's not. in your files."

As Ben walked back to the Forge apartment, he mused, shaking his head. *Of course, you're going to find out who the dog walker is. On film and in photographs, you're going to see him coming out of the embassy and going into the embassy, just as I did today. He's an embassy flunky with the unenviable task of exercising the ambassador's Borzoi. Must be on the bottom of the pecking order.*

Back at the apartment, he found a note from Laura. "Off to an event tonight, then to my apartment. Don't call. Busy tomorrow. Let's talk tomorrow night."

Think time. Ben changed into a pair of jeans, opened a beer, and sprawled on the sofa, lights off, the apartment dimming as night fell.

The keytainer! It wasn't lying in the street. It came off the grille or the bumper of Root's car. Was pulled off by Handler as he squeezed by. He knew the car. Headed straight for it when he could have taken an easier path. So they knew Root was coming. Did they know the street? The film will tell us if Dog Walker shows up on other streets. How far do you have to walk a Borzoi before it dumps?

Another pull on the beer. Eyes closed.

So how did they know? There's no reason for Root to put the keytainer on the grille or bumper of his car. Under the fender, maybe, but not on the outside. Whoever did it was instructed to do it to facilitate its collection. Which means the Russians are onto the FBI filming schedule. Bennett told me that Hoover had cut back the hours, staggered the filming times after taking heat from Bobby Kennedy. Two pricks squaring off against each other. Did Handler get a signal from the safe house. or was it a coincidence that Root parked within a few doors of it? I'll ask him tomorrow. There are no coincidences.

Another swallow. Ben thought back to events in Princeton a few Saturdays ago. *Krentz! Krentz and his spotless workbench, with a stack of keytainers sitting there in plain sight! Krentz! No coincidences. There has to be some connection between Lieutenant Colonel John No-Middle-Initial Krentz and the nitwit farm-kid-turned-failed-traitor Alvin Root. Worlds apart. Smart versus dumb. High-ranking officer versus grunt.*

Tilted up for the last taste.

Do I want another one? What I want is to understand how Krentz managed to put one of the three keytainers I saw stacked on his workbench on the front grill of Alvin Root's car. Krentz: the man who they say hates Germans, yet owns a classic German car. Krentz! What did you send to the Russians?

Ben got up and went to the refrigerator for another beer. Sat down again. Now in the dark.

So many more questions. Who convinced Root to make a visit to the Russians? Nadine was gone. So who? How and when did Krentz get the keytainer on Root's car? How did he know Root would be going? And finally, what was in the keytainer? It sure as hell wasn't a key.

Out loud: "At least not a key to a damned Porsche."

A keytainer! Krentz, who are you? What key are you hiding? Krentz, what are you giving them?

Another pull on the beer. He closed his eyes.

I've got to re-envision what I saw in Krentz's garage.

Ben sat thinking for another fifteen minutes, recalling Krentz's garage, the workbench, the neatly organized tools, the keytainers. He stood and dropped the empty beer bottle in the garbage container below the sink.

Krentz! What are you doing? And why?

CHAPTER TWENTY-SEVEN

Making Haste

October 25. 1962

The call went through. On the other end, the receiver was picked up, but no greeting ensued.

Handy began without preamble. "Events are starting to move very fast, as you predicted. Kosarov's suspicions have been aroused again, and he appears to be determined to unmask Oppor. Against diplomatic rules, he sent an embassy clerk to New Jersey in an attempt to confront Lieutenant Colonel Krentz. The connection never occurred and a disaster followed. The clerk was stopped for speeding on the New Jersey Turnpike and all hell broke loose when the police discovered they had a diplomat traveling outside his permitted distance. The journalist we spoke of, Ben Oliver, may have tipped the police. There may be an opportunity to use Oliver to move things along. It is really quite remarkable to me to observe it happening, but again, you were right. In some ways, Russians and Americans are no different. Kosarov the Bolshevik acts like a capitalist, aggressively pursuing reward and fame, always pushing, in a big hurry; Oppor, from the heart of America, like a good communist, keeping his head down and informing on everyone and everybody. It is really too rich!"

Handy listened as, at last, the other party spoke. Then, with a sigh, he responded. "I agree, my friend. It is time. Yes, we can use Oliver to keep Kosarov headed in the right direction. It's remarkable, really, when you think about it. Kosarov has been trained and trained and reminded that intelligence work must be precise and operate at or below the legal limit. Yet he pushes his clerk to race to Princeton and race back, and bang! He is arrested for exceeding the limit. Kosarov himself is exceeding the limit. I think his ambition has passed his discretion and is now accelerating away into the distance. Excuse the metaphor, although I think it apt. So, we harness his dereliction, this quest of his, to our advantage. Floka-pa-ka, comrade."

"Do svidaniya, comrade!"

Dial tone.

CHAPTER TWENTY-EIGHT

Invisible Handy

October 26. 1962

Before driving back to Washington, Ben had called the Forge to check for messages. Benita, the always pleasant receptionist, told him that a Dr. Newlin had called. The message asked Ben to call him at home that evening. Benita read him the number.

Back in the Forge apartment suite, Ben showered, ate the takeout dinner he'd picked up at a nearby restaurant, and settled in. He picked up the phone.

"Dr. Newlin, Ben Oliver returning your call. Is this a good time?"

John Newlin was a tenured Georgetown professor in the field of American history. At the public library the prior afternoon, Ben had found Newlin's book on the Allies' wartime conferences spanning the period 1942 through 1945. Ben had scanned the index, text, and photographs for about an hour.

"Ideal, Agent Oliver. Here's what I found in my files. The rosters of the official attendees at major conferences are, as a rule, quite accurate and complete. But of your two inquiries, there's a bit of confusion about both." Newlin paused for a moment.

"Please go on."

"Well, regarding a Captain Jay Handy, his name appears on the roster for the delegation at Malta and Tehran, but not at Yalta. He does not appear in any official photographs released from the archives. I thought it possible that someone compiling lists might have written Jay instead of the initial 'J'. But in checking any other first names—James, John, Joseph—I found nothing."

"Have you ever run across a reference to Captain Handy in

doing the research for your books?"

"I reviewed my notes. Nothing came up. But in doing so, I did find the second man you asked about in your inquiry, Hardison McIntyre. His name does not appear on the rosters for Malta or Tehran, and not in the official delegation at Yalta. I find that strange."

"In what way?"

"While his name is not on the roster, he does appear in photographs, specifically in the background of a group of U.S. attendees gathered around FDR, apparently his aides. The picture caption identifies him as one J.H. McIntyre."

"Any luck on the third name?"

"Oh, yes. Almost forgot. Glad you reminded me. Lieutenant Krentz was present at Tehran and Yalta, an official interpreter. I found a reference to a comment by Stalin who publicly chided his own interpreter at the closing session, to the effect that the American interpreter Krentz spoke better Russian than they did English."

"Any photographs of Krentz at Yalta with the others?"

"He appears in the background of two formal shots of the closing ceremonies, and is captioned as Lieutenant John Krentz, US Army Signal Corps."

"In researching the conferences for your book, did you ever run across anything else about Krentz?"

"Nothing other than his presence at official sessions and one remark by Henry Stimson that the team of interpreters performed, in his words, admirably. Of course, you wouldn't expect much publicity or exposure. After all, interpreters are supposed to be discreet and fade into the background."

Newlin paused, then proceeded. "One rather odd photograph, though. Actually, two photographs."

"Odd how?"

"Well, I have a large collection, pretty much everything taken at every session, and some candid shots of delegates and staff on the grounds of the Livadia Palace. People smoking on the walkways or on the lawn in small groups during breaks from sessions. The Livadia Palace has four distinct façades from which to enter and depart. The design was a whim of the czar who had it built. Two photos show Stalin and his entourage emerging from one façade on their way to the façade where the conferences are staged. Their path took them on a walk that led around the building ninety degrees. It's obviously morning. While a dozen aides surround Stalin, two more are lagging behind by several steps, oblivious to the camera, deep in conversation, the taller of the two leaning down as if to catch the words of the shorter man.

"Here's what's strange. One you can identify as a Russian major, from his shoulder boards; the other, the shorter man, a lieutenant. The major's uniform bears a number of decorations, suggesting he is a veteran of significant combat. The lieutenant, who appears to be in his twenties, is relatively undecorated, but wears a patch over his right eye and is on crutches."

"I don't understand. What is it that's odd?"

"Sometime after the conference, someone present identified the taller man as Colonel Machentirov. There's no identification of the younger Russian officer."

"I'm not sure where you're going with this."

"Sorry it's taking me so long to get to the point. The younger Russian officer, despite the eye patch, looks the spitting image of an American interpreter who appears in several pictures at Yalta. A Lieutenant John Krentz."

Hardy's 'Wall of Fame' shows a picture of him alone with Roosevelt at Yalta! But he's not part of the official party? Who would fail to list someone who has access to the president? And if Krentz was there, how could Hardy fail to notice someone front and center at the sessions? And why not tell me he knew Krentz when I told him about the background investigation? He can't have forgotten. He never forgets anything. I wonder if he knew the late and most mysterious Handy? And what's this resemblance of Russian officers in Stalin's shadow with Hardy and Krentz? This, I have to ask Hardy.

The previous afternoon, Ben had an appointment at the Army Records Center at the Pentagon. There, he'd badged the captain in charge of providing access to military personnel and was quickly shown to a microfiche reader.

There was one for each letter of the alphabet. Settling in

front of the screen, Ben didn't have far to scroll, with personnel listed in descending alphabetical order.

Passing Habicht, a dozen Hallorans, and two Hamdens, he came to Hanft. Too far. Backspacing, he double-checked. No Handy. He scrolled further. No Hendy. No Hindy. No Hundley. Back and forth, no Handley. No Hansley. No Hensley.

Try Handel. Handle. Handler. Even Chandler. Nothing.

Gaining permission to move to other microfiche readers, Ben scrolled past Chandy. Chanley. On and on. Then to the next machine. No Tandy, Sandy, Landy.

I remember Krentz's high school teacher—Landy. He identified a Jay Handy checking Krentz for a clearance in 1943. Handy existed then. Does he exist now?

CHAPTER TWENTY-NINE

Dead Drop

The barnyard was filled with vehicles; New Jersey State Police patrol cars and several unmarked sedans sporting multiple aerials that were obviously for the brass. Oliver approached a crime scene tape and badged the officer controlling entrance.

"Wait one moment, please, Agent Oliver."

Almost instantly, a large, bear-like figure strode toward him. Colonel Norman Schwarzkopf, commandant of the New Jersey State Police, said, "Good morning, Agent Oliver. What brings you here?"

A legendary World War I soldier, Schwarzkopf had retired from the military police and had been, for many years, retained by five New Jersey governors as the state's top law enforcement officer—"New Jersey's Hoover," read the descriptions following his press conference quotes in the *Newark Star Ledger*.

Over the course of various background investigations, Oliver had met Colonel Schwarzkopf. Not often, but when he routinely visited the NJTP's "Red Squad" to check on whether the subject of his investigations was cited in their files, when a name came up positive or "pink," the clerks always referred him to Schwarzkopf, who would call for the file, read it in his presence, and then decide how much to tell him. The colonel had some notoriety in the press, and had been involved in investigating the kidnapping of the Lindbergh baby in 1932.

Like Hoover, Colonel Schwarzkopf had a bulldog appearance, and that was accompanied by bulk. He looked like, and was, a big, tough guy. He stared down Oliver.

"I'm here to see Alvin Root," Oliver said. He assumed Schwarzkopf would think it was for Army business. "What's happened here? Is he under arrest?"

Schwarzkopf responded abruptly. "No. Follow me."

Oliver ducked under the tape. As they marched across the barnyard, Schwarzkopf fired questions at him.

"When did you see Root last?" Before Oliver could answer, "What do you want with him?" Then, "Is he still on the Army's shit list?"

As they marched, Oliver responded, "I talked with him two days ago. Arranged to do a follow-up interview with him today. Just cleaning up some details from his case."

Schwarzkopf had been informed of Root's case and his dishonorable discharge. Undoubtedly, Root's name, now a New Jersey civilian, had gone into the Red Squad files.

They arrived at the foot of the silo. "Did you climb up here with Root in the last week?"

"No, I talked with him on the phone yesterday. He said he was getting ready to paint the interior of the silo. I said I'd drive up to see him. Some follow-up questions."

"Follow me."

They clambered up the welded metal steps, the ladder on the outside of the silo. Twenty-four feet up, they arrived at the open top. A row of welded steps on the inside matched those on the outside, leading down to the silo floor.

Root lay splayed on the floor, attended by two policemen and a civilian taking his photograph from different angles—the medical examiner or coroner.

"He fell?"

Schwarzkopf gave him a sour look. "There are fingerprints on the steps that aren't his. I'm inclined to think he was encouraged over the edge. Given a push. So he couldn't talk with anyone anymore, including you."

"Maybe a helper's prints?"

"Unlikely. The neighbor says he was working alone. Thinks he was working alone."

Working alone? As in working alone with the Russians, or with his missing girlfriend Natalie? The Russians had no need to kill him. He wasn't worth it to them. A one-time fling, sadly for Root, of little intelligence value. And yet, they had paid him, essentially for dross. And now this.

They climbed down. Schwarzkopf asked Oliver to provide details on his last meeting with Root to a police stenographer and listened as he did so.

As Oliver finished, Schwarzkopf's gruff voice took over. "So, what do you think happened here, Agent Oliver?"

"I think he fell. He was a dopey kid. Not very smart. Probably not paying attention." *His silence shouldn't be of any value to the Russians. None.*

"Well, another day, another tragedy."

"Too true." As Ben left, he turned back to Schwarzkopf. "Congratulations, Colonel. I heard Norman Jr. received an appointment to West Point."

"That he did," the colonel replied proudly. "The next Schwarzkopf, ready to carry the colors."

As he approached the turnpike entrance, Ben stopped and went to the coin dispenser, and loaded up on quarters for the phone booth by the toll plaza. When he reached the Institute for Defense Analysis, he asked for Chris Iverson, the security officer, his regular contact there. In response to his question, Iverson chuckled.

"Ben, John Krentz is one well-connected officer on the rise. This afternoon he received orders releasing him from Fort Dix. Amazing, given he's maybe the only senior officer in the Army with a directive to travel. He came by here to get something from his temporary office. He was in and out of here in under five minutes."

"Any idea where he is headed?"

"I asked him. His response, with a small smile, was it was top secret."

In minutes, Ben rang Bonnie Ellison's doorbell.

"Hi, Bonnie."

"Hello, Ben. Looking for John? You just missed him. He left an hour ago."

"I know. He asked me to come by a pick up some stuff from his workbench in the garage. He was running late and asked me to grab stuff and save him some time."

"Well, all right. But he did pack a lot of things in the Porsche before he left. Blankets. A parka and an overcoat. Two thermos bottles." She led him through the hallway to the internal garage door.

Inside the garage, it took him no time at all. His eyes swept the workbench. There was a small gap. Along with John Krentz and his pristine Porsche, all the remaining keytainers were gone.

CHAPTER THIRTY

Tehran Conference

Tehran, Iran
November 28 - Dec 1, 1943

On November 26, advance parties from the three participating nations—the United States, Great Britain and Russia—arrived in Tehran and met to review the logistics for the conference set to start in two days once Roosevelt, Churchill, and Stalin had arrived.

Representing the US Army's Signals Corps was Captain Jay Handy, a tall and lean officer in his 40s with a precise bearing. He conveyed an aura of quiet competence; the appearance of a natural leader. Having arrived a day earlier, he was dressed in a neatly pressed uniform, in marked contrast to his Russian and British counterparts who came directly to the Soviet embassy, which had been agreed to as the conference setting.

As the advance staff reviewed the logistics, the need to find housing for various personnel became apparent, as all three embassies would be filled to overflowing with the visiting teams of military aides and diplomatic officers supporting their leaders.

The Russian advance leader proposed that, as each country's translators and interpreters would have to work closely together, they should share a single housing unit. Captain Handy quickly agreed, stating the Canadian embassy, just three buildings away from the Russian embassy, had volunteered to house up to twelve attendees.

"Why not set up a billet there so the translators could get to know each other, become more familiar with their individual styles? I myself will also serve as a reserve translator, as I speak Russian."

All sides concurred. Later that day, four translators from

each nation arrived and were directed to their shared quarters.

CHAPTER THIRTY-ONE

Fancy Footwork

Captain Handy leaned over the back seat to speak to the driver.

"Sergeant Grant, see if you can pull up to the front of the embassy circle and then move about two car lengths past the entrance. See the cobblestones in the roadway right in front of the path to the door? Just past them so the Russians, who should be right behind us, will park right on the cobbles."

"Roger, sir."

The team of American interpreters was just approaching the front walk of the embassy when the massive Russian Zil braked to a stop behind Handy's car. Exiting the rear door, a slim young man in civilian clothes offered a hand to a young woman, helping her out of the Zil. She took several steps, lurched, and would have fallen had it not been for the attentive young man, who seized her arm. Both looked down to see one of the young woman's shoes off her foot, its heel stuck in the uneven cracks between the cobbled drive.

He gallantly sought to retrieve the shoe, wrenching it from the crack. The heel gave way, partially separating from the shoe, twisted at a slight angle. The young woman put the shoe back on her foot and gingerly walked into the embassy, supported by the young man's arm. The rest of the delegation silently followed, the driver bringing along the team's four suitcases.

Witnessing the scene from fifty feet away, Handy turned to a young woman in the group who caught his silent signal and acknowledged it with a brief nod. She turned to their driver at the open trunk, fetched out an over-sized handbag, looped it over her shoulder and led the team into the building, trailing the Russians by a hundred paces. Ahead, she could see the Russian woman hobbling along, favoring the undamaged shoe on her other foot.

Leave it to Handy, she thought. *Recruiting cobblestones to create an opportunity. This is going to be fun!*

CHAPTER THIRTY-TWO

The Interpreters Meet

Escorted by a cultural affairs attaché, Signals Corps Captain Handy escorted his US team of three interpreters into a conference room in the Canadian embassy. Around the table sat a Russian Army officer and three others in civilian clothing—two men and a woman, all appearing to be in their early twenties.

The attaché began. "Please join the others at the table. Welcome to the Canadian embassy. On behalf of Ambassador Everitt, it's our pleasure to provide you with hospitality during the upcoming conference, which we recognize as of vast importance…"

As the attaché continued on in embassy-speak, Handy examined the visages and reactions of the Russians. They sat expressionless as the attaché murmured on.

Handy readily identified two of the four Russians, matching them to the intelligence he had gleaned before the conference. About the youngest Russian male and the young woman sitting next to him, Handy had no prior information. But he remembered his briefing files. *Kosarov, likely KGB, identified as embassy attaché in Paris in the 1930s, observed regularly in Moscow at Soviet receptions and conferences, but not in the role of interpreter.*

"After this meeting, I will show you to your accommodations here in the embassy. But first, let me suggest we go around the table and have each of us introduce ourselves."

At this came a glower from the Russian obviously in charge, but no dissent.

"I will begin. As you know, I am Phillip Thackeray, born in Toronto, graduated from McGill University in International Studies. I joined the Diplomatic Corps eleven years ago, and this is my third posting. Been here about four months. Previously, I served in South Africa, and before that, in Aruba. I speak English, French, Spanish, and a small amount of Russian. And here in Persia, I am rapidly learning Farsi. Should any of you wish to see something of Tehran while here, I am happy to show you the sights. The highlights, as it were." Thackeray turned, smiling at the Russian. "Mr. Kosarov, how about you start for your side?"

"I am Ivan Kosarov, Team Leader of the USSR Translation Team." He looked mildly annoyed.

Unruffled, Thackeray pressed on. "Perhaps a little more about yourself, Team Leader Kosarov?"

"I have Russian, of course; Mandarin, Cantonese, English. No Farsi."

Thackeray: "And where else have you served Russia as an interpreter?"

Kosarov: "For various directorates in Russia."

Giving up on getting more, Thackeray moved to the younger man on the Russian team, nodding at him. The young man quickly looked at Kosarov, who gave him a curt nod.

"I am Evgeny Nolikin, from Moscow. A graduate of the Soviet Language School, with English, French, and German. I have translated at conferences among the Allies since a year ago."

Handy made mental notes. *Twenty-five to twenty-seven, slight in build, 5'10", maybe 140 pounds. Fair hair, blue eyes that show some intelligence. Obviously wary of Kosarov. Impression: Newly assigned to Kosarov's unit. Like so many Russians, terrified of saying or doing the wrong thing. Unlikely to be in intelligence.*

Surprising Thackeray, Kosarov, and the entire table, he continued, gesturing to his right.

"And this is my fiancée, Svetlana Orlova, a fellow graduate of the Soviet Language School. We were teamed together at school and then in our assignments in Moscow, where we have an apartment."

Thackeray turned to the young woman who was looking down and blushing.

Twenty-four to twenty-six; 5'6", trim, light-brown hair, blue eyes; hard to assess her figure beneath classic Russian sackcloth tunic wardrobe. Surprises me. She is no mouse. What's the attraction to the milk toast Nolikin?

"Welcome, Miss Orlova. And you speak…?"

"I have Russian, Polish, English, and Spanish."

"And German, as does your husband-to-be?"

She blushed "Yes."

Thank you, Thackeray. You're doing my work for me, thought Handy.

"And you grew up where, Miss Orlova?"

"Just outside Moscow."

The attaché moved on to the last Russian, a stocky, swarthy man in his forties.

"I am Victor Shermets, from Leningrad. Also of the Language School. English, also German."

Also a liar. You were Cultural Attaché Alexei Prokov in Amsterdam, where you spoke Dutch and French with ease. KGB all the way. What cultural attaché is not? A.K.A. Leonid Gogol in Madrid, where you managed quite well in Spanish. I make you out to be the KGB watchdog in the group—except that spot's already filled by Kosarov. Must be doubling up? Do they have doubts about Nolikin and Orlova? Or do they need an extra hand for some spying at the conference?

Thackeray, continuing to carry Handy's water, asked, "And your postings, *Gospodin* Shermets?"

"Mostly Moscow."

Thackeray smiled. "And now, our American interpreters." As he turned toward Handy, Shermets, to his discredit, actually leaned toward them as if to catch them out.

"I am Captain James Handy, US Army Signal Corps, leading the US interpreter's team. From study at the Army Language School, I have German, French, and Russian." He smiled. "Alas, no Farsi."

Kosarov interrupted. "And where have you served, Signals Captain Handy?"

"Just about everywhere. US, Army posts in the US, in France during World War I. Now in Washington."

"Never in Russia?" inquired Kosarov. "You seem familiar to me. Perhaps in Moscow?"

Handy grinned. "Always wanted to visit Moscow. Admirable architecture, I hear."

Thackeray intervened. Turned to the young man to Handy's left.

"I am Lieutenant John Krentz, also US Army Signal Corps. I am from New Jersey, went to college there, then entered the Army and was posted to the Language School. I have Russian, German, and French. This is my first assignment at an international conference."

Kosarov, too, made his mental notes. *Twenty-four or twenty-five, six feet, sandy hair, brown eyes, 180 pounds, looks like an athlete. Doesn't seem at all cowed or impressed by his surroundings.*

In Russian: "I trust you will put your study of Russian to good use this week. How extensive is your Russian vocabulary?"

Krentz replied briskly in Russian. "I have read and can recite from many of the Russian classics—Pushkin, Gogol, Tergenev. I expect to be able to capture the essence of your delegation's remarks throughout the conference."

Thackeray laughed. "All Greek to me, I'm afraid." He resumed and finished up with the two other American team members. Then, with a twinkle in his eye, he closed the meeting.

"Now, before I show you to your quarters, I suggest you all exchange a few words with each of your fellow interpreters, get to know each other just a little bit better. After all, you'll be working side by side, nonstop, over the next few days."

Everyone stood. Thackeray immediately corralled Kosarov and Shermets. As if on cue, the American interpreters stepped over to the young Russian interpreters, and extended handshakes.

In Russian, Captain Handy spoke to them both. "Let us strive for a successful outcome as we translator for our country's leaders."

As Nolikin assented and began to respond, John Krentz

turned to Svetlana Orlova and took her hand. "Congratulations on your engagement! When do you and Interpreter Nolikin plan to marry?"

Orlova blushed again. "Oh, we haven't set the date yet. So much to do so soon. It is not yet convenient."

"Well, these things work out. It's not every day that you are sent to interpret for the three most powerful leaders in the world."

"It is quite an honor."

"Have you interpreted for Moscow leaders before? Secretary Stalin perhaps?"

"No. But I have heard him speak when I was translating at a meeting of Soviet republics. He is most impressive."

"A Russian committee needs a translator? I would think everyone in attendance spoke Russian."

"Not on that particular occasion."

Thackeray rounded up the interpreters and herded them out of the room and to their assigned rooms on the upper floors of the embassy.

As he saw Handy, the last of them, to his room, Handy beckoned him inside, out of the hallway, and closed the door.

"Many thanks, Phillip. You were very good at drawing them out."

"Think nothing of it, Handy. That's what diplomats do."

Spies, too.

• • •

There was the usual milling around in the hallway as people and bags found their rooms. Svetlana Orlova and Evgeny Nolikin turned at the approach of Roberta Green.

"Excuse me, Miss Orlova. I am Roberta Green, a transcriber. We noticed that you damaged your shoe outside on the cobblestones. Lieutenant Krentz and I."

"Yes?" asked a quizzical Orlova.

Roberta smiled at the Russians. "Well, Lieutenant Krentz thought that your shoe size and mine look about the same, and I have an extra pair of shoes you might like to borrow. It's not likely you can get yours repaired overnight here in Tehran."

Reaching into her voluminous handbag, she extracted a pair of low-heeled pumps, and offered them to Orlova.

"But how will I return them to you?"

"In two days, at the end of the conference. Your damaged shoe will likely be repaired by then."

After looking down the hallway and not seeing Kosarov, Evgeny stepped forward and accepted the offered shoes. "You are very kind, Miss Green. Thank you."

Orlova softly echoed Nolikin, "Thank you."

An American officer looking at my feet? Guessing my shoe size? What is that all about?

Slipping the offered American shoes on her feet and holding her damaged pair in her hand, she and Nolikin turned, entered their room, and closed the door.

CHAPTER THIRTY-THREE

In a Persian Garden

Shortly before midnight, Handy knocked softly on Krentz's door. When he opened it, Handy pointed to Krentz's pajamas. "Either change or put some clothes over those. We're going for a short walk."

They exited the embassy's rear door into a walled garden and crunched along the moonlit gravel path that circled it. The spice aromas of the Orient washed the nighttime air around them.

At the farthest point from the embassy, Handy gestured to a bench. "Lean in. No sense in being overheard if there's anyone out there in the dark."

"What's up?"

"Report back from queries to the Moscow military attaché. I just decoded it now. Are you ready for a shocker?"

"Come on, Captain. It's past midnight."

"Svetlana Orlova, nicknamed Lana, is very connected in Mother Russia. She is the youngest child of Gennedy Orlov, a longtime member of the politburo."

"And that explains why she gets this plum assignment. How about Evgeny?"

"Evidently, what privileges she gets, he gets. Looks like Daddy blesses the coming union."

"You'd think a heavyweight like Orlov would encourage a union with a more dynamic suitor. Someone in Stalin's circle or a KGB up-and-comer."

"Well, as the saying goes, love is strange. Maybe she's found something in Nolikin we don't see?" Handy laughed and shook his head. "Or maybe it's our own macho military egos telling us she'd be much better off with the likes of us."

Krentz gave Handy a look that could have meant "indeed she would."

"So what's next?"

"I want you to be attentive to both the lovebirds, and see what you can learn about Daddy's daughter and her husband-to-be. Particularly her husband-to-be. It's hard to believe Nolikin's anything but an interpreter. He certainly doesn't walk , talk, or act like a spy."

CHAPTER THIRTY-FOUR

Eggs with FDR

November 1943, American Embassy, Tehran

"Good morning, the illusive and mysterious Jay Handy," boomed the president. FDR sat at the breakfast table and beckoned Handy to join him. "You're looking sharp today in civilian clothes. I'm surprised you're not in uniform for this shindig."

"Keeping a lower profile. Don't want the Russian security folks worrying about this particular military man."

"I get it. So how is your personnel project going?"

"Still in the early stages, but looking good, sir. Very promising."

Handy paused, causing FDR to look up.

"Don't be coy. You look like the cat that swallowed the canary. Tell your president what tickles you so."

Conspiratorially, Handy drew his chair closer. "Last night, after the dinner speeches and all the toasts, there was a moment when Secretary Stalin beckoned to the Russian interpreter, a young woman he knows, signaling her to come up to his table. She takes a few steps and he waves at her, points to our interpreter, Krentz, who had been seated to her right, indicates he wants them both up there. They chat for a few minutes, mostly Stalin and Krentz, and they return to their seats. The head interpreter Kosarov looks in a panic. Can't figure out what happened. You know how paranoid the Russians are."

"So I'm told. And what was the conversation about?"

"Krentz reports that Stalin wanted to know where he'd learned his Russian. Swore he heard him speak at first that Krentz was Russian-born. Said it was the first time he'd ever heard an American speak Russian perfectly."

"How amusing! Your man, getting high marks from

Russia's biggest cheese."

"Well, it does bode well for what we have in mind for him."

"And that is?"

"I think I'd like to have him sit in on another conversation with Stalin again. One where we control the subjects discussed."

"And how do you propose to pull off a feat like that, the devious Captain Handy?"

"Mister President, you'll be the second to know."

CHAPTER THIRTY-FIVE

Departure

Tehran, December 1943

Tehranis awoke to a sunlit morning. Awakening the conference delegates were the calls to prayer broadcast from loudspeakers mounted on the minarets.

The conference had ended. Stalin, Churchill, and Roosevelt had departed, their personal staffs shepherding them away. Remaining were those from the three Allied nations who would pack up the respective governments' paraphernalia and disband the logistics for the conference. Among them were the interpreters, emerging from their assigned wing of the embassy into the Italianate courtyard shaded by colonnades and palm trees.

Three Jeeps—Lend Lease had provided thousands to the Russians—awaited the interpreters and their luggage. A Russian soldier leaped from each driver's seat to relieve the interpreters of their luggage, and began to stack the suitcases in the back of their vehicles.

Evgeny Nolikin and Svetlana Orlova approached Captain Handy, who was overseeing the Americans' departure.

"Excuse me, Captain."

Handy turned to Nolikin. "Good morning, Mister Nolikin. Beautiful day for a departure."

"Ah, yes. We're looking forward to returning to Moscow."

"And good morning to you, Miss Orlova."

They stood awkwardly, looking around.

Handy asked, "How may I help you?"

"We're looking for Miss Green."

"I'm afraid you've missed her. She is traveling with President Roosevelt."

Orlova stepped forward. "She was kind enough to lend me a

pair of shoes at the beginning of the conference and I wish to return them to her." She offered a soft bag to Handy.

"Tell you what. I think Lieutenant Krentz is your man. He'll see her long before I do." He turned and called out to Krentz, who was handing luggage to the driver. "Lieutenant, please join us."

Krentz stepped over to Handy and the Russians, and shook hands, first with Nolikin, then with Orlova. Shyly, she explained the need to return the borrowed shoes.

"I'd be happy to deliver them to her in Washington as soon as we get there."

Orlova started to hand the soft bag to Krentz, but it began to slip from her grasp as she again seemed to slip on the cobblestone driveway. Krentz deftly caught the bag. Gripping her arm, he steadied her on her feet. Blushing, she thanked him, murmuring, not really looking at him, and it was left to Nolikin to repeat the thanks for the favor.

Krentz squared up. "It was a pleasure to work with both of you. Perhaps we'll work together at another conference."

Nolikin agreed. They shook hands again, and he led the awkward Orlova to their jeep.

The Russian jeep pulled out first, moving out of the palace grounds followed by the British. Climbing into the back of their jeep, Handy looked at the seated Krentz, who held the soft shoe bag.

"Better check the bag, John. For a microphone or a bomb."

Krentz looked. "Just shoes. But ah, a note." He took it from the envelope and read: "Thank you for your kindness."

"That's it? Not addressed? Just thank you for your kindness?" As the jeep got underway, Handy observed: "You can't have everything. But on the whole, I'd say the shoe ploy was a big success."

CHAPTER THIRTY-SIX

The Pianist

Fort Belvoir, Maryland
December 19, 1943

"Did my good friend Frankl send you?" The large, shambling man smiled broadly, leaped up from a table laden with enough food for four, and extended his hand. "I am Haenfstengl. Call me Putzi! Frank and I were at Harvard together. Class of 1903!"

As Handy shook Haenfstengl's hand, the he introduced himself and his colleague. "I'm Captain Handy and this is my aide, Lieutenant Keller."

"Have some lunch," boomed Ernst Franz Sedgwick Haenfstengl, one-time Hitler confidant, Harvard graduate, and now prisoner of war, turned over by the British and on loan to the U.S. government.

The Roosevelt Administration had commissioned a noted psychiatrist, Walter G. Langer, to compile a psychological profile of Hitler for use in predicting his behavior as the tides of war changed in the Allies' favor, and *der Führer* was put on the defensive.

Langer had briefed Handy, describing the large, flabby, self-indulgent Haenfstengl as a wealthy, coddled dilettante who had gone from financing the publication of *Mein Kampf* to becoming one of Hitler's inner circle. Hitler's "piano player" sneered at his detractors. Putzi had always been the life of the party. With an American mother married to a German art dealer with galleries in Berlin, Paris, and New York, Putzi spent his time as a college undergraduate composing music and orchestrating on-field routines for the Harvard Marching Band.

Years later, as a Hitler acolyte, he'd recycled his music and love of pageantry into the Nazi Party's vivid military parades, vast Wagnerian choruses, and Nuremburg extravaganzas. Like many early Nazi adherents, he'd fallen from favor, fled to England, and was now singing for the psychiatrists. Despite his buffoonery, Haenfstengl 's close observations of Hitler for 14 years had contributed some useful insights into the Langer Report.

Handy led Putzi to believe he and his assistant were part of the Langer team, and yes, he brought greetings from President Roosevelt.

"I haven't seen him since our days around the piano at the Harvard Club in New York in the early 1920s. You tell him to arrange for me to get out of here and come for dinner at the White House. I'm sure he has a piano there. You know, I once introduced Hitler to one of the Bechstein daughters. But they made no music together. Pffft."

At Haenfstengl's invitation, they sat at the table and talked while he ate most of the food on it. They were following up on some history, some questions, Handy said. The affable Putzi regaled them with story after story, plunging into mammoth detail.

"In the early days, before he became chancellor, I even showed Hitler how to be discreet when dealing with conspiratorial matters." Putzi rambled on with little prompting, occasionally breaking away from his narrative about Southern Germany, interjecting vignettes to show his visitors how close to Roosevelt he was, and how he looked forward to a reunion with "my fellow Harvard alumnus."

Finally, with the food consumed and Haenfstengl winding down, they took their leave.

"Tell Frank I await his call!" Putzi cried gaily.

In the parking lot, Handy turned to the young lieutenant. "Jackpot. It was worth the bombast and bullshit after all. What did you get?"

"At least four ideal locations for dead drops in Munich. A couple of possible safe houses. And the names of dozens of Nazi flunkies who are cut from the same cloth as Putzi. They're in it for the takings, not the politics. Perfect for recruitment."

"And your tape recorder was running the whole time?"

"On all cylinders."

"Maybe you can play some of it for Putzi's good friend Frank."

"The very next time he pipes me on board the Sequoia for cocktails."

The things I do for the smallest scraps of intelligence. This buffoon is typical of what's wrong with Germany. People of his standing, with all manner of money, fall in love with a rabble-rousing politician and they practically handed him the chancellorship! God help us if that ever happens here.

• • •

"I just have a hunch that Stalin is not that kind of a man ... I think that if I give him everything I possibly can and ask for nothing from him in return, noblesse oblige, he won't try to annex anything and will work with me for a world of democracy and peace."

— Franklin Delano Roosevelt, 1943

• • •

CHAPTER THIRTY-SEVEN

Boat Building

October 20, 1944
Lake Hopatcong, New Jersey

"Okay, here's the challenge," said Handy. "There's a five-story building on the sloping banks of a 100-yard-wide river that freezes solid in the winter. The building has guards on the main floor at the lobby's front door to inspect any authorized visitors, but no patrols on the river side. I have a team that can gain access to the building to remove a document by rappelling up the rear of the building to the roof at night, preferably while it's snowing. They can get in and out in about twenty minutes. What I need is a way to get them to the building and away from it on the ice. Can you design a simple, two-man iceboat that I can build on the spot?"

Charlie Grant, retired Army Master Sergeant and iceboat builder, scratched his head. "How sturdy?"

"It only has to last for one night, but it has to bring a crew of two from two miles away, and then take them back two miles."

Charlie pointed to a black-and-white photo on the wall of his garage. "You could do it with a rig like this one." The photo showed a 10x15 box mounted on runners with a single mast and triangular sail. "Pretty basic."

"Can you make a set of runners for me and provide a sail and tack if I provide the box?"

"Sure. Runners like these?" Grant pointed to an iceboat on a trailer in the garage bay.

"A little shorter. Maybe two feet shorter."

"I have a set I can cut down for you."

"And the mast and sail?"

"Pretty standard. Mast about twelve feet."

"Too high. Have to negotiate under two arched stone

bridges crossing the river. No more than ten feet clearance off the ice."

"The shorter the mast, the smaller the sail, the slower you go."

"Speed is not an issue. Being able to slide up the river and beach on the bank is what I need. It's plenty windy at night, usually fifteen to twenty miles an hour."

"When do you want the runners and sail rig?"

"As soon as I can get them. I've got to ship them and need two weeks to get them there."

"Where's there?"

CHAPTER THIRTY-EIGHT

On the Neva

November 12, 1944, Leningrad

The militia captain followed the bank down to the river. At the edge where the bank met the river ice, there were two deep gouges, parallel and three feet apart, some six feet long. The falling snow, falling for an hour, had lightly covered the frozen river, but the grooves on the bank had not yet been filled in.

A night watchman, a resident of the apartment house across the river, had called it in at 2:30 a.m. Returning from his shift, he'd looked out the window at the snow and had seen a dark, blocky shape on the far bank, below the five-story Archive Depository building. *Looks like a small construction shed.*

After showering and brewing some tea, he looked again. Even though the snow was increasing, he could see the shape was gone. *How does a construction shed get up and leave on its own?* He picked up the phone.

While he waited, he finished his tea, then uncorked a bottle of vodka to further warm himself, as the apartment building superintendent regularly turned off the heat at night. Ten minutes later, the militia had arrived at his apartment door. He led them to his window, pointed to the far bank of the Neva, and told them what he'd seen.

The captain wrote in a notebook, requisitioned the vodka bottle, and took the stairs to the ground floor. From his window, the nightshift worker watched the militiamen cross the river on the ice.

The militia captain's crew of three found two sets of footprints going up the bank to the back of the Archive Depository, and the same set returning. No, the nightshift worker had not seen anyone. Who would choose to go out on a night like this? It was twelve degrees and the wind was blowing steadily along the Neva. It felt like zero.

The captain and crew walked around to the front of the depository, which faced one of the most famous avenues in Leningrad, *Dvortsovaya Naberezhnaya,* the Palace Embankment. Along its length lay the palaces of the czars, including the Hermitage, which could be discerned through the snow, some three hundred yards away.

The two depository guards responded to the militia pounding on the front door. Lights came on. The militia trooped in. No, they had had no incidents. Had no visitors. Had heard nothing.

The militia captain insisted on a floor by floor search of the building. Two hours later, finding nothing missing, nothing awry, they returned to the river, its icy surface now swathed in two inches of snow.

The captain had requested a broom from the depository guards. He instructed one of his men to sweep the entire path of original footprints from the river to the base of the depository. At the base of the foundation, the snow was discolored. Yellowish.

The captain reached into the outer pocket of his greatcoat and found the vodka bottle. Uncorking it, he took a long pull, then passed it among his crew. Shivering, he muttered, "No report. Probably some drunks. Including our caller."

Within moments they had departed, and in a few more, their footprints and the two unexplained grooves on the banks of the Neva had been obliterated by the snow.

CHAPTER THIRTY-NINE

The Hero Buys the Drinks

November 20, 1944, Moscow

The young soldier shook his head, chased away the vodka-induced cobwebs, cleared his vision. Yes, he saw it.

"Sergei, look! At the bar. Look at the medal!"

The two men gazed at the officer standing at the bar with a medal hung on a ribbon at his throat. He held a glass and surveyed the smoke-shrouded room. Spying the two young soldiers, he lifted his glass toward them, and a bottle of vodka. A toast. An invitation?

Mikhail clambered to his feet and beckoned toward their table and its third chair. The hero strode over, vigorously shook their hands, and boomed, "Comrades! Join me in a toast to the *Rodina!*"

Glasses filled to the brim, the young men downed their drinks.

"I am Vasily Krenev. And you? Who are you? Where do you serve?"

The young men quickly identified themselves and their unit.

"Sergei Bulov, Third Infantry."

"Petr Sertin, Third Infantry, sir."

"Don't 'sir' me. I am Vasily."

Awed, they fell into a conversation, Vasily asking them to recount where they'd served, which front, learning they were on a brief leave from their unit and due to return the next day.

How often does a conscript like me meet a Hero of the Soviet Union, thought Sergei as Vasily refilled his glass.

"Here, Petr. Don't fall behind." Vodka poured to the rim.

Four hours later, Sergei awoke, shivering, in the dark.

Where am I? he thought. He rose and immediately stumbled over someone lying next to him. It was Petr, coming awake, aware of the cold. He looked down and found himself in his underwear. In the dim light, he saw that he was in what appeared to be a room filled with crates of empty bottles. *Must be the storeroom behind the bar*. He looked down at Petr, who was also in his underwear.

"Petr, we must get dressed and get out of here."

"What happened? Why are we here?"

"We must have had too much vodka. I think they let us sleep it off here in the back room."

"Well, let's get dressed and get out of here."

They looked around for their uniforms, but they were not in the room. Sticking his head out into the bar, Sergei saw that it was early morning, and just a few patrons remained in the usually crowded room. He called to the bartender, who came over to him.

"Where are our uniforms?"

The bartender shrugged. "The colonel took them to be cleaned. He said he would return with them this morning, but he hasn't shown up yet."

Sitting in the storeroom in their underwear, drinking coffee and nursing their hangovers, Sergei and Petr waited for another two hours. Then they asked the bartender for the phone and called their unit. Within a half hour, one of their mates showed up with fresh uniforms.

"What happened to you idiots?"

Sergei rubbed his unshaven jaw. "Don't ask me why, but a Hero of the Soviet Union stole our uniforms."

CHAPTER FORTY

Intelligence Briefing

December 12, 1944
Warm Springs, Georgia

"How are you feeling, Mr. President?"

Immersed in the sulfur pool, Franklin Roosevelt looked up, and his trademark smile lit his face. "Handy, you old codger! You've come to cheer me up, I hope."

His visitor disrobed and slid into the steaming water. The two shook hands.

"So, you received my summons. I wasn't sure where in the world you were," the president said.

"Wild Bill asked me to help him sort out some folks in the Balkans. They were supposed to be giving the Germans fits, but they preferred to squabble among themselves."

"So, what did you do?"

"I promoted the leader causing the most trouble. Gave him a title, some money, and moved him to Zagreb. Problem solved."

"You make it sound too easy. I'm sure there was more to it than that. Here, crank that thing and get me out of this boiling pot before I turn into a white prune."

Roosevelt nodded to a contraption with a crank mounted on the pool's edge. Handy climbed out, turned the handle, and slowly the president rose out of the water, still seated in a metal chair. Handy handed him a towel. Instantly, an orderly appeared with more towels and with terry robes for both men.

Dried and toweled, an orderly pushed the president's wheelchair into a glass-in sun room. Handy followed.

The president spoke to the his Filipino steward. "Juan, please bring us some lemonade. Handy, make yourself comfortable."

He sat on a rattan sofa next to the president, who lit a

cigarette.

"So, how much of your time do I have?"

"As much as you want. The war's progressing nicely without me right now," Handy replied.

"Good. I want your very quiet advice on a major decision I'm going to have to make as soon as the war is over—and that could be by June."

Juan returned with a pitcher of lemonade and a tray with two glasses, then withdrew.

"Captain, as soon as the war is ended, I'm going to shut down Bill Donovan and the OSS. And I'm going to replace it with a new intelligence agency. What I want from you is some thinking on how it should be set up, how it should work."

"Why is Donovan walking the plank?"

"A bunch of reasons. He's a damned fine man, done a lot of good. But he's broken a lot of eggs and a few too many balls. If they found him dead in the hallway with a knife in his back, there'd be hundreds of suspects, from the military chiefs to Henry Stimson to Edgar Hoover."

Roosevelt drained his glass. "Bill asks for forgiveness, not permission. And the aforementioned are all permission men. So, whatever he does, he accomplishes with either minimal or zero cooperation from the others. And they begrudge him not only his successes, but his flamboyance. There's a reason they call him Wild Bill."

"Anybody ever fire a Medal of Honor winner?"

"I'll be the first. You must know that I know how to deal with Medal of Honor winners, Captain. Oh, I'll have some sweeteners for him. He won't like it, but I'll do it. But the key isn't shutting down the OSS. It's what comes next. Making sure we get the right organization up and running, and the right people running it. You follow me?"

The captain grinned. "I do. You know me, I'm a lot like Bill Donovan. I'll try wild ideas, and sometimes make them work. You can get away with it in wartime, but once the dust has settled, we'll need an intelligence arm to deal with threats we see coming—like the Russians and those that crop up that, right now, are not even on the horizon."

"Everybody in the so-called intelligence business sees it coming. They're all gearing up to claim the mantle. Stimson, Hoover, a couple of generals, one admiral, one pilot."

"Let me be candid about two of them. Twenty years ago, Henry Stimson made one of the most incredibly stupid decisions about intelligence gathering in the history of the country—perhaps the most stupid—when he shut down the code breakers in 1929."

The president beamed. "Ahh, the Black Chamber. Henry said, 'Gentlemen don't read other gentlemen's mail,' or something to that effect."

"You remember. And as a result, the country was in the dark about who was doing what to whom for a decade, and when we finally woke up, the world had Hitler and we didn't know a damned thing about German rearmament until it was too late and the die was cast."

"And despite it, all these years later, Henry's turned out to be a pretty good diplomat."

"If you say so. Not my bailiwick."

"So, that brings us to the acquisitive Mister Hoover. He wants to manage all post-war intelligence operations. What's your take on him?"

Gathering his thoughts, the captain poured more lemonade for both of them. After a long sip, he said, "In the years ahead, we'll need to understand European, Asian, and Middle Eastern countries a lot better than we do now. Has Mr. Hoover ever set foot outside the United States?"

Roosevelt beamed and they clinked glasses.

"Touché! My sentiments exactly. He is dangerous enough in his current capacity. But he would be a danger to you, me and the entire country if let loose on the world. I'd like to replace him as well as Donovan, but Wild Bill first. All in good time."

"I understand the need for a new centralized intelligence agency once the war is over. But I have an additional idea for you to chew on."

"And that is?"

"Why not hedge your bets and lay the groundwork for a back-up plan for when your new intelligence agency stumbles, lays an egg, or just plain screws up?"

The president looked hard at the captain. "Tell me more."

CHAPTER FORTY-ONE

Livadia Beach

Livadia Beach, Ukraine
December 29, 1944

Emerging from the fog that lay on the surface of the water, the three men paddled their rubber raft toward the shore with oars wrapped in muffling cloth. Making the beach at 0300, they silently dragged the raft up from the edge of the lapping waves and offloaded shovels. No one spoke. One stood watch with a submachine gun as his companions dug a pit six feet deep in the dunes just above the shale beach.

All three manhandled a heavy metal coffin from the raft, lowered it into the grave, and filled it back in. Smoothing the sand around the grave's perimeter, they then took measurements of its location, running a tape measure from a nearby row of palm trees above the dunes, sketching a rough map by hooded flashlight. Within minutes, they were gone, swallowed by the fog.

CHAPTER FORTY-TWO

Yalta Harbor

February 3, 1945, onboard the USS Intrepid
Yalta Harbor on the Black Sea

"You wanted to see me, Captain Handy?"

"Yes, Mr. President."

"Skip the title, soldier. We go back too far."

"Okay, Frank. If you say so."

"I say so. Martini?"

Without waiting for a response, the president wheeled over to a low bar and began filling a cocktail shaker he removed from a small freezer. A film of ice appeared on the shaker, courtesy of immediate exposure to the controlled air onboard the battleship.

Handy looked out the porthole at the Livadia Palace, the spotless grounds marked by three towering palm trees and a vast lawn that swept down to the oceanfront.

Observing him, Roosevelt asked, "Know anything about that pile?"

"Two things. One, that Czar Alexander had it built, but his grandson Nicholas was so enamored of Italian architecture, he tore down the original and rebuilt it from the ground up—all eighty-one rooms—in 1911. Krasnov was the architect."

The president wheeled over to deliver the drink. "Here, try this. Five parts gin, one-half part vermouth, one-half part small olive. And the second thing?"

"The Russians have wired the entire place. You will not be able to have a private conversation anywhere in the building except in the Russian suites, and maybe not even there. The damned palm trees are probably riddled with microphones to catch anyone talking on the lawn."

"Verdict?"

Handy took a sip. The martini was superb. "Not strong enough, Frank. You're losing your touch."

Roosevelt flashed his famous grin. "Cheers!"

Handy put down his glass. "Here's the bottom line. The Russians have been working hard for the past ten years, maybe even longer, to penetrate our security, trying to find a way to pry loose intelligence on our intentions, strategies, plans."

"I concede it. I was dead wrong about Stalin last year."

Handy repeated what the president had said just a year ago: "I just have a hunch that Stalin is not that kind of a man ... I think that if I give him everything I possibly can and ask for nothing from him in return, noblesse oblige, he won't try to annex anything and will work with me for a world of democracy and peace."

"That was then. What we know, from our studies, is that the Russians play a long game when it comes to espionage. They plug away at a target nation, someone they think is their enemy—actually, they think everyone is their enemy no matter what the current situation, because ultimately, Stalin and his cadre are all paranoid about Russia's weaknesses—and they are willing to invest ten, fifteen, twenty years to get an agent in place."

"I read what you sent in about Sorge, their man in Japan."

"Perfect case in point. So, here's what is most likely. In the next few months, certainly before June, Germany will be done, and our troops will be nose to nose with the Russians, probably in Berlin."

"Stimson has put together a team to work on how we cut up Germany after the war."

"Stalin will try to get a spy on or around that team, so they can learn what we plan."

"Like another?" The president was already rolling his way back to the cocktail table. "What do they want?"

"In the simplest terms, they will encourage us to break Germany up into seven or eight small states, none capable of defending themselves or ever rising up again as Germany has done twice in this century."

"Cold enough? And our position?"

"Stimson and Morgenthau will go at it. Stimson will argue for a unified Germany, occupied jointly by four powers—Russia, Britain, France, and us—to keep it under control. Morgenthau will push for the seven small states position. Germany goes away, and Russia gets weak little countries on its western border to go with Poland, which they will certainly control."

"Are you suggesting Morgenthau is sympathetic to the Russians?"

"By no means. He is adamant that the Germans never again are a strong nation capable of destroying their neighbors or their Jewish citizens."

"So, how does it come out?"

The president cocked his head. "What do you think, Captain?"

"Germany needs to be a big, unified nation we rebuild as a buffer to the Russians. Otherwise, they'll end up beating down our doors in Boston. We can use the upcoming deliberations to launch a scheme to screw up the Russians and their paranoid desire to embed a spy in our midst."

"And how do you propose to do that?"

"I propose to give them what they want."

A bemused Roosevelt looked over the rim of his glass at Handy. "Which is?"

"Their very own American spy."

Intrigued, the president leaned forward. "Pray tell."

"Because once they have recruited a spy and that spy delivers solid, actionable information, while they continue to recruit many others for gathering low-level intelligence, they have always shown a single-minded focus where they concentrate a huge amount of effort on having that one spy slowly and steadily rise to a position of power. They put a lot of their eggs in one basket. And that is their weakness—over-reliance on one individual."

The president's eyes gleamed. "You are a devious bastard."

"That I am. The better to deal with Stalin and all the paranoid creeps that will succeed him."

"So we do exactly what?"

"We give them the best traitor they ever had."

"Doesn't that mean giving them secret information?"

"You bet it does. Tons of it. But much of it they will get eventually, because as a democracy, we're a sieve. All kinds of stuff gets out. Stupid, sloppy bureaucrats give it away. Newspaper and radio reporters insist on spreading it all over the pages and the airways. But the day will come when we'll need a trusted traitor to give the Russians something huge we want them to have. Information so false that it completely screws them up."

"Ah, disinformation!"

"Better than that. Time and again, the Russians act on information from trusted spies whether it is accurate or not. When they totally believe in the man, they totally accept his reports."

"And you envision..."

"Do you doubt that we are on a collision course with the Russians? That they will be content with what they've won in the war?"

"Oh, I've learned my lesson. They're coming at us, all right."

"Well, when they do, I want them to have a source deep in our government that they can believe one hundred percent. Even when that source is telling them day is night and black is white. We're going to need that, sooner or later. Maybe a few years from now. Maybe sooner."

"How do you propose to do it? To give them their spy?"

"Not a spy. A traitor. I want to help them recruit a young career Army officer. Someone who will rise over time in the Intelligence arm of the military, gaining access to secrets."

"Where and when would you propose to go about it?"

"Where the Russians will be trying hardest very soon."

The president looked at Handy quizzically. "In the very near future, in beautiful downtown Berlin."

"Well, however you plan to fox them, keep me informed."

"Absolutely not. The less you know, the better. And you're not going to know the identity of the agent we pick. All I want from you is a signature on a piece of paper authorizing him to give information to the enemy."

They talked on for a few minutes. Then it was time to go to the conference to meet with Winston Churchill and Joseph Stalin, where it would be agreed to split Germany and Berlin into four occupied zones.

CHAPTER FORTY-THREE

Livadia Inspection

Yalta, the Crimea, February 4, 1945

The middle-aged Russian officer walked up the path to the east façade of the palace at a leisurely pace, his hands clasped behind his back as he looked over the immaculate grounds. Dozens of Russian soldiers were feverishly grooming the landscaping for the conference set to begin the following morning. In his wake, a young Russian lieutenant propelled himself along with the help of a cane. A leather case was slung over his shoulder, slapping at his side with each lurch forward.

As the two of them stepped into the south façade of the palace, a guard snapped to attention when he saw the insignia on the officer's uniform: major general.

"At ease. I am Duganov, from the Inspector General's office." He nodded toward the trailing officer on crutches. "My aide, Lieutenant Rostov."

The guard ogled the trim young man, taking in his eye patch, an empty tunic sleeve pinned neatly to his side, and the medal at his throat—a Hero of the Soviet Union.

"I must examine the apartments for a final security check before the secretary and his party arrive. I have but a few minutes. Please direct me."

Responding to the imperious tone, the guard immediately escorted them deeper into the palace. As they walked, the general interrogated the guard. "I am aware that the Livadia Palace has four distinct façades and that the support staff will enter and occupy the south façade. Which façade will house the English, and which the Americans?"

"Sir, I believe the English are on the west, and the Americans on the north."

The general stopped and turned on the guard. "Believe? Or

know? I'm not interested in guesses."

"Sorry, sir. I know."

"When I ask you a question, be precise."

"Yes, General."

The guard led them down long, high-ceilinged hallways hung with tapestries and portraits of the czars and their families. Since the 1860s, Livadia had been the favorite summer retreat of the czars. In 1909, Nicholas II had commissioned Yalta's leading architect, Nicholai Krasnov, to build a new palace in the Italian Renaissance style, amused by the notion that each façade should bear a distinctly different ornate look. Construction lasted almost two years, with the site teeming with engineers and laborers. The cost was astronomical.

The guard escorted the officers, walking slowly enough so the heroic young lieutenant could keep up. *He must have been at Stalingrad. An eye, a leg wound! But certainly fought bravely. My God! A Hero of the Soviet Union.*

Arriving at immense double doors at the end of the hallway, he motioned to a fellow guard to admit them. The suite, too, had towering ceilings and tall, glass-paned doors to terraces. Heavy drapes hung from the ceiling, pulled back to let in the waning afternoon sunlight.

A half-dozen servants were readying the three-bedroom apartment. Two were on short stools cleaning windows; a young woman was arranging flowers on a large dining table that could easily seat twenty; another was setting a fire in a massive fireplace. Still another was provisioning a bar, placing wine bottles in a dry sink, and lining up bottles of vodka and brandy along its back. Already, there were dozens of tumblers and wine glasses arrayed in an open cabinet above the sink. A maid peeled citrus skins into long, continuous curls, fed them into vodka bottles, recorked them, and submerged the bottles into the ice-filled sink.

The general and his hobbling aide stood watching the activity until it was done. Unsettled by the watchful eye of a senior officer, the staff hastened to complete their tasks, then scurried from the room.

The general turned to the guard. "I wish to see a floor plan of this apartment."

"I will have to get one. It will take but a moment."

"Make haste, comrade. I do not have all day."

The moment the guards left, the lieutenant hobbled over to the double doors and closed them. The general stepped to a paneled wall to the left of the massive fireplace and examined it closely. He reached up to a knot in the dark-stained wood and pressed it. A soft click produced a slight shift in the wall, and with a push inward, a small, low doorway appeared in the center of the paneling.

"All yours, Lieutenant."

Krentz straightened, removed the eye patch, tossed his cane inside the secret room, and turned and stood in front of the General.

" Captain Handy, I think my arm has gone to sleep. Can you unstrap me?"

Quickly, Handy stripped the leather case, removed the medal from around Krentz's neck, and unbuttoned his tunic. In seconds, he unwrapped the apparatus that had concealed Krentz's "missing" arm. Krentz began to massage his still-cramped arm.

"Finish that inside. Time to disappear. Good luck!"

Krentz put the leather case inside the room, snapped a short salute to Hardy, and, ducking his head, stepped through the four-foot-high entry, then closed it behind him. Hardy heard a soft click, and confirmed the doorway had aligned precisely with the rest of the paneling. He moved to the double doors and opened them.

A minute later, the guard came down the hall at a near trot, a roll of plans in his hand, to find the general out on the terrace.

"Sir, the plans."

"Place then on the table. Tell me, what is the plan to secure this terrace when the Secretary Stalin and his aides are in residence?"

The guard unrolled the floor plans and pointed to specific locations on it as he answered. "Once the secretary arrives, a platoon of guards will surround the building, with a half dozen positioned thirty yards off the terrace. Then, his group of eighteen will enter the building. The secretary and three aides will come to this apartment. Six guards will be on duty in the hallway throughout the night. The rest of his party will go to quarters on the second and third floors of this wing."

"And in the morning? When they leave for the conference?"

"Half the guards will go with him. The rest will remain here to maintain security."

The guard stood silently, wishing this visit to be short, while the general perused the plans on the table for what seemed like ten minutes.

"Very well. I am finished. I am ready to leave."

"Excuse me, General, but where is your aide, the young lieutenant?"

"I sent him away on another matter. He left just after you went to get the plans."

As the general strode down the hallway, the guard practically ran to keep up.

Thank God this is over.

CHAPTER FORTY-FOUR

The Czar's Cell

How does he do it? wondered Krentz as he sat in the secret room. *How did he ever find out about this bolt hole?*

Indeed, Handy, the ultimate Russofile, had unearthed details about the history of the Livadia Palace. Just as soon as he had learned, at the conclusion of the Tehran Conference, that Yalta would be the venue for the next meeting of the Allied leaders, Handy had turned to his prodigious academic sources. Within days, he had found the architect Nicolai Krasnov, who, come the Revolution, had quickly vacated Yalta, moving to Crete, where he lived in modest retirement. Yes, he had maintained all his architectural files, and with little persuasion, consented to an interview.

Within an hour, Handy had learned of the secret room designed for the Czar Nicholas. "Even in 1909, he knew that the Revolution was coming and took this small precaution with the designs of the Livadia," reported Krasnov with a sad smile as he accepted Handy's generous check for the Livadia architectural drawings, assuring Handy he would maintain silence about both the secret room and their transaction.

Exploring the room by the dim light that filtered in from a vent in the high ceiling, Krentz confirmed what the drawings had shown. The room, remarkably clean and dust-free, a tribute to the building prowess of Krasnov's artisans, was a 15x12 rectangle with a sofa, two chairs, a partial sleeping loft, and a toilet behind a screen in one corner. Amazingly, there was water in the toilet and tank. Referring to the original drawings, Krentz located three small black metal discs on the wall that backed the larger apartment's fireplace. Each disc covered a spy hole that could be lifted to peer into the main apartment. Handy had been specific in warning that there could be no light of any kind in the secret room when lifting the discs. Otherwise, a beam could literally leap through the pinhole and alert those present in the apartment. *Unbelievable, the czar thought he could hide if the palace was overrun. But how could he get away? Once occupied, how could Nicholas or anyone else with him get out?*

John Krentz continued his examination of the room. In a small closet, he found several sets of men's and women's clothing. Not elegant, but peasant garb.

Perhaps you thought you might dress down and make your way out of here? Foolish to even think it possible!

Checking his watch, Krentz saw it was nearing 5:00. Carefully folding his uniform, he stood on a chair in his underwear and pulled on a chain hanging from the vent, closing shutters over it and darkening the room. He crawled into the bed in the corner, and within minutes, was asleep.

He set no alarm. He was certain that when Stalin and his entourage arrived next door, he would come wide awake.

CHAPTER FORTY-FIVE

Livadia Morning

February 4, 1945, Yalta, the Crimea

The morning of the Allied conference dawned crisp and clear as the delegations began to assemble. Long before the arrival of the principals, various aides began to filter in through the west façade's portal to the central conference room.

Captain Handy informed the American interpreters that Lieutenant Krentz had taken ill the previous evening and might or might not be joining the group that morning. He had assigned an alternate interpreter to Krentz's position.

After reviewing the protocols and sequence of opening remarks by the Allied leaders, he excused himself a half hour before the scheduled start to go "check on Krentz." His entourage surrounded Stalin who, wearing his marshal's uniform, strode into the Yalta sunlight from the south façade. As they turned onto an immaculately raked gravel path that led to their left toward the east façade, the crunch of ten pairs of approaching boots alerted the Honor Guard at the east façade to snap to attention.

No one concerned themselves with the lone Russian officer who emerged from the south façade a minute after Stalin's departure. The young officer, walking awkwardly with a cane, slowly headed straight ahead on the path to the palace gardens. At a point some two hundred yards from the palace, in a well-screened corner, sat a small shed. After checking that the garden was unoccupied and he was unobserved, Krentz ducked his head and entered the shed.

The waiting Captain Handy quickly closed the door. Krentz began talking as he first removed the medal sash around his neck, followed by the Russian uniform. Handy handed him the trousers and blouse of a freshly pressed U.S. Army uniform with Signal Corps badges on the epaulets. Krentz sat to replace the Russian boots.

As he completed his report, tied his tie, and slipped on the jacket, Handy was stashing the cane and Russian clothing in a dirty burlap bag and wedging it into the darkest corner of the shed behind other bags of fertilizer.

Handy asked a few specific questions, then headed for the door. He turned back.

"Well done, John. Count to thirty and follow me out. Open the door a crack and look straight across at the group of trees thirty yards away. I will signal you from there to clear the area. See you at the conference."

• • •

Handy entered the west façade of the palace and was quickly ushered into the bedroom, where President Roosevelt was getting dressed with the assistance of his White House valet, who traveled with him.

"Thank you, Miguel. Give us a moment, please."

The moment the door closed behind the departing aide, Handy handed the president a slip of paper. It read: *I will whisper in your ear, in the event the room is bugged.*

The president nodded.

Leaning close, lacing his hand on the president's shoulder, Handy's immediate reaction wasn't good. The president looked gaunt and tired; his body under the suit coat felt flabby.

In the president's ear: "Our man heard much of what Stalin and his team discussed. Stalin despises Churchill; that you know. Believes the English are devious and perfidious and essentially still czarist in their attitudes, even after all these years. In one tirade, he roared about their temerity in attempting to aid the czar and the White Army with the 1920s expedition. He thinks you are gullible, feels he will be able to get you to agree to…"

For five full minutes, Handy repeated Krentz's report, the president sitting stone-still, occasionally nodding. When he finished, the president seized a nearby note pad and began writing.

He handed this note to Handy. *I was naïve before. You were right. He's not to be trusted. My warmest thanks. I now know what I shall do—and what I won't. Thank you, old friend.*

"My pleasure, Mr. President."

The president beckoned to Handy to lean down. He spoke into his ear. "I remind you...call me Frank."

• • •

Krentz trotted into the west façade of the Livadia Palace, just ahead of the arriving British delegation who, trailing Churchill, came around the gravel path from their façade of the palace.

Standing near the conference hall door engaged in conversation, Evgeny Nolikin and Svetlana Orlova saw him first. Concern on their faces, they immediately turned to him. Nolikov spoke first, in English.

"Lieutenant, we heard you were ill. Are you all right?"

He certainly didn't look it; wan, red-eyed, and apparently unshaven, although in a neatly pressed uniform.

"We wondered about you," Svetlana said softly, also in English.

Respond to any inquiries in Russian. It will make their watchers less suspicious. "I'm all right. I had food poisoning, but I'm feeling better now."

"We're glad you're back, both of us," Svetlana offered softly.

"Thank you, Svetlana, Evgeny."

Krentz quickly located the alternate, who rose and surrendered his place at the interpreter's small table set alongside the main conference. Krentz scanned the agenda sheet to refresh his memory on the sequences. The agenda called for him to move in between Roosevelt and Stalin as they exchanged comments.

Roosevelt ignored him. Stalin looked at him, gave him a brusque nod, and turned away to speak with an aide. Resisting the urge to lean toward the secretary's words and eavesdrop,

Krentz was close enough to breathe in the vodka fumes that lingered from Stalin's virtual all-nighter.

The man is an amazing engine. He operates on no sleep, an unending quantity of alcohol, and an aura of fear. But now, he is doing his smiling bear, "Uncle Joe" routine. Not the sneering schemer of last night.

Stalin turned to Krentz in full Uncle Joe bonhomie.

"Interpreter, ask the president if he enjoyed a good night of sleep in a former czar's bedroom."

Before Krentz could respond, Churchill banged a gavel twice on the table. Before the echo of the gavel had faded, he growled, "Let us begin."

CHAPTER FORTY-SIX

Dacha Toasts

Moscow, February 12, 1945

Handy shivered as he trudged through the falling snow in a borrowed overcoat toward the restaurant. He had walked for almost thirty minutes, doubling back on his path to confound anyone following him. Twice, he had been able to use small alleys to scuttle away from pursuers, real or imagined, and now was within half a block of the restaurant.

As he approached, a figure swathed with a muffler around his face approached him from the side. "Can you direct me to the Kremlin?"

"It's three blocks behind you. No, make that four."

"Change of plans. Don't go in. Walk on about two hundred yards to the corner. Turn left. Get in the back of the car idling at the curb."

Before Handy could determine more, the man was gone.

Sure enough, the car was there. Before he closed the door, it was off, wipers beating furiously against the driving snow. Fifteen minutes and many turns later, the Zil, a bulky Russian limousine, wound up a snowplowed driveway through birches and sighed to a stop in front of a countryside dacha. The moment Handy stepped out of the Zil, it drove around a circle and departed back down the driveway.

The path showed a single set of footprints through six inches of snow leading to the front door. Handy stomped the snow off his boots on the front porch.

The door opened and he stepped into a warm, steamy entranceway. A tall man stood there, his hand in the pocket of a double-breasted jacket.

"Hang up your coat right there." Taking his hand from the pocket, his host gestured to a rack on the wall.

A fire was crackling merrily in a large fireplace, Near it, a low table was covered with small plates of food, small glasses, and the perennial vodka bottle.

Handy looked at his host with raised eyebrows.

"I have borrowed the dacha from a friend. Only he doesn't know it. So he is unable to tell anyone we are here."

"And should we be discovered? Say, the owner walks in? What then?"

"It is unlikely, as he is in Tashkent this week. Not due back for four days."

"But if we are interrupted?"

"Ah, then I will have to report that I have recruited you, and that I was debriefing you. Extracting all manner of intelligence."

Handy smiled. "But we are allies. Surely, Russia would not spy on the United States!"

"No more than the United States would spy on their Russian allies."

"I take your point."

"Please, join me for some sustenance and a toast."

They toasted each other with a small glass of vodka.

"To allies."

"To allies. As far as it goes."

"It must go farther than the fall of Berlin and the end of the Third Reich."

"How much farther?"

"I would say considerably farther. Say, on one level, this level, perhaps indefinitely."

"Let us hope so."

They fell to eating lunch, and after a moment, the Russian resumed.

"So, as to our proposition, do you have a suggested name for me?"

"I do. And you one for me?"

"You first."

"Lieutenant John Krentz, U.S. Army Signal Corps. He will be posted to Germany after the war as an interpreter. It is likely Lieutenant Krentz will be present at many meetings of the Allies as they administer what's left of Germany."

"I recall the man. He is known to the Praesidium."

"Yes, I hear Secretary Stalin admires his facility with Russian."

"I can confirm that."

"And your candidate for me?"

"Ah. I am going to make it easy. Evgeny Nolikin. Also an accomplished interpreter. Known to Krentz. And on the list to serve in Germany after its fall. I wouldn't be at all surprised if it turns out they will live and work very closely at many Allied conferences."

Handy stood. "A very interesting combination." He paused. "And you're certain Nolikin has no idea of your plans for him?"

"He is innocent of any knowledge of this conspiracy. Can you say the same for Lieutenant Krentz?"

"He is."

The Russian refilled their glasses with ice-cold vodka, and raised his. "May it be a long time before either of them find out."

CHAPTER FORTY-SEVEN

FDR Funds

Washington, February 20, 1945

He could tell the president was in a good mood.

"A cocktail, Captain Handy! Bourbon Manhattan isn't it?"

"Mr. President, why is it we only meet at cocktail hour?"

"Simple. I am not interrupted as I am all day long. It's quiet time. And few if any of the little pitchers with big ears on my doting staff are here to see you come and go, much less eavesdrop. A dash of bitters?"

They touched glasses, tasted, and made true appropriate noises of satisfaction.

"So, give me your assessment of how our little project is going," the president said.

Hmmm. 'Our' little project! He is enjoying this far more than I thought—and far more than I am. Then again, all he has to do is run the country. I, on the other hand, have to keep this whole interpreter gambit moving forward while keeping its goals from everyone and their uncle, including my superiors, who have the unbridled power to court-martial me and lock me up for infinity.

"Pretty well in fact. That is, so far, so good. As long as we continue to make our interpreters available to the Russians, it is only a matter of time before they will attempt to suborn one of them."

"And what are the odds it will be the candidate you've selected?"

"Mr. President, I have a plan."

"Captain, you always have a plan. Can I freshen that up for you?"

"Thank you. Speaking of plans, how goes the discussion about the reorganization of intelligence services after the war?"

"God! Those senators do go on about topics about which they know very little. Kind of like some of our generals, if you ask me."

"You know that I think your decision to create the OSS was a great stroke, no matter how much Donovan has come to annoy the British."

"Alas! Not just the British. And occasionally, me."

"That's why I ask. I remain concerned about the same subject that we've discussed now for two years. Intelligence services, by their very nature, have limited shelf lives before they are either reformed or disbanded or rebuilt."

"So, we're about to start a new cycle?" the president mused.

"Indeed, but this time, for this next cycle and the one to follow it, I suggest we may want to keep our project operating *outside* of any new organization, for I envision it as being valuable to the country for decades."

"And your concern in handing it over to a new agency is…"

"The juicier the secret, the more ambitious a program, the more everyone wants to be in on it. Cleared. Privy to its big secret. And as that happens, security goes downhill and the odds of it being revealed go up geometrically."

"Ah," the president nodded. "You told me the story of Russia's man in Japan, Sorge. How long did that operation run?"

"Thirteen years!" Handy said. "Thirteen extraordinary and very lucrative years. The Russians effectively owned all Japanese intelligence worth having for almost that entire period."

"We have discussed this before. This trip down memory lane have a reason?"

"It does. I think we're ready to put the operation in gear."

"Tell me what you have in mind, how long it will take, what it will cost, and how in God's name to keep it from all the Army brass and intelligence types lining up to give Donovan the heave-ho."

"I will. But remember, all the brass and the spies aren't planning on giving Donovan the gate. They're counting on you to do it for them."

The president raised his martini glass. "A toast to democracy! That's why this job is so much fun."

"And there's a bonus. You need to get me a little start-up money."

"How much?"

"Fifty-thousand now. Another $50,000 in 1946."

"What about 1947 and beyond? Remember, I'm not running again in 1948."

"By then, the operation will be self-funding."

The president rubbed his chin, musing. "All right. The funds will come from private sources. Let me know when, where and how you want the $50,000."

"As soon as possible, in my hands and in small bills. In other words, nothing on paper. And nothing traceable." Handy looked at FDR, whose eyes were gleaming over his glass. "And Mr. President, I'm going to need an authorization for the operation from you in writing."

FDR pulled a mock look of disappointment. "What? After all these years, you don't trust me?"

"At some point down the road, I may need to show it to the president. And as you just said, after 1948, that won't be you. If everything goes even close to plan, I may not need it until the 1950s. Maybe the 1960s.

The president grinned. "Point taken."

CHAPTER FORTY-EIGHT

1945
Money Transfer

Berlin, July 18, 1945

Captain Jay Handy sat side by side with Lieutenant John Krentz and another young officer, a Lieutenant Forrest, at a dining table in the Army mess hall. It was vacant, early afternoon, well after lunch and before the early dinner rush. They could hear the clatter of cooking pots in the kitchen as the cooks prepped for dinner.

"It's a simple exercise, Krentz. When we compromise someone, we do it with money, and the passing of that money works best when it's in the most ordinary places. No skulking around back alleys. We do it in what can best be called plain sight. But because no one is expecting it, it works. When there is a natural, unforced opportunity, you sit next to the target in a public place—a bar, restaurant, among people all around. And hip to hip. Below the level of the tabletop, you pass information or money. The key is to determine that no one on your opposite side, the side away from your target, has a view of your activity. The easiest way is to sit up close to the table. Just like every mother tells a teenager. Get your belly close to the table edge, and you create an area for the exchange that others can't look at, across or down. Follow me?"

Handy placed a packet of U.S. dollars on the table; a brick of $20 bills bound by several rubber bands. Sitting side by side, Handy's right knee was inches from Krentz's left knee.

Lieutenant Forrest raised a hand. "What if you can't arrange a situation where you can conveniently meet to sit next to each other?"

"In the particular case, it will not be an issue. We intend to make the switch at the Two Joes with a Russian officer at a communal table."

"So, this is not an exercise—it's real? We've recruited a Russian officer?"

"We'll have one when the transfer takes place. But it has to go perfectly. Once you feel secure that no one can see what you're doing below the table, you set the money on your thigh. But no switch unless I give you a signal. If I fail to nod, simply abort. Return the packet of money to your pocket, and after a while, get up and vacate your spot at the table. We'll do it another time instead."

"Who's the target?"

Handy smiled thinly. "Let's wait on that. I'll let you know just beforehand. Meanwhile, I want you to practice using a deck of playing cards. You have some?"

"No, I don't."

Handy slid a deck to Krentz. "Now you do. Practice on each other. Both of you. Both of you be prepared. If a situation presents itself and one of you isn't available, I want the other ready to go. Use my office. Lock yourself in when you do. Behind the door is a Russian officer's uniform, jacket, and pants. Alternate wearing it. Let me know when you're really comfortable with making the transfer with ease. At that point, I'll bring in the cameraman."

Surprised, both officers looked at Captain Handy.

"We plan to immortalize the transfer on film, as a present to our newest defector. A little reminder of our generosity."

CHAPTER FORTY-NINE

The Two Joes

Neiselstrasse, Berlin, July 20, 1945

In an area twenty blocks square, only two buildings remained standing in the aftermath of the unrelenting combination of Allied bombing raids and advancing Russian artillery. Around them was block upon block of rubble—charred and twisted timbers, scorched concrete, and shattered bricks by the thousands. Each block was scavenged daily by surviving Germans, alone or in groups of two or three, sifting bricks in hopes of unearthing anything of value for barter—anything to trade for food, clothing, and medicine.

Each flattened block had a low pyramid shape. As the scavengers worked at the edges from curbside, they tossed debris into the center, and so the profile emerged, a shallow hill with four discrete sides. A CBS correspondent described the scene to his listeners in America as "Prussian pyramids."

Of the two buildings the bombs had miraculously bypassed, the first was a four-story apartment house constructed in 1919 that had been singed by fire, but not hit by ordnance. Its exterior was blackened brick. Perhaps the post-World War I construction design had been sturdier than its former neighbors.

There were no occupants to be found when the city was taken. Undoubtedly, they had joined the thousands of Berliners who had fled before the arrival of the first Russian troops, whose rapacious reputation had preceded them. Wise decision or not, accommodations were at a premium, so the Allied Control Commission, conceived at Yalta, had convened in a church, also left standing, off the cratered K-Damm. Continuing the arrangements begun in Tehran and repeated in Yalta, they assigned the apartment building to the four teams of Allied interpreters from Russia, the UK, the U.S., and the newly-added

French. Each would interpret at meetings in the four Berlin sectors controlled by the four Allies. The commission assessed that the structure, quickly given the named the Babel Building, would house interpreters in the upper floor walk-up apartments (sorry, no elevator), and the lobby and ground floors were consigned as rooms for meetings where translators could easily attend.

The second building, two blocks east, was equally scorched on the exterior, but like its fortunate neighbor, remained intact. A former two-story restaurant, it had a large bar area and dining table in two sizeable rooms on the ground floor, and offices on the second floor.

Veteran field commanders reminded the commission that victorious occupying troops needed ways to blow off steam, shake off the terrors—and adrenaline—of battle, and reacquaint with more peaceable pastimes, which, in the case of soldiers everywhere, meant alcohol. Astonishingly, the commission appointed a pair of officers, one Russian, one American, in charge and within days the interior was refurbished, supplies from a brewery also spared from the Allied bombings were secured, and a sign erected over the front door that read: Allied Victory Hall.

Within days of its crowded opening—amazingly, no fights or brawls, just a lot of serious drinking, atonal singing, and sodden declarations of unbreakable friendships—unidentified night visitors painted over the sign to read: GI Joe & Joe.

In short order, beer-drinking American troops had discovered vodka, which the Russian officers could somehow continuously provide in vast quantities, so the renaming stopped. But soldiers being soldiers, they manufactured red shorthand and simply referred to the watering hole as "the Two Joes."

The idea of weaning soldiers from war with whisky may have been time-tested, but it didn't take long before bragging and boasting rights between the Americans and Russians inside the Two Joes emerged as a nightly drinking war. If you simply wanted a beer or some vodka but no fireworks, you stopped by early—and left early. If you stayed late, it frequently turned riotous—and you were either sorted out or arrested by the MPs from your respective army.

So, the saloon operated for a brief time, until the tensions between the conquering Allies mounted. Within a few days of its opening, the French and British troops stopped coming, so it became the focused drinking battleground between the Russians and the Americans.

Russian intelligence officers were directed to frequent the GI Joe & Joe, and to identify possible recruits among the Americans. Night after night, they sat thigh to thigh, ten or twelve wedged into tables for eight, drinking, drinking, drinking, and probing. Always probing. Looking for a potential spy.

And among them—usually early to stop in, and wisely, early to leave—were the Russian and American interpreters who, after all, were billeted just two blocks away at the interpreter's building on Neiselstrasse.

CHAPTER FIFTY

Dueling Henrys

Berlin, July 20, 1945

Those familiar with the views and personalities of the two cabinet members expected fireworks. The two Henrys would go toe to toe.

Few observers would disagree: Secretary of War Henry Lewis Stimson was a prig. Formal, stiff, imperious, and humorless were adjectives that crossed the lips of admirers and detractors alike. None doubted he was a conservative Republican, a rare and sole species among the Roosevelt inner circle.

Garrulous, passionate, a liberal Democrat to the core, Henry Morgenthau arrived for the conference on defeated Germany's post-war reorganization with a long history of fighting for the persecuted. As US Ambassador to the Ottoman Empire, he had been in the thick of efforts to stem the slaughter of Jews and minorities in Armenia. None doubted where his voice would be heard in discussing Germany's annihilation of its Jewish citizens, much less the treatment of Jews throughout the third Reich's once-conquered neighbors.

As the attendees met, it became clear the conclusions would go the full fifteen rounds. "Stimson is looking out for American businesses," said some. The president had sent Morgenthau to represent the American Jewish community.

At issue was: How should Germany be restructured? Stimson, the hawk, pled the case for a single German state, able to rebuild its industry with central planning. Morgenthau argued that Germany should never be in a position strong enough to start another war after having done so twice in less than half a century.

The commission went at its work, day in and day out, with

the "clean" Germans selected by the Allies sitting in silent attendance, waiting their constitutional fate. A French representative was also present, added once the French joined as late members of the Allied Control Commission.

The interpreters were kept hopping, with four languages involved, every utterance translated and relayed. And, as they did so, the pace of the conference slowed to a crawl.

CHAPTER FIFTY-ONE

The Prussian Pyramids

Berlin, July 20, 1945

The air was acrid. The underlying smell was stale beer. The cheers were ragged and the singing loud and off key. Another typical night at the Two Joes. With combat-weary Russian and Americans now free of the rigors and adrenaline of following orders and advancing against enemy fire, perhaps to death or injury, the letdown was relief and the desire to celebrate their survival.

Boredom had replaced unceasing alert, and nightly consumption of large quantities of alcohol resulted. Add the pall of smoke from burned Balkan tobacco and the familiar smell of Camels, mixed with vodka, beer, and bragging rights, and the result was a cheerful hostility, ready to boil over at any time.

When it did, MPs from both armies cracked skulls with batons and dragged the semi-conscious out the doors. A scratchy Victrola and crackly speaker spewed out music unfamiliar to both allies.

Six interpreters sat at a corner table, raising their voices above the din to converse among themselves. Evgeny Nolikin was the least plastered. Enjoying a buzz from the vodka toasts but drinking far less than his fellow Russians and the three Americans, he watched and listened as Lieutenant John Krentz went about getting thoroughly drunk.

Krentz had foregone beer to participate in every toast the Russians proposed, and was matching their best drinkers shot for shot. As he steadfastly progressed toward oblivion, his volume increased.

Krentz cursed the Germans in phrases even the Russian interpreters were hard pressed to decipher. From what they gleaned, Germans, according to Krentz, were lower than whale shit, a race of sadistic murderers, every one of them should be locked up, and most of them hung.

"I piss on all Germans. Piss on them. All Germans."

Nolikin was not the only one who found Krentz's rant repetitive and tiring. Captain Jay Handy made several attempts to rein him in and to slow down his drinking. But Krentz was a man on a mission. After two hours, his comments were slurred, he was dropping words, stopping, repeating himself, and insisting, pugnaciously, that everyone must agree with him. He suddenly rose, steadying himself on the tabletop at the expense of beer sloshing out of steins and vodka bottles tipping over. He mumbled he was going to "shake his snake, bleed the lizard," and went reeling off toward the back door of the Two Joes that exited to a raised deck with a set of stairs that led down to the street level and a line of privies.

When Krentz lurched through the door, Evgeny Nolikin rose and followed. And then Jay Handy rose, following him.

A fight had broken out several tables down, and by the time Evgeny skirted it and got to the deck, Krentz had already negotiated the stairs. Reeling unevenly toward the outhouses, he wove past them and headed away from the light spilling from the Two Joes. Nolikin called out, but Krentz slogged on, oblivious. Nolikin ran down the stairs, and at the bottom, called again, but to no avail.

By now, in the evening gloom, Krentz had stopped and was standing, looking up at the low summit of the pile of rubble that formed one of the many Prussian pyramids. Off into the distance lay block after block of more shallow pyramids.

He's literally going to piss on the pyramids, and by extension, the Germans! Nolikin opened his mouth to call to Krentz.

Suddenly, Krentz was not alone. Emerging from out of the rubble were three—no, four—figures who fell upon him as he stood there, with blows that drove him to his knees.

From the deck, Handy called out. Then, spotting Nolikin below, yelled his name. Nolikin looked up to see Handy draw a pistol and toss it down to him.

Catching the pistol, Nolikin whirled and ran toward the

marauders, yelling at them in German. They paid no heed, and were now pummeling and kicking Krentz, who was on the ground. Nolikin stopped, aimed hesitantly, and fired two shots. One of Krentz's attackers fell away, writhing on the ground.

The remaining threesome turned from Krentz, gathered their fallen comrade, and quickly carried him off, out of the light and around the corner of the pyramid. Gone.

Nolikin and Handy rushed to a semi-conscious Krentz, who tried to sit up but promptly fell over on his side. Handy removed the pistol dangling from Nolikin's hand.

"Good shooting, Evgeny! Call an ambulance. Tell them to make it quick. Krentz looks in bad shape."

Krentz looked up, trying to focus, squirming in pain. Up on one wobbly elbow, he said, "Fucking Krauts!" Then he keeled over again.

CHAPTER FIFTY-TWO

A Gift of Science

July 22, 1945

Returning to his apartment in the early evening, Evgeny Nolikin found an envelope that had been shoved under the door. Svetlana had not yet returned or she would have picked it up. The envelope bore only his name.

The letter inside was in English. As soon as he read it, Evgeny's heart began to race.

Karl-Heinz Bork, a German physicist, is hiding at a farmhouse three kilometers outside Plotz in the Russian Zone. He has been secreted there by American intelligence officers who plan to smuggle him out of the zone and to the West.

An ardent Nazi, Bork fled from Peenemunde where he was in charge of a team developing the next series of V-2 rockets being fired at Great Britain.

You can find him at the house of Wulfrin Mueller, on the road to Dorter, heading west from Ploltz. Thanks to the advancing Russian Army, the physicists ceased their vile rocket work and fled. It's imperative that he be captured before he finds a way to escape his crimes.

If you wish to receive additional information of this nature about Allied intelligence activities, open a numbered account at any bank in Bern with a deposit of $200. Write the account number on a slip of paper and leave it in the urn atop the gravestone of Sgt. Claude Fronzi, Section 6, row 14, of the American cemetery in Berlin.

The letter was signed *Oppor.*

I don't want anything to do with this, thought Nolikin. Putting his coat back on, he hastened to Kosarov's office.

The KGB man read the letter twice before wheeling on Nolikin, demanding the circumstances of its delivery. Nolikin stammered that he had simply found it pushed under the door sill to his apartment.

"Who could have written this? Likely a provocation! Could it have come from the Americans?" Sarcastically, he added, "Perhaps from your friend Lieutenant Krentz?"

"I rather doubt it. He's still in the hospital. He's in no shape to climb five flights of stairs to the apartment."

Kosarov paced. "Go back to your apartment. Question Orlova. Ask her if she knows anything about this letter."

Aha! You dare not question her yourself! You know not to tread there. "But she had not returned when I found the letter."

"Nonetheless, ask her. And report her answers to me."

Nolikin left, just as fearful as he had been when he'd arrived.

Kosarov remained in his office, smoking one cigarette after another, reading and re-reading the Bork letter. He summoned an aide, Kavchek, and ordered an immediate search of the NKVD records on wanted and missing Nazis.

"Now!" he bellowed at the back of the startled Kavchek, who hastened away.

Kavchek was on his way back to Kosarov's office when he was intercepted in the hallway by a tall Russian Army colonel who called out to him. "What's kept you, comrade? What do you have on the Nazi Bork?"

Kavchek looked hesitantly at the looming figure, not certain who he was.

The officer snapped his fingers, as if summoning a serf. "Come, what do you have? Do you have an answer or not?"

Kavchek quickly handed him a copy of the search-and-seize report on Karl-Heinz Bork.

As the officer scanned it, Kavchek noticed that his tunic was laden with decorations. But above all, he noticed the Order of Lenin.

Finished scanning the document, the officer barked, "Task accomplished. I shall take this to Comrade Major Kosarov. Dismissed."

Before Kavchek could register a comment or a salute, the officer whirled and marched off down the hall. He stepped into the smoke-filled office to find Kosarov with his back to the door, feet on the desk, in deep contemplation.

"Comrade Major Kosarov."

The barked greeting brought Kosarov out of his chair. Instantly, he saw the bemedaled tunic of his guest.

"I am General Machentirov. I require your immediate attention. Put that foul cigarette out!"

Obeying, Kosarov found the search report thrust into his hands.

"So, do you have a lead on this man or not?"

Kosarov recounted the information in the note, describing its contents as unconfirmed.

Machentirov again thrust out his hand. "The letter!"

He stood reading it, not moving at all. Kosarov waited silently for what seemed like several minutes.

"If this Bork is where the letter says he is, we must have him." He turned and fixed a stare on Kosarov. "A Swiss account number will be provided to you within the hour. Ready an arrest team—at least three men—and be prepared to leave for Plotz. It is fortunate that the writer of this letter sent it to Interpreter Nolikin and that he was quick to bring it to your attention, and you to one in records. I expect you to do a precise job to capture this Nazi prick. If he's there, you know what to do. If he's not, forget the bank account. We'll use it for another operation. Any questions, comrade?"

Their discussion was over. The general turned away and in two strides was at the door.

"Go get the bastard!"

Kosarov moved to his desk and picked up the phone to rouse his arrest team. As soon as he completed dialing, he looked up, but the Hero of the Soviet Union had disappeared.

Forty-eight hours later, the NKVD delivered a shaken and shackled Karl-Heinz Bork to a Russian weapons research facility deep in the Ural Mountains.

CHAPTER FIFTY-THREE

Bedded Down

U.S. Army Hospital, Berlin, August 23, 1945

Krentz awoke as he had the past two mornings, stiff, aching, and twinging every time he shifted in the bed. He eased onto the floor and shuffled to the bathroom. In the mirror, he saw that he had a shiner and a yellow-blue-brown bruise over his right eyebrow. He felt like a mummy, his torso taped tightly. To the mirror he mouthed, "Fucking Krauts."

Back into the bed. No easy task. A painful, slow-motion effort. He ate a tasteless breakfast, continuing the unbroken tradition of bland that is typical institutional fare. *Cardboard,* he thought.

After breakfast, his first visitor arrived. As with the prior morning, it was Captain Handy. "And how is our intrepid, boozy battler this morning? Mending, are we?"

"Get me out of here, Captain. I'm going bananas with the boredom and the lousy food."

"Another day or two. I brought you a radio."

"Great. I can listen to Armed Forces Radio. America's contribution to thousands of years of European culture."

"Sarcasm does not speed the healing process, Lieutenant. Have the MPs been around to interview you about the incident?"

Krentz pointed to his wrapped chest. "You call this an incident? Yes, they were here yesterday afternoon. What could I tell them? It was dark. I got jumped. I went down. I went out. I woke up here."

"They ask you about the boozing?"

"Didn't have to. They deal with incidents seven days a week at the Two Joes. Whose idea was that place, anyway?"

"FDR's, I think."

"Well, he's lost my vote."

"Lieutenant, Roosevelt's been dead for months. They really must have rung your bell."

"Speaking of 'they'...any arrests? Find any Krauts in the Pyramids with bullet holes in them?"

"As the sheriff laments in the oaters, the bandits made a clean getaway."

"Hard to believe. And the sleuths among our crack MP squad found nothing?"

"Affirmative."

A pause.

"I brought you some reading material." Handy dropped some magazines and a pair of books on the bedspread.

Rather than read, Krentz dozed, then arose, and repeated his arduous routine of climbing out of bed and going to the small bathroom. His leg bruises were losing yellow and gaining blue. Once back in bed, Krentz had just begun contemplating the magazines Handy had left, when his next visitor stuck his head around the door jamb.

"Lieutenant Krentz, may I come in?"

With Krentz's nod, Evgeny Nolikin stepped into the room.

"How are you feeling?"

A slight smile. "I'll live. As you can see, they've used enough tape on my ribs to hold me in place for years. In any case, they tell me you're the hero that ran off my attackers. Thank you."

"I'm no hero. Captain Handy tossed me a pistol from the upper deck. I fired a couple of shots over their heads and they ran."

"I heard you winged one of them."

"No body. I'm not much of a shot. But I wasn't trying to hit anyone. Just to get them to stop kicking you."

"Well, it worked. I'm grateful."

"I bring you greetings from Svetlana, who wishes you a swift recovery."

"Please thank her for me."

"She would have joined me here today, but is interpreting at a conference in Munich. Hopefully, she might come with me to see you within a day or two, when our schedule permits."

"You'd better check before you come. I'm trying to get out of here in a day or so. It's pretty boring."

"I'm no doctor, but you're not going to be interpreting anytime soon. Not with that wrapping."

"I'll be taking recuperative leave for a few weeks. Not sure where, but it won't be in Germany. I've had it up to here with our Teutonic hosts."

"What are your choices? Mountains? Seaside?"

"I think the ski season is out of the question this year. And I can't imagine lying in the sun with this tape job on. I'd end up with one weird suntan, and I am definitely not going in the water in this rig."

"So, what other choice do you have?"

"Maybe the Austrian countryside. I have a friend with a nice, quiet place there."

"Well, I hope you'll return before long. It'll be good to be working with you again, seeing you recovered." He paused. "Svetlana and I are also going on leave. She goes to Moscow this week and I will follow next week. We are both anxious to see our families and friends." He reached into a briefcase. "I thought you might like to borrow some books from my library. You might enjoy a little Pushkin prose and to read about the Pugachev Rebellion."

"Why, thank you. I will certainly enjoy them. A chance to keep my Russian up to speed."

"Lieutenant Krentz, your Russian is far better than my English."

"I'm not so sure about that. You know, given that we've known each other for over two years, I think you could call me John and I could call you Evgeny. At least away from the office."

Nolikin nodded. "I would add Svetlana to that, John. Lana. She would like it too."

"Please give her my regards, Evgeny. I look forward to seeing you both when we're all back from leave."

"Do svidaniya, John. As you know, it really means more than goodbye. It's like *a bientôt* in French. Until we meet again."

They shook hands and Nolikin departed.

CHAPTER FIFTY-FOUR

The Second Letter

Nolikin found the next letter shoved under his door a week later. *My God, they must have opened the Swiss account! But why use me for a delivery boy?*

The note read:

Deposit $1,000 in the Swiss account to receive a copy of the minutes of the first three commission meetings being held between the Americans and the British to determine how post-war Germany is to be organized. US Secretary of War Henry Stimson favors creating a strong central German government while US Secretary of the Treasury Henry Morgenthau is adamant that Germany be broken up into a series of small states, none capable of rearmament or future aggression toward any European countries.

On confirmation of deposit, you will find the documents in an envelope taped behind the cistern in the men's toilet at the Two Joes.

— Oppor

Again, Dimitri Kosarov subjected Nolikin to a withering cross-examination, but the interpreter could provide him no thread of who might be the source of these intelligence reports.

Kosarov immediately dispatched a man to the Two Joes to determine how best to mount a surveillance on the men's toilets with the intent to identify the source, but found the documents already taped behind the cistern. After reading the contents, there was no doubt about it: Oppor had provided gold. He made a note to deposit $1,000 into the Swiss account.

CHAPTER FIFTY-FIVE

Visiting Nurse

Despite his pleas, the doctors would not release Krentz the next day, and he continued to lie uncomfortably in bed. After sleeping on and off, he opened Evgeny's book on Pugachev and began to read. Immersed, he looked up at the soft knock on the door.

"Miss Orlova. Please come in."

Svetlana wore a kerchief covering her hair, and a light sleeveless dress to cope with the warm, humid Berlin summer. Carrying a briefcase, she sat primly on the chair next to Krentz's bed. She seemed somewhat embarrassed or flustered, glancing briefly at Krentz's taped chest.

"Are you comfortable, Lieutenant?"

"John, please. Not very." He paused. "Lana."

She looked at him sadly. "The war is over and still there is so much violence." She sniffed. Dabbed at a tear with a handkerchief.

Uncomfortable with her crying, Krentz forced a smile. "Cheer up. Evgeny came to my rescue. It could have been a lot worse, but he came through in the clutch."

"I don't understand 'the clutch.' What is the clutch?"

"It's an American expression. It means solved the problem, or did the right thing at the right time. Evgeny did the right thing and stopped the attack on me."

She was still teary. "But look at you. You must be in pain."

"I'm feeling better every day. It will just take time for the bruises to go away. My ribs are bruised, but not broken."

A small smile curved her lips. "I'm glad to hear that. We will think about you while we are in Moscow. We have much to do there. And Evgeny is under a lot of pressure here. It will be good to get away."

"What kind of pressure, Lana?"

"Constant supervision. Criticism. Demands he do more."

"But he's a superb interpreter. Top-notch."

"I know. He plans to find out in Moscow if he must meet all the additional demands being made on him."

"Complaining? Is that a good idea?"

"No. Inquiring. He is very diplomatic. Not crude like so many others." She stood, leaned in, and kissed Krentz on the cheek. "Thank you for being such a good friend to Evgeny."

"And you, I hope."

Lana sniffled and nodded, looking out the window.

"Here." Krentz reached to the side table and pulled a Kleenex from a box.

Lana kept her back to him, disregarding his offer.

"Evgeny is a good man." He smiled at her, and moved to sit up and get out of bed.

She finally turned from the window. "Please, John. Conserve your energy. It will all work out. It must."

Krentz tried to allay her obvious distress. "In any case, we're all going away for a few weeks. I'm going to Austria for a short rest. When we return, everything can get back to normal."

Lana wiped away a remaining tear. "I don't know if it ever will, but I truly wish it could be so."

"I hope to see you before you go to Moscow."

"Perhaps it is possible. Perhaps not." Then, as she turned to go, she gently touched his arm, and in Russian said, "Do svidaniya."

CHAPTER FIFTY-SIX

The Third Letter

When the third letter appeared—this time in the outer pocket of his raincoat hung in the cloakroom outside an Allied Control Commission conference room—Nolikin knew for certain that Kosarov had opened the bank account.

Who chose me to be the middleman? It can't be anyone I know. None of the British. None of the French. And it surely is not an American interpreter. Except for Krentz, that whole group seems to bristle around any Russian they're forced to work with. But Krentz? He hates the Germans passionately, despite the fact he is always polite to everyone. Reserved, yes. Deep, some say. But quietly patriotic to the American cause. It must be someone who knows my schedule. Where I'll be and when.

Kosarov hammered home the exact same point.

"Why you? Why are you the messenger? Who knows your schedule? Where you'll be? When you'll be away from your apartment When you'll be at a conference? Who?"

"Easily one hundred people, comrade. Maybe more. Dozens of people in my building see me come and go. Schedules for conferences requiring interpreters are posted outside conference rooms throughout the Four Powers sectors. Maybe two hundred people. Three hundred. More."

"But it's an American. That cuts the numbers down, yes?"

"How do you know that? The letters are in English, but a Frenchman could write them."

"Aha! But no Frenchman attended the US-British meetings on Germany's future organization."

"Comrade, I beg to differ. The French were provided the minutes."

Kosarov snarled. "But not the Russians, right?"

"Comrade, I am an interpreter. Again, I do not have any

training in security matters."

"If I have my way, that is about to change. You must become more aware, Comrade Interpreter. I have sent an urgent request to Moscow for you to undergo indoctrination in security matters so that you may assist in the discovery of this man's identity."

"Why do you have to know it? If the information is accurate and valuable, be satisfied that you are getting it for a good price and leave it at that."

"Why do you defend this American traitor?"

"I don't. Are you trying to catch him? If you do, won't that stop his flow of intelligence to us?"

"When I catch him, I'll see to it we keep on getting the intelligence—but not be lining his pockets."

"How do you even know it's an American, or a man? Perhaps it's a female stenographer making copies of memos and minutes."

"Do you have a particular one in mind? I've seen a few joining you all for drinks at your chummy corner at the Two Joes."

"I don't know all their names."

"Well, from now on, make a point of learning them and making a list for me after every occasion."

"I don't go there all that often. Maybe once a week."

"Starting right now, go four times a week. Five. I need names."

CHAPTER FIFTY-SEVEN

Threat Level

The next letter revealed the location of a second German scientist in hiding after a flight from Peenemunde. And a demand to deposit additional funds in the Swiss account.

"Why you...Comrade...Interpreter...Nolikin?" Stretching out his words with significant pauses between, Kosarov practically sneered.

"I don't know. It is not addressed to me. It was just there, shoved under the apartment door."

"In a building riddled with other foreigners—foreigners from decadent capitalist regimes that engage in all manner of provocations. This is a stupid English trick."

"But this time written in German, not English or Russian."

"Do not state the obvious, Comrade Interpreter. How many people have regular access to your building?"

"Just interpreters for the Four Powers in the Allied Control Commission. Four English interpreters who live in two apartments on the second floor; three Americans who live in two apartments on the third floor; four French in two apartments on the fourth floor; and my floor, the fifth."

"Where you and Comrade Interpreter Orlova share one apartment, and interpreters Bulov and Shamsky occupy the other?"

"That is correct, Comrade Kosarov."

"What about the first floor?"

"It is a general area for official use by all. There are three conference rooms, a transcription room with typewriters, and a kitchen."

"And who has access to these facilities besides the interpreters?"

"Couriers coming and going. Several typists. Cooks."

"And do they frequent the upper floors?"

"There is a locked door at the bottom of the stairwell. Keys are issued to the tenants of the eight apartments."

"Who else?"

"I have no idea. Perhaps the control commission officers who commandeered the building."

"Americans! You must be very careful what you say in your apartment. It is undoubtedly wired. They listen to every word you say."

"But Comrade Kosarov, nothing we say in our apartment is of any consequence to the Americans or the British. We don't have secrets to discuss."

"Don't be naïve, Comrade. Everyone has secrets. Even you."

Evgeny Nolikin blushed.

"See?" Kosarov took a slightly more conciliatory tone. "Come, comrade. You must assist the *Rodina*, be vigilant and guard against imperialist plots and provocations."

"But if the note is not a provocation, someone is telling us where an enemy scientist is hiding. How is that provocative? That could be seen as being vigilant and helping the *Rodina*."

"Are you telling me you wrote this letter?"

"Oh, no. Not me. Comrade, I came to you the moment I found it."

"Very well. But Nolikin, you must help me learn who the author is. I will deal with the contents of the letter. You must be on the alert. I know you and Comrade Interpreter Orlova are exposed to the imperialist interpreters and are required to work with them." He continued, "You must be my eyes and ears. Watch them carefully. Report to me anything suspicious they do."

"How do I do that? I'm not trained for surveillance work."

"Watch them openly. Have a beer with them after a translation meeting. Have dinner. Observe them. Don't write anything down. I will seek you out and you can report to me."

"I'm not sure I would be any good at this. Perhaps you should request this from someone else better suited to this task."

"For you, my request is not an option." Kosarov glared at Nolikin. "In fact, it's not a request. It's an order.

Comrade…Interpreter…Nolikin."

CHAPTER FIFTY-EIGHT

Kosarov Steams

Another letter arrived. Details of U.S. Army troop dispositions in the U.S. zone. A reminder that only deposits in the Swiss account would keep more information coming. This time, another $500. Dreading the response, Nolikin nonetheless wasted no time in taking it to Kosarov's office.

After a quick read while Nolikin stood waiting, the squat NKVD man pounded the table in frustration. "Guess for me, Interpreter Nolikin," snarled a stymied Kosarov. "Who sends these reports to you and why? The style of writing is as terse as the first letter on the Nazi rocketeer. Who? Could it be one of their interpreters?"

"I don't think so. Most of those I've met are indifferent to politics. They operate as specialists who are only here because of the war. The military interpreters long for more comfortable assignments, like the Pentagon in Washington. The civilians want to go to the UN in New York."

"They tell you that? Which ones?"

"All of them. No one says it exactly. That's just my opinion."

"Give me facts, comrade. Not opinions. Opinions can cause you trouble."

Nolikin couldn't wait to get away from the rabid Kosarov.

For the duration of the month-long conference, the letters kept coming to Nolikin, who was obliged to turn them over to Kosarov and bear his withering interrogations. But when Kosarov staked out Nolikin's apartment, the letters stopped. When Kosarov called off the watch of the Babel Building, they resumed.

Discussion raged among the Allies about steel production. Chemicals. Electricity. Returning refugees. The homeless. POWs. Political parties. Pharmaceuticals. Human rights. And in the end, despite the efforts of the Russians and their unnatural ally Morgenthau, the conference concluded with the decision that Germany should remain a single nation, not broken into a collection of small states.

The Russians complained loudly that the only reason the U.S. had supported a unified Germany was to thwart the Russians and place a sizable nation on its flank. The Americans denied it vehemently. Everyone knew better.

CHAPTER FIFTY-NINE

Crime Scene

"Show me where you were standing, Comrade Interpreter," Kosarov commanded.

The following morning, the moment Nolikin had reported the events of the prior evening, Kosarov had rushed them both to the back deck of the Two Joes.

Nolikin pointed down the wooden stairway. "From here, we saw a group of four men assault the American interpreter Krentz. Out there." He pointed to the corner of the pyramid pile of rubble. "I called out, and ran down the stairs to go to his aid, several others behind me on the steps."

"Others?"

"Interpreters. We had all been at the same table inside."

"Russian interpreters?"

"Interpreter Bulov; a new French interpreter, Marcel Duval; two Americans. Interpreter Sampson and Captain Handy."

"Go on."

I had just reached the bottom of the steps when Captain Handy called to me from this deck. He tossed me a revolver. I caught it and ran at the attackers and fired two shots."

"How far away were you?"

"Perhaps twenty meters."

"Perhaps? Be accurate, comrade."

"Yes, twenty meters."

"And were you not concerned you might shoot Interpreter Krentz?"

"He was on the ground. His attackers were taking turns kicking him. I aimed at them."

"With what result?"

"One of them fell down. The others stopped kicking Krentz. The picked up their comrade and dragged him away, out of the light."

"Then what?"

"I ran forward with the others who had come down the steps behind me. Krentz was still down but moving. Trying to get up."

"Did anyone pursue the attackers?"

"I don't think so. We were focused on assisting Krentz. Someone behind me called for the military police and an ambulance."

"In what language?"

"English."

"The pistol. What happened to it?"

"Handy took it back from me. I was glad to be rid of it."

"Did he ask you for it?"

"No, he just took it out of my hand."

"Again, Nolikin! The group of you around Krentz—how many Russians? How many Americans?"

"Bulov was there. The Frenchman Duval. A couple of others from the Two Joes. The American Handy. Two other American officers."

"Their names and rank?"

"I don't know. It was very traumatic. It's not every day you see someone so brutally attacked."

"Really, comrade? You interpreters live a sheltered life."

"Not that night we didn't."

"Come. We inspect." Kosarov led the way down the steps and marched toward the rubble pile. "Show me where the attack took place."

Nolikin stopped near the corner of the old pyramid. "About here." He pointed back at the second-story deck at the back of the Two Joes. "Those spotlights lit the area to about here. It was right on the edge of the light."

On the ground, the crushed brick was marked by dozens of footprints. Kosarov knelt and gathered loose brick shards with his hands.

"Krentz was lying here?"

Nolikin nodded.

"And was there blood?"

"On his face and arms. And on his jacket."

Kosarov rose. Wiped his hands on his trousers. "And in what direction did the attacker go?"

Nolikin pointed.

Inspecting the ground again, Kosarov moved slowly off, hunched over. Nolikin followed.

"A blood trail. It would appear you hit actually hit someone. Astounding! From that distance. Have you had weapons training?"

"No, comrade. That is not part of the Language Institute curriculum."

Kosarov froze and wheeled on Nolikin. "You would be wise to watch your sarcasm, comrade. This is serious business."

Nolikin looked away. "My apologies, comrade. All this is outside my experience. It's unnerving. I hope I never have to shoot at anyone again."

"Much less hit your target with a chance shot," Kosarov sneered. "Best you stick to being an interpreter, comrade. Leave the shooting to others."

CHAPTER SIXTY

Staff Changes

August 15, 1945

The interpreters assembled in the Babel Building's largest conference room.

British, French, Americans, and Russians sat as a Russian member of the Control Commission took the podium.

In Russian, he said, "Today, I am announcing one temporary change and one permanent change in the delegation of interpreters assigned to the Allied Control Commission by the Union of Soviet Socialist Republics. Interpreter Evgeny Nolikin is currently on leave in Moscow. His leave has been extended for a month. Until his return, Pyotr Malinofsky will serve as one of the USSR's four interpreters and will occupy Nolikin's apartment. Comrade Malinofsky, please stand. Svetlana Orlova has been promoted to serve as a senior interpreter on the staff of Foreign Minister Vyacheslav Molotov. Her posting takes place immediately and she regrets she will not be able to return to Berlin to thank her colleagues for their help or to say farewell. However, her former fiancé and now husband, Evgeny Nolikin, will be returning to Berlin within a few weeks and will bring you personal notes she has written to each of her interpreter colleagues on the control commission.

"Upon Interpreter Evgeny Nolikin's return, his temporary replacement Pyotr Malinofsky will assume Madame Nolikin's position as a permanent member of the Russian delegation. I'm certain all of you will join me in congratulating the Nolikins on their wedding, wishing them a long life of happiness and many children. That concludes my remarks. Please take this opportunity before you leave this meeting to introduce yourself to Interpreter Malinofsky. Thank you. Meeting adjourned."

CHAPTER SIXTY-ONE

Kubelwagen

August 1945

Captain Jay Handy sat in Krentz's Kubelwagen, a reclaimed German jeep-type vehicle.

"Anything wrong with driving American?" Handy asked.

"I had a chance to grab this for next to nothing and I took it."

"Looks like you've made some improvements."

"I have. Let me show you," Krentz said, and fired up the engine.

"Air-cooled. Does it run as good as it sounds?"

Krentz pushed the stick shift into first and wheeled away from the Babel Building. He drove cautiously along the Marktstrasse, which was, like most Berlin thoroughfares, pock-marked by shell bursts that were rapidly deteriorating into impassable potholes. Priorities had led to the repair of major arteries connecting Berlin to other German cities. Once Krentz arrived on a ramp to the once-vaunted Autobahn, he opened the throttle and the Kubelwagen surged ahead down the wide and newly repaved roadway.

"Jeeeez-us, John. What's under the hood?"

"Under the back seat, actually. It's a modified Volkswagen engine with bigger carburetors and special cams."

"And where in God's name did you find these parts in bombed-out Berlin?"

"I didn't. They were installed in Austria."

Handy shook this head in mock disbelief.

The Kubelwagen sailed along. The speedometer needle topped 125 kilometers per hour.

"You're going to reinjure your ribs if you hit just one bump in the Teutonic tarmac."

"I'm fine. Feeling better every day. Tape's been off for a week."

"Can you stop this rattletrap?"

Krentz obliged, reining in the Kubelwagen to a crisp, smooth, and abrupt halt.

Handy removed his outstretched hands from the windshield. Flexed.

"Point taken," Krentz said.

Krentz ran at a more reasonable pace to the next exit. Pulling off the Autobahn, he rolled to a stop along a deserted rural road.

Handy was first out, walking off his adrenaline-induced stiffness. He circled back to Krentz, who had opened the rear trunk lid and was checking the engine.

"Can we sit and talk at a standstill, John?"

Krentz held out his hand toward the Kubelwagen. "Be my guest."

Handy began. "We don't need to guess whether Malinofsky is NKVD, and if not one of them, installed for the express purpose of keeping an eye on their interpreters and spying on the rest of us."

"You believe everything you heard in today's announcement?"

"Largely, yes. Reports from Moscow confirm that Orlova has been assigned to the Foreign Secretary's staff, and it is in the public record that Evgeny and Svetlana registered to be married at Moscow's City Hall. We don't know if they are on a honeymoon or where. The biggest unknown is why Evgeny is held over for a month. We don't think he has run afoul of the NKVD or has some political difficulty, but it is highly unlikely given he is now Gennedy Orlov's son-in-law."

"You think he'll return to Berlin?"

"Given what we know, I'd bet on it."

"Why the rush to get married? They'd lived together for about two years."

"Actually, twenty-seven months. Sometimes, these things are decided for them. Maybe Orlov decided it was time. His generation of Russians love grandchildren. He has none. It could be that simple."

"Nothing's ever that simple."

"We'll know more as soon as Evgeny returns to Berlin, won't we?"

Krentz shook this head. "I repeat: Nothing's that simple."

"Well, John, you could be right. After all, they are Russians."

CHAPTER SIXTY-TWO

Evgeny's Return

October, 1945

On the first evening of Evgeny's return, the Russian interpreters and a gathering of other Russians celebrated, taking him to dinner in one of the black-market restaurants the authorities encouraged by looking the other way. Then, a dash to the Two Joes where they tried to close the place. That was hard to do, as it was still going strong three hours after their late arrival.

Across the room, Handy watched as Nolikin begged for release and the festivities broke up. Nolikin, gracious as the center of attention, managed to remind the ringleaders that they all had to work the next morning. A few agreed and formed an amoeba-like group that worked its way through the crowd to the front door. But a hard core of celebrants stayed rooted to their drinking spots.

Some Russians can drink themselves blind and still function in the morning, thought a watchful Handy.

Handy noticed with some surprise that Dimitri Kosarov sat among the revelers. The usually scowling Russian was animated and seemed a happy participant, but constantly stared at the American and British officers at the table.

Handy caught the eye of one of the uniformed American officers and summoned him with a wave. The officer rose from the table with a "Save my seat, I'll be right back," and headed for the bathrooms, trailing Handy. After a few minutes, he returned to the table and sat back down next to Kosarov. As he engaged in conversation with the squat Russian captain, several camera flashes went off, and the raucous officers bunched together for a group portrait.

Desperate for excuses for overindulgence, the thirstiest of

the Russians tried again the next evening, but the occasion fizzled out after dinner and a few drinks. Handy watched again, and was glad of the prospect for a good night's sleep.

On the third afternoon, the American interpreters ran into Evgeny by chance as he entered the lobby of the Babel Building, by now, shortened to "the Babel."

With much backslapping and calls of congratulations, and laments for the absence of the blushing bride, they proposed a spontaneous dinner on their floor in the apartment shared by Daves and Edgerton across the hallway from John Krentz.

Welcoming a respite from the exhausting Russian approach to any occasion, Evgeny agreed, and after a brief stop in his third-floor apartment, walked up two flights with a handful of envelopes.

Whether by sleight of hand or dumb luck, Joel Daves had opportunistically secured a case of French wine as a result of inviting the fourth-floor French interpreters to participate. They were required to bring some additional items, particularly French, and produced some cheeses and a baguette. It had taken the French less than a month to find a way to deliver forage to Berlin and to start up a bakery to address their daily obsession for fresh bread. The Gauloises were a given and the smoke lent a Parisian air to the gathering. Daves wondered if they'd ever get the smell out of the draperies.

Truly glad to be back in Berlin, Evgeny made it a point to have a personal conversation with every interpreter present and to hand each a small addressed envelope bearing Svetlana's handwriting. He was nearly overcome when a British interpreter, Raleigh Vanover, called for quiet and presented the group's wedding gift, a silver bowl engraved with each interpreter's signature. Evgeny thanked them profusely, and then found himself holding a single envelope addressed to John Krentz.

He inquired of the assembled, and learned that Krentz was due back late that evening. A few moments later, as if on cue, Krentz poked his head into the apartment, and seeing Evgeny, strode in and gave him a hearty handshake and a slap on the back.

"Congratulations on your marriage," he said solemnly.

One of the Frenchmen proposed they all have a sip out of the silver bowl, and a chorus of disappointment rang out as they discovered the wine had been exhausted.

And presto! A bottle of champagne appeared, the cork was popped off, and the bubbling contents tumbled into the chalice. They passed the bowl around, oohing and aahing until it arrived at Evgeny and John Krentz.

"Finish it off, you two!"

They did.

CHAPTER SIXTY-THREE

A Brief Note

October 20, 1945

Dear John:
I miss seeing all of you and my sadness is erased only by the sheer intensity of the work here at the Foreign Secretariat. Please offer Evgeny your continuing friendship. I am certain our paths will cross again, hopefully in the not-too-distant future.
Yours, Lana

• • •

Handy put down the note Krentz had passed across the table.

"Do you make anything of it? Is there any hidden meaning here? Some message we're missing?"

"Captain, I have to tell you, I'm somewhat weary of scrutinizing and analyzing every scrap of dialogue and writing and facial expressions from Russians, in search of ulterior motives and messages. Svetlana Orlova liked her job here, enjoyed the perks, the status, and exposure to brass and top pols, and I imagine she relished the camaraderie and casual friendships only possible among Westerners."

"Now you're the one overanalyzing."

"Undoubtedly, I am. Anyway, Evgeny's back and looks like a load has been lifted off his shoulders. Besides getting married, his visit must have been a success in Moscow."

"He's now an official member of the Orlov family, and soon to be a father, too."

"What?"

"Our embassy's Russia-watchers in Moscow tell me

Madame Orlova is expecting. That ought to make everyone happy all around. Lana. Her father. Evgeny."

"But why didn't Evgeny tell us tonight?"

"Let's assume his wife and father-in-law will determine when they wish it to be public. I believe it works the same way in our country, John."

A few weeks later, Evgeny announced that Svetlana was pregnant, and endured a Russian celebration that was a repeat performance of those nights heralding his return. He planned to return to Moscow on leave just before the baby was born.

The Americans interpreters all congratulated him individually and wished him the best.

CHAPTER SIXTY-FOUR

Cozy Notes, Continued

Evgeny was the recipient of two more anonymous packages in October, one in November, and two in December. Each contained information the Russians welcomed, each confirming data they'd already acquired from other sources, or opening up an avenue they were anxious to exploit. Each included a demand for payment into the anonymous Swiss account.

Dutifully, Evgeny bore the envelopes to Kosarov, who responded not with thanks, but with withering interrogation of the source, but to no avail. Evgeny never saw who left the unmarked envelopes. Sometimes he found one in the inside pocket of his overcoat. Anyone could have placed it there when it hung on the rack outside a Berlin conference room. Fifty people, maybe more, had attended the conference. One was slipped into a folder he'd left on a table after a conference. He found it when he returned moments later to reclaim the folder.

Kosarov ranted. But Evgeny knew that even with all his sulfurous rage at the unknown source, Kosarov was benefitting from the envelopes.

Evgeny didn't know much about other NKVD agents, but felt Kosarov must be leading the pack in terms of information gleaned from the person or persons unknown who were funneling a regular supply of secrets through him.

The latest letter divulged another Nazi hiding in the Russian zone. Another coup for Kosarov when he'd be captured.

With the next letter, Evgeny didn't even open it. By now, he recognized the shape. Same size, same type envelope. He simply carried it to Kosarov, who made him stand by while it was opened, read, dissected. Then Kosarov would question him yet again. "Where do they come from? Who do you think is sending the letters? Why?"

Evgeny was called to interpret at a conference sixty miles

south of Berlin. When he returned to the car for the ride back, the driver handed him an envelope someone had placed under the windshield wiper blade. This time, there was writing on the envelope: Personal for Interpreter Nolikin. He didn't open it, but ordered the driver directly to Kosarov's office.

Examining the contents, Kosarov whirled on Evgeny. "It has to be another interpreter. That's who was there. Which Americans were interpreting at the conference?"

"None. It was in the French zone. A meeting between Russian and French military staff."

"So, obviously you suspect a Frenchman!"

"I don't suspect anyone. I don't understand why it's me receiving these letters—or who is sending them."

"Listen to me, Comrade...Interpreter...Nolikin. You'd better start understanding. Think! Think! Don't keep whining at me. Use your celebrated skills as an interpreter. Interpret who's doing this. I must know!"

Kosarov was practically frothing at the mouth. Evgeny agreed he would think harder, but couldn't wait to get out of Kosarov's sight.

CHAPTER SIXTY-FIVE

Tea Cozy

January 1946

Dimitri Kosarov left suddenly for Moscow "to attend an important security conference." The morning after his return, he summoned Evgeny Nolikin to his office.

"Sit, Interpreter Nolikin. Would you care for some coffee or tea?"

Expecting the usual tirade, Nolikin was surprised by the softened tone. *Warm, no. But making an effort as best he can to be pleasant. What a change. What's going on?*

"Yes, tea, please."

They sat, sipping.

"Any more packages come your way?"

"No. If they had, I would have delivered them to your office immediately."

"Any of the interpreters away from Berlin while I was? Americans? British?"

"Several. I believe on assignment in their respective zones."

"Lieutenant Krentz?"

"I believe he was in Bavaria for six days."

"The British?"

"Always one in Berlin, but they're all moving around to different conferences." *You must know this from your agents. They watch everyone. What are you waiting to ask me...or tell me?*

"It has been decided that we will, for the time being, reduce our efforts to learn the identity of the ally providing you with regular information. After analysis, it is clear that the information is genuine. No disinformation. We have confirmed it by other sources. It seems you have an admirer who is making substantial gifts of intelligence."

"I'm not in position to judge. I'm an interpreter, not an intelligence analyst."

"True. Nonetheless, it is decided that you must continue to do as you have done before, making no effort to learn the identity of the man delivering the gifts."

"Does that countermand your repeated requests for me to learn who he is?"

"Yes and no, comrade. More tea?" Kosarov poured. "You need not work hard to find out. But should an inkling come to you, of course you will share it with me, yes?"

Ahh, you've been told to lay off by your superiors, but you still hope for glory. Of course, you want it both ways. "But of course, Comrade Kosarov."

"Excellent, Nolikin. Biscuit?"

CHAPTER SIXTY-SIX

1962
Money Talks

October 26, 1962

Kosarov sat in the twilight. He could see for several hundred yards in each direction, observe anyone approaching his park bench. From a bag, he tossed bread crusts to the pigeons who marched on his bounty in droves. Twenty. Thirty. Then forty.

Capitalist pigeons. Greedy bastards.

He dug out some more scraps from the embassy kitchen.

From behind him: "Nice touch, comrade! Good cover."

And there in the gloom stood Comrade Machentirov, shrouded in an overcoat. He stood in the shadow of an elm some ten feet away.

"Don't look my way again. Just report, comrade. Look straight ahead and speak slowly and distinctly as I ask you questions."

Kosarov remembered his past meetings with the ominous KGB general. He waited without speaking.

Machentirov began. "The crisis mounts, Kosarov. It is imperative that you expose your special source. Learn what decisions the American imperialists are ready to make. If they are prepared to strike the Motherland with a pre-emptive nuclear bombing, we must know it. We must."

"Comrade, I have been instructed to refrain from trying to identify Oppor. Directly, by my superiors."

Machentirov spoke clearly but did not raise his voice. Unstartled, the pigeons continued to squabble and peck at the crusts around Kosarov's feet.

"We must have any information he can give us. Every shred. We have no one closer to the levers of power than Oppor. His intelligence has been pure gold for seventeen years! Seventeen! You of all people should know that. You've been harvesting it. And you've been recognized, rewarded, and promoted for your role in securing priceless information."

"But comrade, Oppor delivers precisely because we do not try to unmask him. If we do, the Americans are likely to find out and his usefulness is gone forever. Why would we risk losing him by exposing him?

"The answer is that we must know, Colonel Kosarov—and I call you by that title for it is the one to which you will be promoted the instant we have revealed the American traitor Oppor."

"But how do we…"

"Listen. You must send a signal to Oppor now. A simple one, that you must meet with him right away. And that at that meeting, you will hand him $10,000."

A fortune! We've never paid him that kind of money before. It's preposterous! "I don't have access to that kind of money."

With a thunk, a banded bundle of $100 bills landed among the pigeons at Kosarov's feet. The birds squawked and fluttered away.

"Now you do. So return to the embassy and send Oppor a message. Or do it however you like."

Kosarov bent to retrieve the packet of money. "How will I get in touch with you, comrade, when…"

"I will find you, comrade, as I always have. Act now! For your country. For your service. For your future."

"What if I can't get a response from Oppor? Then what?"

But his queries went unanswered.

Kosarov slowly turned around to confirm what he already knew. The general had gone.

He picked up the $10,000 and put it in his overcoat pocket. He looked left and right along the path. No one.

He tossed the rest of the bread crusts among the returning pigeons, then rose and walked slowly out of the park back toward the embassy. The pigeons barely shied away as he rose, then closed in again on their feast as if he had never been there at all.

CHAPTER SIXTY-SEVEN

Finding the Key

October 27, Washington

On the radio, the music stopped in mid-song, followed by an announcer's voice.

"BREAKING NEWS! TENSIONS REMAIN ON HIGH ALERT IN WASHINGTON AS THE KENNEDY ADMINISTRATION ANNOUNCED TWO SEPARATE INCIDENTS AND THE U.S. CONTINUES TO MONITOR THE GRAVE CRISIS UNFOLDING AROUND THE INSTALLATION OF SOVIET MEDIUM-RANGE BALLISTIC MISSILES IN CUBA. LATE YESTERDAY AFTERNOON OVER THAT QUARANTINED ISLAND NATION, A U.S. RECONNAISSANCE FLIGHT WAS SHOT DOWN BY ANTI-AIRCRAFT BATTERIES ON CUBA'S NORTHERN SHORE, ACCORDING TO UNCONFIRMED REPORTS. THE FATE OF THE PILOT AND CREW ARE UNKNOWN. IN A SEPARATE CONFRONTATION, AIR TRAFFIC CONTROL IN JUNEAU HAS STATED A U-2 WEATHER SERVICE PLANE FLYING OVER THE BERING SEA BETWEEN RUSSIA AND ALASKA WAS INTERCEPTED BY RUSSIAN MIG JETS WITH WARNING SHOTS FIRED. THERE ARE NO FURTHER REPORTS ON THE OUTCOME OF THE ENCOUNTER. THE PENTAGON AND THE WHITE HOUSE HAVE DECLINED FURTHER COMMENT AT THIS TIME. STAY TUNED FOR CIVIL DEFENSE INFORMATION AND UPDATES AS THEY OCCUR."

The music resumed. It was 9:00 p.m., Saturday night. Ben had driven directly to Washington from New Jersey and was holed up in the Forge apartment. No sign of Laura Prentiss.

Around the sofa where he sat were dozens of yellow balls— pages from a legal pad he had written on, scratched out, torn out, and dropped to the floor.

He turned out the lights.

Think! If Krentz is their agent, who is his handler? When did it start? Probably Berlin. Which means it could be Nolikin. Except Krentz couldn't be an agent. Couldn't have climbed so far up the promotion ladder. He's an actor. His teachers said so. No, make that a remarkable actor. Fooling the Army for how long? Not seventeen years, surely. But he flipped out in Germany years ago. Hating Germans with a passion. Such passion coming from a cool character. Was that an act?

What did he send the Russians in the keytainer? Why take the risk? There was no other way. One-way communications. They couldn't reach him, so he had to improvise. They tried, sending an embassy employee to Princeton to make contact. I spotted that, not knowing at the time that they hadn't connected.

That's why! His message had to get through. You'd think with the missile crisis, the Russians would have more important issues than getting a message from Krentz. Unless...

Ben rose from the sofa and paced for a few minutes, drinking a glass of water. Then, back to the sofa, still in the dark.

Root. Did the Russians kill him? Why? What did he know? He only met them once. Kosarov for a minute, and that was just for a moment, before. Kosarov left and went into the park. The park! The park where Root told them Nadine had gone while he was in the embassy. I was going to ask him about it. But the Russians didn't know I was going to see Root. Nobody at the Forge did, except Laura. Jesus! Her panties are still in my jacket pocket!

Ben leaped up, turned on the light, and went to the closet. He pulled the panties from the pocket of his sports jacket, opened the trash bin under the sink, and dropped them in. Laura wouldn't tell anyone, he hoped.

Ben dialed the Forge. Reached the night clerk.

"Hi, Benita. It's Ben Oliver. By any chance is Mr. McIntyre there tonight? Well...I need to reach him. It's important. I see...should he come in or call in, would you ask him to call me right away? Thanks."

The clerk had reported that Hardison McIntyre had been called away and was not expected back until Monday. "Oh, and there was a message, a note left for you from a Mr. Bennett. Laura said she would take it to you at the apartment."

He looked around. Kitchen. Hallway. Living room. Bedrooms. No message left anywhere. Ben lay down, but his mind raced and he remained awake, no sleep, turning, half-dreaming, going over and over the same ground. Near dawn he drifted off, only to wake up to early morning sunlight streaming through the open drapes.

Quickly, he dialed Tom Bennett's home number. Bennett picked up after one ring.

"Tom, what's up?"

"Did you get my message? I left it for you at six. At the Forge."

Benita had just told him Laura had his message from Tom. Where was she? Why hadn't she shown up?

"I didn't get it. Screw-up."

"Well, here it is. You're amazing. Right on the money. It's a straight replay of the first time. We found footage of Root's car—that beat-up Chevy—parked along a street, and sure enough, the Russian dog walker comes along and does exactly the same routine. Crosses the street, passes in front of the car's grille, and retrieves a keytainer."

"How do you know it was a keytainer?"

"Before and after. We blew up the scene of the grille before the dog walker made his move and then took another close look after he'd gone. First the keytainer was there. Then it wasn't."

"Very good. Keep it under your hat until I get back to you."

"As they say in those long commercials, 'wait, there's more.'"

"Come on, Tom. I have to go."

"Listen! I went back over all the footage from his first visit, the day Root went into the embassy. And you'll never guess who turned up on it."

"Who?"

"An old friend of yours."

CHAPTER SIXTY-EIGHT

The Lodge

October 28, 1962, Catoctin Mountains, Maryland

"Heavenly shades of night are falling,
it's twilight time…
deep in the night…"

"**WE INTERRUPT THIS PROGRAM WITH A SPECIAL BULLETIN. RUSSIAN PREMIER NIKITA KHRUSHCHEV HAS JUST ANNOUNCED ON RADIO MOSCOW THAT HE HAS AGREED TO REMOVE MISSILES FROM CUBA. CORRESPONDENTS IN THE SOVIET CAPITAL CONFIRM HEARING THE ADDRESS, BUT HAVE RECEIVED NO FURTHER DETAILS FROM TASS, THE RUSSIAN NEWS AGENCY. REPEAT: RUSSIAN PREMIER NIKITA KHRUSHCHEV HAS JUST ANNOUNCED ON RADIO MOSCOW THAT HE HAS AGREED TO REMOVE MISSILES FROM CUBA. WE'LL BRING YOU FURTHER NOTES AND DETAILS AS THEY UNFOLD.**"

"…with you at twilight time."

Ben left the radio on, but turned the volume down as he sped toward Hardison McIntyre's lodge in the mountains sixty miles northwest of Washington. Ben remembered the turn-off road from a past visit, particularly because it was what he called "a Porsche road"—one in which you could drive all out, diving into the corners at speed, knowing there was almost no chance a car was coming the other way. And it was inviting him to go fast, surfaced in fresh macadam.

Hardy had obviously been able to afford a top-notch paving job, so Ben drove fast, powering through the ever-rising turns, braking hard before the switchbacks, then getting back on the throttle and keeping it down until the next turn, calculating the line he'd take through it to roar out the other side.

It's about seven miles up to Hardy's lodge at the summit. As I remember, about thirty-five turns. At the bottom, just off the highway, a narrow, low-walled bridge over a stream some hundred feet below, then a hard 180 degree uphill left. Remember to take that one slow on the way down.

Running between fifteen in the tightest turns and up to seventy on uphill straightaways, Ben neared the top in under five minutes. Rounding a corner, he caught a glimpse of a vertical plume of smoke, then the chimney it rose from.

The road began to level out, and Ben eased the Speedster around the last corner and rolled to a stop in the flat parking area at the foot of the three-story lodge. A nondescript Buick four-door was parked there at the base of the steps leading up to the main door. No other cars were visible.

Not the kind of car Hardy would drive. If he's here, and I'm betting he is, his car will be parked around the side of the lodge in the basement-level garage.

Up the steps quickly, Ben knocked on the door and waited some thirty seconds before Hardy opened it.

"Ben, come in. What brings you here?"

The living room boasted an extraordinary view; a wall of glass looking off into a seemingly endless view of the Catoctin Mountains.

"Don't mean to intrude, Hardy, but a lot's going on and I wasn't able to raise you."

"What's going on that's so important that you would intrude on me here?"

"For openers, a good chance of World War III. I'm surprised you're not at the Forge, with Washington keyed up and the military at DEFCON Two."

Hardy said nothing.

"Do you have guests, Hardy? Why not bring them out so you can introduce me?"

Hardy gave Ben a long look, then walked to a closed door off the living room, opened it, and spoke quietly. Leaving it open, he returned to the living room, and indicated a sofa.

"Take a load off, Ben. May I offer you a drink?"

"Sure. A Coca Cola and an explanation."

"Well, here it is."

Hardy turned and gestured toward the doorway. Evgeny Nolikin and his daughter Natasha stepped into the room.

"I believe you've met the Nolikins."

Ben rose. "Yes, at the embassy reception. Hello."

Evgeny nodded, but neither he nor his daughter spoke.

Ben turned to Hardy. "So, are you an official greeter for Uncle Sam? Or just offering hospitality to passersby?"

"It's a little more complicated than that, Ben."

"I'd agree. Suppose everyone sits down and I tell you what I think is going on. Save a lot of time."

Sipping his soft drink, Ben began. The room was very quiet.

"I applaud you, Evgeny, for voting with your feet and for doing the right thing for your daughter." He turned to Hardy. "You, I applaud for being a very clever man. While I assume Evgeny doesn't know the whole story, do you have an objection if I spell it out for him? After all, he was present near enough at the beginning."

Evgeny looked up. "The beginning?"

"Yes, Tehran, 1943."

Evgeny looked at Ben, then Hardy, then back to Ben, a puzzled look on his face.

Ben looked at Hardy. "May I?"

Hardy nodded.

"In 1943, Hardy here was a captain in the Army Signals Corps, but used the name Handy for an operation mounted against the Russians."

Hardy remained silent.

"Hardy a.k.a. Handy engineered the three Allies to house their interpreters in a single billet, first at Tehran, then at Yalta. It worked so well, the interpreters performed so well as a group, it was only natural that the Allies would agree to continue the practice with the occupation of Berlin in 1945."

Evgeny looked at Ben, wide-eyed, but said nothing.

"You were not the subject of the operation, but a means to help it succeed. Through you, the GRU and the NKVD received intelligence passed to you from an anonymous source."

"It is true, I passed the information along—first, about a Nazi scientist hiding near Peenemunde. I gave it to the NKVD. If I had not and they found out, they would have killed me."

"I imagine that they asked you constantly to look for informants among the Americans and the British, but I doubt they leaned on you too hard, given the status of your fiancée's—and later, your wife's—family."

Nolikin nodded. "But we were always pressed. Weekly. Sometimes daily. Constant pressure."

"So through you, they had latched on to an anonymous source. But they couldn't find out who it was. Only that the information was correct—and valuable. Because you received and passed on reports on the Stimson-Morgenthau Committee deliberations on German reorganization, they accepted the intelligence and kept you in place as a conduit. All the while trying to find out who was supplying it."

"Yes. As an interpreter and then later, a cultural attaché, it was arranged for me to be assigned to an embassy or Russian facility where the information could be sent to my attention. But they never found out who was sending it."

"But you suspected, didn't you?"

Again, Nolikin was silent.

"The information was so good, the source began dictating where you should be posted to facilitate getting the information to you. As frustrated as they were at their inability to find out who it was, the NKVD agreed. That explains your diplomatic postings, which were always close so the Russians could place you to the source's request. It didn't always work, but most of the time it did. Berlin. Belgium. Moscow. Cairo. Frankfurt. Washington."

Hardy looked at Ben, somewhat shocked. "And how did you learn where Evgeny has been stationed?"

"I'm a reporter, remember? Actually, I didn't even give it a thought until I found out that you knew John Krentz during the war. And once I figured out why you never told me that after I revealed my interest in Krentz, I began to wonder. And dig. That led to you and to everyone around the two of you in 1943, then 1945. And that led to Evgeny and Svetlana and the Berlin compound where they all lived."

"What's Krentz have to do with it?"

"Please, Hardy. John Krentz is your agent, the one you run, the one who has been feeding information to the Russians through Evgeny since 1945."

Hardy sighed, then smiled grimly. "I underestimated you, Ben. You're a pretty good spy for a journalist. You've drawn some pretty wild conclusions and dug up some past connections, but you're way off the mark."

"Spy catcher, actually." Ben turned and spoke to the half-open doorway of a bedroom. "Suppose we invite the man of the hour to join us."

Everyone froze. Then the door was pushed open and Lieutenant Colonel John Krentz stepped into the room.

CHAPTER SIXTY-NINE

Exposition

"Hello, Ben," Krentz said, not smiling.

A nod. "Lieutenant Colonel. Why not take a seat and hear the rest. I'm almost finished."

Krentz sat at the end of the sofa next to the Nolikins. Natasha's gaze switched back and forth between her father, Krentz, and Ben.

"Ben gestured toward Hardy. "Just so you know, I'm not armed and I am assuming that no one here is, either."

The three men nodded.

"So let's not get all excited about this voyage of discovery. I think it has a good chance of having a happy ending—for some."

Hardy threw his hands in the air. "Lose the melodrama. No one needs to shoot anyone here."

"Good. To continue, over the years, off and on since 1945, the lieutenant colonel here steadily rose in the ranks and occasionally made anonymous gifts of intelligence to you, Evgeny, and you dutifully passed them on to the NKVD. And, not incidentally, preserved your special status as one of the few Russians who can travel abroad and have his daughter visit him frequently. Quite unusual in the world of Russian diplomacy. No one held hostage back home."

Natasha looked at her father with a long, serious glance, but registered no shock or any outward emotion.

Ben swung on Hardy. "So here we are, seventeen years after Krentz's first gift of intelligence to the Russians and the world is poised to blow up. And the Russians desperately want to hear from their American source. One of the best they ever had. They need to know what he knows about American intentions. They know his intelligence has increased in value over the years as he's risen to positions of prominence. They suspect, but aren't one hundred percent sure it's Krentz, but hope it is, as he has made it all the way to the door of the National Security Council where life-and-death decisions are made. Only he's somehow in the wrong place at the very time they need him at the NSC. He's at Princeton, getting a master's degree at the Woody. Which explains why the KGB can't use Evgeny to ask him the sixty-four-million-dollar question: Is the US going to blow the Motherland to Kingdom Come?"

Ben looked at Krentz. "Princeton is out of bounds. The Russians can't go there. It's outside the diplomatic travel circles around Washington. The Army freezes you in place. Has you report temporarily to the G-2 at Fort Dix. You can't go to Washington, where I assume there is a dead drop arrangement, a place to collect a list of questions and then leave answers."

Ben looked at Evgeny who said nothing, but looked away from his gaze.

Right on the money!

"The Russians send one of their guys—listed as an embassy driver, but we know better—to Princeton, because Dimitri Kosarov is narrowing down his search for the source and you are now in his sights. The embassy driver stalks you at an event on campus during Yuri Gagarin's visit, but doesn't connect. I happened to be there. I recognized him from my embassy visit. I called the New Jersey State Police and they bagged him on the turnpike. Potential communications line broken. Somehow, you hear Alvin Root joking about selling secrets to the Russians. Maybe you overheard him at the G-2 office at Fort Dix, maybe off the base. You tell Hardy."

Ben pointed at Hardy. "You decide to turn Root's joking into reality. Use him as an unwitting courier. A mystery woman shows up in Trenton, meets Root in a bar, and by the weekend, she's convinced him to steal some code book pages, pretty low-level stuff, get in the car with her, and drive to the Russian embassy in D.C.

"She goes for a walk in the park while Root goes into the embassy and peddles the code book pages. Kosarov, the top spook at the embassy, isn't aware of what's going on until after Root leaves. He goes ballistic when he finds out. Knows the

FBI is surveilling all visitors to the embassy, photographing license plates of cars parked within eight blocks of the building. If they catch Root, they could turn up Krentz, who may be the Russian's source. But they're desperate. The missile crisis is building. They want information from their unimpeachable source, the one that's given them gold for years. Will the U.S. trigger a war? Is there already an American atomic weapon concealed on Russian soil? In Moscow? They are crazed. Send you a message. Use an agreed-upon method to send information to the embassy. The FBI hasn't acted on Root. They must have missed his car. You..." Ben pointed to Krentz. "...attach a message to Root's car without his knowledge—the keytainer—and off he goes to the embassy again, unaware that he's a courier for critical information.

"This time, several things happen. He parks within a block of the embassy. The FBI photographs his license plate. He walks into the embassy with more code book pages, for which he is paid another $75. Amazing! Kosarov sends the dog walker out with the ambassador's Borzoi. I'm on the street with Laura Prentiss from the Forge, headed for the embassy, and we witness the dog walker cross the street, squeeze between parked cars, and grab the keytainer off Root's bumper. I confirm it by looking at the FBI film. The minute I see that, I remember where I saw keytainers recently—on my visit to a Princeton garage to look at John's Porsche. It clicks. Could this be a message from you to the Russians?"

Hardy interrupted. "This is all very fanciful, Ben. I think you are suffering from an overactive imagination."

"The one that suffers is Root. He's arrested by the FBI. They turn him over to the Army, which in this case is my counterintelligence field office. We begin to interrogate him. He eventually confesses. Can't really ID the so-called girlfriend. The Army screws up. Holds him for more than seventy-two hours without charging him. The court-martial is over before it begins. He got $150 from the Russians, a dishonorable discharge, and then he got dead. I was on my way to talk with him when he was dropped forty feet to the concrete floor of a grain silo."

Ben stopped and stared at Hardy. "Do you want to tell the rest? How you set this whole series of events in motion nearly twenty years ago?"

"I'm not inclined to aid and abet your unfounded suppositions."

"Well, suppose this: You put a long-term double-agent operation in play. Knowing the Russians would try to recruit US Army officers in Germany during the Four-Power occupation, you offer them a young lieutenant, one who exudes hatred for the Germans, and through Evgeny offers them information harmful to the defeated Germans. In fact, Krentz first gives up a Nazi scientist, the scourge of Peenemunde, who someone—probably you—had stashed in a farmhouse in the Russian zone while all the other scientists were being smuggled into the American zone."

All eyes in the room were on Ben. No one moved a hair.

"You're on your way. Krentz and Evgeny are allies, work closely together, live in the same building, drink together at an Allied pub. Evgeny rescues Krentz, drunk behind the pub, from an attack by Germans living in the bombed-out rubble. You arrange to get Krentz assigned as an interpreter to the Stimson-Morgenthau Committee, and lo and behold! Evgeny receives a report on its deliberations. The Russians think they have a source worth nurturing, especially as he goes up the promotion ladder."

The front door banged open. Laura Prentiss kicked it shut behind her with her foot; her hands were too busy holding a pistol, which was aimed straight at Ben.

CHAPTER SEVENTY

Intrusion

"Well, well, what have we here? A hotshot soldier and a Washington power player past his prime?" She spoke without turning her gaze or gun from Ben Oliver. "And you, Ben. A very enterprising snoop. Thanks for leading me here." Still holding the gun, she nodded her head toward the Nolikins on the sofa. "Why are they here?"

Hardy responded quickly. "Weekend visitors."

If they keep quiet, maybe she won't make the connection, Ben thought. Turning his back to her, he faced Evgeny and Natasha, putting a finger to his lips. *Silence.*

"Nice move, Ben. Good evening, Cultural Attaché Nolikin. Or should I say Defector Nolikin?" Laura gestured with the pistol barrel. "Sit still. Don't move an inch, and maybe you won't get hurt."

Ben spoke to the room. "Laura is the mystery woman I was talking about. But then again, Hardy, you are to blame."

"What?"

Laura waggled the barrel of the gun. "Please continue with your fairy tale, Ben. I've found the first part most entertaining."

"You don't need a gun, Laura," said Hardy softly.

"Oh, but she does. You see, there's a lot more to Laura than you might see on the surface."

"Why, thank you, Ben."

"Laura's ambitious. A trait that appealed to you. She'd do anything that made her shine in the boss's eyes. Happy to please you, Hardy, so you sent her to Princeton to coax Alvin Root to make a trip to the Russian embassy."

Laura said, "I doubt you can prove a crime, Ben."

"You became a criminal when you did a deal with the Russians. While Root was in the embassy, you met Dimitri Kosarov in the park, agreed to work with them."

"Prove it."

"I don't have to. The FBI has you on film going into the park, Kosarov going into the park ten minutes later. Root was dumb enough to tell him you had brought him from Princeton. He figured out you had more brains than Root had, and went looking for you."

"You're dreaming this up. Coincidence. I went for a walk in the park. That's all."

"And then there's the film of Kosarov coming out of the park with you just forty seconds behind him."

"Fantasy! That doesn't prove anything."

"When I identified the Russian safe house two blocks from the embassy, I sent you to call the FBI. They show up ten minutes later and the Russians had beat it out the back. Only you and I knew about it. You tipped Kosarov."

"Somewhat circumstantial, Ben."

"Then why are you holding a gun?"

"Just want to be sure of the lay of the land. The air is a little thin up here."

"But you're not afraid of heights, Laura."

"Which means?"

"You're the only one I told I was going to New Jersey to interview Alvin Root again. You got there first, climbed the silo ladder, and helped Alvin take a dive. You knew if I talked to him, he would confirm you went into the park. Maybe he even saw you with Kosarov."

"You're dreaming."

"Have you met Colonel Fuentez?"

"No, I haven't."

"You soon will. Homicide detective, New Jersey State Police. He has a partial palm print from the silo—and it isn't Root's."

"This is all conjecture and bull crap."

Ben sat down. Hardy and Krentz remained standing.

"So what now, Laura?"

"I want to hear the end of your story." She looked at Krentz.

"One moment. I need to catch my breath."

"How about I shoot someone? Would that speed things up?"

CHAPTER SEVENTY-ONE

Revelation

Ben stood up and moved toward the glass wall with his back to the room. He looked down and saw that the tires were flat on the Buick. Laura's sedan was parked next to it. And he saw the phone lines to the house were on the ground. He turned back to face the room.

What is she going to do? She has to know she can't kill all five of us. I think she followed me here because she saw me closing in on Krentz. She couldn't know that the Nolikins would be here. She wants to unmask Krentz and prove her worth to Kosarov.

"Okay, I'll wrap it up for you, Laura. Since 1945, John Krentz has been a double agent, offered to the Russians by Hardy, who has been his handler on a long-term intelligence operation culminating in a crisis situation just like the one we've got now. Sometime recently, either John sent them something that scared the living daylights out of them and they're scrambling to back out of the Cuban crisis, or they couldn't find him and they've assumed the worst. Either way, he's queered their plans and they've backed down. They've agreed to pull the missiles out of Cuba."

Laura stared at Krentz, her eyes narrowing.

"So you are 'Oppor,' the agent Kosarov is obsessed with. I can't wait to tell him it's you."

Hardy shook his head. "He's going to have bigger problems than learning about Oppor's identity after the fact."

Ben said, "I suggest you put the gun down and let Hardy work out a deal for you with the FBI."

Her response was to turn toward Krentz and pull the trigger. He went down. On the floor, he grimaced, holding his right thigh.

Everyone in the room was frozen, agape.

"He's not going to die. He's just not going anywhere. And that bullet wound is evidence to the Russians that what I found here and what I tell them is the truth." She moved to the door and pointed the gun at Ben. "Keys to your Porsche. Now!"

Oliver dug them out of his pocket and tossed them to her.

"I appreciate the driving lesson you gave me. It'll be a nice ride." She smiled, but without warmth. "My getaway car."

And she was gone.

From outside they heard two shots. Ben looked out the window. Laura's sedan now had two flat tires. And then he heard the revs as she started the Speedster and came wheeling around the corner, across the parking lot, then plunged into the first downhill corner, disappearing from sight.

CHAPTER SEVENTY-TWO

The Chase

Ben pushed Krentz's Porsche around another downhill turn, tires shrieking, a minute behind Laura. A lifetime.

The moment the door had closed on Laura, everyone except Ben, still at the window, had rushed to aid Krentz.

"I'm all right. Hit a bone in my thigh. Need a tourniquet. Ben, chase her. Catch her in my car. In the garage. Keys are in it."

Hardy opened a drawer and handed Ben a small automatic pistol, then led him to the interior stairs to the garage. "Stop her from getting to the Russians. She'll look for a phone about two miles down the road from the end of my driveway, going west."

Krentz's Porsche was just like Ben's, only more so. Bigger engine, bigger brakes. Faster. But would it be fast enough to overtake Laura and her one-minute head start?

Remember the understeer. If you start to slide in a corner, keep the hammer down. Let off the accelerator and you take weight off the front wheels and spin out. If Laura remembers, I'll never catch her. She had a day to practice it at Lime Rock, but that was largely on the flat. Downhill turns, that's way different. Keep from losing control and you'll catch her. Hard left-hander. Starting to slide. Rear end coming back in. Brake before the corner. Back on the gas. Shift down. Brake. Turn hard. Rear starting to slide out. Back on the gas. Straighten the wheel.

After the first three turns, Ben found a rhythm and gained familiarity with the more powerful Super 90 Porsche. The engine sound was different with four cams instead of two, but the driving principles were the same.

Halfway down the mountain, across a long traverse, Ben glimpsed Laura in his Porsche disappearing into a hairpin some 100 yards below.

I must be three turns behind her. About twenty seconds to make up. If I make up more time, she'll see me, hear me on her tail. Will she speed up?

Another minute elapsed. Three more turns and Ben was entering the hairpin that had swallowed Laura. Then, he accelerated across another traverse, braked, and again turned sharply downhill. Tail out, tail back in. About a mile to the end.

Around the next bend and there she was, 100 yards ahead.

What do I do? Can't drive with one hand, try to shoot out a tire. I would never hit it—or anything. Press her. Get close and when we leave the driveway, run her down on the paved county road. Ram her? Shoot out the tire then? That's the best plan. She'll have had no time to reload. Has three bullets left. I've got six. Good odds.

Glancing back, Laura picked up her speed and slid around another bend. Here the descent was more gradual, the turns easier to negotiate. But even as she increased her speed, Ben narrowed the gap between them, the edge in horsepower to his advantage.

With two turns to go, he had closed to within thirty feet. He caught glimpses of her face—a grimace—in the Speedster's rearview mirror. She dipped into a soft downhill right-hand bend, braking late. Ben closed to within fifteen feet.

Engine roaring, Laura turned left into the sharp downhill turn before the bridge and slid toward the edge of the graveled road. She corrected with a twitch of the wheel. The Porsche came back on line. But she looked up, saw the tight end of the curve coming, and hesitated for a second. Lifted off the gas. As the Speedster began to slide onto the concrete bridge, Ben hit his brakes in the turn, and muscled his fishtailing Porsche, sawing the steering wheel and standing on the brake pedal to cut his speed in half.

The Speedster careened across the concrete bridge surface at a thirty degree angle, and it seemed to Ben's mind that it was moving in slow motion when it hit the low bridge railing hard. The Speedster's momentum caused it to rise and begin to turn over, much as a high jumper turns over to clear the bar. With its entire underside exposed—pan, axle, shocks, wheels—Laura was no longer visible.

She must be looking straight down into the chasm. Jesus!

He braked to a stop at the entrance to the bridge. Ben sat and watched as the Speedster hung on the railing, then disappeared over the side.

Somehow, its engine had stopped. The car made no sound as it fell, but the impact, a hundred feet down, made up for it. Seconds later, what was left of the Speedster exploded.

Laura's words ran through his mind. *Well, well, what have we here? A hotshot soldier and a Washington insider past his prime? Don't turn around yet. I don't want to startle you, but I'm wearing a bathrobe.*

Ben sat for a moment, eyes closed. Then he put the Porsche into first, drove across the bridge, not looking down, to the highway, turned left and found a phone where he called for an ambulance for Krentz. He then turned Krentz's Porsche around and drove slowly back up the hill, again crossing the bridge without looking down.

CHAPTER SEVENTY-THREE

The Tip-off

Back at the lodge, as they waited for the ambulance, Ben told them about Laura and the bridge. He handed the keys back to Krentz, who was lying on the sofa, his pants leg cut away, a tourniquet in place.

Krentz nodded at the improvised bandage. "Courtesy of my old commanding officer."

Nolikin and Natasha had retired to their bedrooms.

"How does the defection go from here?" Ben asked Hardy.

"We'll keep them out of sight for a few days. Originally planned to keep them here, but now that won't work. We'll be hosting the local sheriff's deputies wanting to take statements. So, I plan to drive them out in a few minutes to a new site."

"I have a question. Did you plan the defection to coincide with the crisis?"

"Emphatically no!" Hardy pointed at Krentz. "John has a soft spot when it comes to Evgeny. Old buddies from Berlin. He took it upon himself to tip-off Evgeny that the Russians would figure out the double-agent game as soon as the dust settled on the missile crisis."

"I didn't want Evgeny and Natasha to be blamed for my actions," Krentz said. "Kosarov, in particular, would be looking for a scapegoat. Anybody to take the blame except himself."

Ben said, "And what about Nolikin's wife, Svetlana? Won't they bear down on her?"

Krentz spoke slowly, solemnly. "Not likely. They've been divorced for eleven years."

CHAPTER SEVENTY-FOUR

Zoo Story

Hardy left with the Nolikins. It was agreed that Ben would wait with Krentz for the ambulance. The parting between Krentz and the Nolikins was private. Evgeny had asked for a few minutes alone with Krentz.

While Hardy went to the garage, Ben and Natasha sat outside on the front porch.

"This is all happening pretty fast, Natasha. How are you holding up?"

"I'm am content with the decision my father made."

"Won't you miss your friends, school in Moscow?"

"Not much. My grandfather wants me to be an interpreter, like my father and mother, and I have their talent for languages. But I think here in America, I might like to be something else."

Astonishing how composed she is for a young lady who has just seen someone shot, and has learned that Laura is dead.

"Any ideas?"

"Perhaps a zoologist. I've been to the Washington Zoo four times. My father took me. I looked at the animals and he looked at the trees."

"Which trees?"

"There's a grove of trees—I believe they are conifers—and there's a bench. I would always walk to the grove from the aviary and find him sitting there, reading or just waiting for me."

Dead drop? Documents stuck to the underside of the bench? Eureka! That's how they did it, until Krentz got frozen in place in Princeton and couldn't make regular trips to Washington.

"Do you think your father is happy to be here?"

She was pensive for a moment before responding. "Perhaps. He used to tell me stories about the Americans he'd met in Berlin and New York and Washington. I think he might have acted sooner, but he would never have come without me."

"And your mother?"

"They are divorced. I live with my grandparents in Moscow, and I see my mother when she is in Moscow, several times a year. I will probably fly up to see her soon."

I'm not going to tell Natasha she may not see her mother for a long time—if ever again.

Evgeny came out the front door looking solemn. He put his arm around Natasha, and shook Ben's hand. "I'm not sure any of us thought this was the way things would turn out, but I thank you for your part. I hope that once we are settled, we might see you again."

"All I did was stir things up. I look forward to seeing you both once you are settled."

Hardy had pulled a car around from the garage. Evgeny and Natasha walked down the steps and got in. Hardy leaned out the driver's window.

"Meet me at the Forge on Monday. We have much to discuss."

He wound up the window and drove down the hill at a sedate pace.

CHAPTER SEVENTY-FIVE

Doubled Over

"How much did you give the Russians over the years?"

Ben sat. Krentz lay on the sofa, his bound leg thrust out.

"After Berlin, where I gave up the Peenemunde scientist, and then information from the Stimson Conference? Whatever Hardy gave me to whet the Russians' appetite."

"How did you keep the Russians from blackmailing you to get even more intelligence? They're not exactly subtle."

"In my letters to the KGB, I said if they wanted to threaten me by exposing me, they would be shooting themselves in the foot; that I would select what I gave them and they could take it or leave it. Through Evgeny, Kosarov pursued me to no avail. He suspected me, but up until the end, he still didn't know who I was. When I told him it was my terms or none, he took it out on Nolikin and went away angry, but when he came back, he said we had a deal. As bad a spy as he is, we made him look good."

"Who do you think agreed to the deal?"

"Someone higher up. Theirs is a byzantine world. No straight lines. Some high intelligence apparatchik in the NKVD. Maybe the GRU. Maybe neither."

"How about a Comrade Machentirov? Hero of the Soviet Union."

Krentz moved his leg slightly and winced. "Sorry. Not a name to me."

"But Comrade Machentirov was identified as an officer present at Yalta. Surely, you must have met him."

"Not that I recall."

Ben shook his head from side to side. "Seventeen years is a long time for anyone playing this game."

Krentz nodded. "A lifetime. But what makes you think it's over?"

"They'll focus on the crisis, why it backfired. Look for someone to walk the plank. Kosarov. His superiors. Two defections on top of it all. Heads will roll. They're bound to blame someone. Possibly Evgeny. Imperialist plot, all that. When they put the heat on Kosarov, he'll finger you, whether he's sure or not. Anyone but him." Ben thought for a moment. "What did you give them to defuse the missile crisis?"

Krentz pulled a wry grin. "Hardy told me you'd ask. Telling you the answer is beyond my pay grade. Ask Hardy. He might tell you."

Ben nodded. "So, how do you convince the Russians that you're not a double, that everything that happened these past two weeks wasn't orchestrated by Hardy, that there is no seventeen-year conspiracy?"

"Again, I refer you to Hardy. And again, he might tell you. Or not. But he and I are going to continue…if we possibly can."

Ben looked at Krentz hard. "You actually love this stuff. The deceit. The conspiracy."

"The chess. You found me out. I really do. And I'm one of those rare people who can pull it off. Hardy recognized that in me when I was twenty-two. It was never just the languages. They were a bonus."

"You know, conducting your background investigation required for the NSC appointment, I talked to a lot of people who knew you, even all the way back to Berlin. One guy, even in Tehran in 1943."

"And did any of those interviews give you thoughts about my loyalty?"

"Not exactly. But what I found puzzling was that everyone who knew you in Berlin and after the war religiously teed up your hatred of Germans."

"It wasn't all made up. They gave all of us a lot to dislike. Evgeny organized a trip for interpreters to a concentration camp. That was the most obscene sight I'd ever seen. Nicely organized by the German Nazi leaders; nicely ignored by German civilians. Anyway, Hardy deemed it an important part of the set-up to let the Russians know in case they discovered my identity as a traitor. My blind hatred would give them a reason for my intelligence gifts. Even if they didn't know who was giving them intelligence, they needed to know why he was. So I wrote about the guilty Germans in my notes attached to the envelopes I left for or sent to Evgeny."

Ben paced. "What made me scratch my head about you, dig deeper, was your affection for Porsches. How does a guy who passionately hates the Germans end up driving one of their most iconic symbols?"

"In Berlin, I drove a commandeered Kubelwagen—the German jeep, also designed by Ferdinand Porsche. Abandoned by the Wehrmacht. It was in a garage that the RAF had failed to flatten. The engine was running on only three cylinders. I'd met the British officers charged with restarting the Volkswagen plant. They gave me an engine out of the undamaged inventory. I found out Ferry Porsche was planning to open a factory in Austria in the town of Gmund, just across the German border. His father was interned by the French, Ferry was in Gmund, so I drove down there. Borrowed a small trailer and towed the VW jeep to Gmund. He agreed to install the new engine and mate it to the Kubelwagen gearbox. While I waited, I walked around the property, an abandoned sawmill with large sheds Ferry planned to convert into a production line. I looked into other buildings and found dormitories for former sawmill workers; the place was way back in the woods, close to the source of lumber but a long way from civilization.

"When I returned to Berlin with a new engine in my Kubelwagen, I told Hardy about the sawmill dormitories and he sent me back to Gmund to convince Ferry Porsche to rent the dorms to us. In need of cash, Ferry agreed and Hardy showed up with about sixty Germans—men, women, and children—a few days later and they moved in."

"Who were they?"

"The scientists from Peenemunde and their families, being smuggled out of Germany and on their way to the US and Huntsville, Alabama."

"Hardy organized that?"

"Indeed. *Reapolitik*, I believe it's called. He also used his clout to get the French to release Ferdinand Porsche from internment. Seems that Renault, the French car company, wanted to keep Porsche on ice. Reduce the competition."

"Hardy had enough pull to relax the French grip on Porsche?"

"I don't know what he had on Renault, but once he had a word with his counterpart in French intelligence, it took about a week, and presto! Papa Porsche was reunited with his son in Austria." Krentz continued. "In any case, we kept the German rocket scientists away from the Russians—with the exception of one extremely nasty Nazi whose whereabouts I gave to the Russians. So, we got rid of a very bad guy and the Russians thought I was a gem. And, as we learned from the others, he was a terrible scientist, given a big job because he was a loyal Nazi. According to reports, he screwed up a number of V-2 launches aimed at Britain because he couldn't calculate trajectories. One of them aimed at London landed seventy miles away in an English grain field. So, we started him on a new career, miscalculating ordnance trajectories for the Russians."

"So, your love affair with Porsches began there at Gmund when Ferry fixed your Kubelwagen?"

"Not at first. Ferry remembered that I had gotten my engine from the Brits at the VW plant and asked if I could get him three or four. They were still a year off from assembling cars and were retooling for a bigger engine. I delivered a half dozen, which Porsche used in prototypes. A few years later, in 1948, I happened to be near Gmund and dropped by. Ferry showed me his first production car, and I was hooked. I bought one of the first Porsches from him. He gave me a very good price, said I'd helped him get started. By then, his father had recovered from his internment and rejoined him in the business. I drove that Porsche all over Europe while I was stationed in Germany, and later Belgium and France.

"Last year, I swung through Stuttgart and visited Porsche headquarters. Ferry showed me the modern production line and then the Porsche model I now own, the Super 90 GT. Four cam. You just drove it, so you know how amazing it is."

They both sat for a moment, thinking about the chase and its end result.

"So, I bought one—again Ferry gave me the 'friends of the family' price and here it is in the USA."

"Why weren't the Russians suspicious of an agent who expressed hatred against all things German, who nonetheless drove not one, but several Porsches and who participated in German-American automobile clubs in the US?"

"You'd have to ask them. But I always thought that someone made the decision that what I gave then was too good for them to start questioning my automobile preferences."

"Someone who accepted your rationale for providing intelligence, that you hated Germans, but looked the other way when it came to driving a German car?"

Krentz produced one of his rare smiles. "Ben, you have to remember that the Porsche family wasn't originally from Germany. Ferdinand was born in Czechoslovakia. When Hitler learned that the designer of the Volkswagen was not a German, he had him made a citizen by act of the Reichstag. The silly fucker."

CHAPTER SEVENTY-SIX

Opening the Kimono

Washington, October 30

Hardy, well dressed and ever the trim patrician, welcomed Ben into his office. On the walls were dozens of framed photographs. Hardison McIntyre with JFK. Hardy with George Patton. Hardison McIntyre with two senators. Hardy in the Rose Garden. Hardy receiving an honorary degree from Georgetown.

Hardy indicated at a pair of comfortable chairs around a low coffee table. "As a friend of mine used to say, take a pew. Coffee?" Hardy looked toward a pot and cups on a tray.

"Sugar and cream, please."

Pour. Pass. Sip. Sip.

"So, you went with John to the hospital?"

Now it's John, not Lieutenant Colonel or Krentz. Maybe he is going to tell all. Unlikely. But maybe some.

"I followed the ambulance in his Porsche, which he has been kind enough to let me borrow. Mine is, shall we say, not recoverable."

"And your weekend? How did you spend it without the same level of excitement?"

"Kicking myself for not anticipating that Laura might be following me. She was one of the reasons I came to the lodge— to tell you that she had gone over to the Russians and that she had killed Root to keep him from telling me more. She feared he would tell me about her in the park and that I would put two and two together. Ironically, I didn't. A contact at the FBI saw her on their films in close proximity to Kosarov. So, I eventually found out anyway."

They thought about that for a moment.

Ben sipped. "So, talk to me, Hardy. Or should I address you as Comrade Machentirov? Pretty ballsy to fly so close to the sun, giving yourself a Russian name the mirror image of your own."

"I admit the conceit. A Russian defector who'd been at Yalta was shown photographs of the Soviet delegation. He must have overheard me use the name and identified me. But he didn't make out Krentz in his uniform with the eye patch and the crutches. It was one of our most outrageous successes, listening in on Stalin and his Yalta strategy and relaying it to President Roosevelt."

Hardy pointed to a framed picture taken with Roosevelt with the Livadia Palace in the background.

"I kept hopping, changing identities and uniforms for the duration of the conference. One hour, Handy, then Machentirov, then myself."

They sipped their coffee.

Hardy smiled. "So Ben, some pretty amazing deductions on your part."

"Journalistic training, really."

"Far more counterintelligence work, I would say."

"Hardy, I will tell you this. After conducting the background investigation on Krentz and observing him at the Woody in Princeton, my antenna told me he was a straight shooter, not a spy."

"Flimsy! Without evidence? On your gut? Intelligence work isn't done that way."

"Not often, but sometimes it is. Krentz didn't look like a spy, smell like a spy, even though you might think he acted like one. He did. But for our side. As it turned out, for you."

"Are we fencing?"

"Not at all. It's important to clear the air. So let me try to do that."

Ben sipped, and said nothing for a moment. Hardy spoke.

"When we met for lunch in Chadds Ford a few weeks ago, I was shocked that you knew who John Krentz was, much less that you were working on the background investigation for his clearance into the NSC. The moment you mentioned his name, it sounded a warning bell. I knew there was a chance you might find something that linked him to Root. So, I offered you an office and some support at the Forge so I could keep an eye on your investigation."

"And the Forge? Is this whole place a cover for intelligence operations?"

"Only one. Except for my handling of Oppor—John Krentz—the Foundation does exactly what our charter says: we study government and make recommendations and propose ideas to both the public and private sector."

Ben waved his hand around at Hardy's office, but meaning the entire Foundation. "Where'd the money come from to build the organization?"

Hardy smiled a wolf's smile. "A good chunk of it was provided by my old friend and enemy, Dimitri Kosarov of the KGB. Through Krentz, I offered him intelligence regularly; Germany, 1945 to 1950; Brussels and NATO, 1951; Korea, 1953; Hungarian Uprising, 1956; Suez Crisis, even the U-2 incident in 1959. And then, now. In all, he coughed up over $200,000. That's a lot of rubles, wouldn't you say?"

Astounding! The operation against the Russians was funded by the Russians! Ingenuous!

They sipped coffee and thought about that.

Ben continued his musings. "I imagine some of the Forge recommendations have a lot to do with matters of national security."

"Absolutely. As are recommendations from a half dozen other foundations like ours."

"Having the unique perspective of seeing what you've been up to for seventeen years with Krentz, would it be safe to say you have good connections with various intelligence agencies?"

"It would."

"So, in 1945, after you left the Army and started the Foundation, did you provide any recommendations to Roosevelt or Truman on how to organize a post-war intelligence agency?"

"I did, and let me tell you how. First off, the Krentz operation began in 1943, not 1945, in Tehran with the first gathering of Allied interpreters. So we're coming up on its twentieth anniversary."

"An extraordinary run. I salute you. But I doubt you'll make it to the twentieth. I give the Russians about two weeks, maximum, before they figure it out, if not sooner. If not already."

"I wouldn't be so quick to write an obituary. It may have more time to run."

"How's that possible?"

"Let me come back to that in a minute. Let us go back to the beginning. Tell me how you think this whole thing got underway."

"I assume you found Krentz—in fact, I came across a teacher of Krentz's you interviewed in 1942, while conducting your own background investigation. He remembered you because his name was Landy and you were Handy."

"German teacher, Raritan High School. Krentz was his best student ever."

"That's what he told me, a month ago."

Hardy smiled. "So how do you think I managed to handle the Krentz operation in the middle of World War II?"

"I would assume a senior Army Intelligence officer authorized it and saw to it you got the logistical support you needed. Traveling with the interpreters to Tehran, Yalta, then Berlin."

Hardy reached into a drawer and removed two envelopes. Handed the first one to Ben. "You could say that from the outset, the plan had White House Interest."

The envelope was engraved with the seal of the President of the United States.

"Roosevelt approved it?"

"Loved the idea. Especially after Krentz unearthed some powerful intelligence at Yalta."

"Which was?"

"I'll leave that to him to decide to tell you."

"You won't?"

"Below my pay grade. Read FDR's letter."

CHAPTER SEVENTY-SEVEN

The Offer

At the top of the letter, in his own hand, was written Warm Springs, Georgia, and the date, April 12, 1945. Roosevelt authorized Operation Two-Time, and directed Captain Hardison McIntyre to manage it, providing a budget of $100,000 to be paid to the bank account of Hardy's choice. *Days before Roosevelt's death.* The signature was shaky. At the bottom of the letter was a set of initials and the same date. Ben pointed to it, eyebrow raised.

"Missy LeHand. FDR's secretary. Witness."

Ben handed the letter back to Hardy, and Hardy handed him the second envelope, also with the White House imprimatur. The lead-off: Warm Springs, Georgia, April 12, 1945.

The letter instructed Lieutenant John Krentz to follow any and all directives to provide and divulge classified information to the Russians for the purpose of deception and disinformation. It closed with a single sentence: "I hereby pardon John Krentz from any court-martial conviction under the Uniformed Code of Military Justice, or U.S. civilian court conviction relating to the matter of providing the above information to any Russian officer or official."

Below Roosevelt's signature, in the lower corner, was a different set of initials.

"And this is?"

"Ramon Ayala. FDR's White House valet. Filipino. In Warm Springs with the president."

"So besides you and FDR, the only other two people who knew about the operation were LeHand and Ayala?"

"They didn't. I masked the letter so they couldn't see the contents above FDR's signature, and they simply initialed to confirm they'd seen FDR sign the letters."

"Very neat."

"They've been in my safe for seventeen years. I took them out this morning. You're the only person who has ever seen them other than successive presidents." He gathered them up and put them in an open safe in the corner, closed the door, and twirled the dial to lock it.

"You may need to show them to some people soon, once the Army begins to investigate how Krentz suffered a bullet wound and the FBI digs into Laura's death."

"I'm not concerned about the latter. I sent a team down into the ravine yesterday and they've managed to police the area."

"Is that a euphemism for removing the body?"

"Among other things, yes. Laura was thrown clear of the car before it crashed and burned. By the end of the day, her roommate will report Laura missing. And if you report your car stolen, it's pretty unlikely that it will ever be found."

"I have a distasteful suggestion, Hardy. It would be better for the Russians' piece of mind if her body was found, say, somewhere around Washington. That way, they can't worry that she's in government hands."

"That's already been taken care of."

"That leaves Krentz. Are you going to put him on ice for a while, or maybe the rest of his life? The Russians are known for stalking their traitors and eliminating them, even if it takes years."

"I'm working on squaring him with the KGB. Meanwhile, he's on leave. Out of the hospital. Off for a week's leave. Left this morning."

You're devious, Hardy. I'm beginning to recognize the pattern. Shortening up your sentences. Looking past me, not at me.

"Hopefully at a place where you can protect him?"

"A place he knows well, and one where it's easy to spot any opposition. He'll be okay."

"And you're not going to tell me where I can find him?"

"Let it rest a week. You can sit down with him upon his return."

Not asking, Hardy poured a refill into their cups, signaling he had more to say.

Ben slowly stirred in cream and sugar.

"I want to talk to you about your book project. Given what's happened, it's become problematic."

"You mean unpublishable?"

Hardy nodded slowly. "I have an alternative suggestion. It seems to me that you have an incredible facility for a unique kind of intelligence operation. You're as cool as Krentz and an opportunity has just arisen here that could use your talents."

"I'm a journalist."

"And a natural as a counterintelligence officer."

"You said 'here.' You want me to work for you?"

"On paper, yes. But actually, I would like you to become my eventual replacement."

"Running a foundation? You getting ready to retire?"

"Only from intelligence work. I've been at it since 1926. For you, I have something challenging in mind: running a long-term operation against the Russians."

"Like the Krentz operation?"

"You could say that."

"My guess is that the Krentz operation is about to be over."

"Assume it is not. Do you truly think the Russians would walk away from a source that is poised to sit in on classified briefings at the National Security Council? They are salivating at the prospect. It's obvious that they tried to rein in Kosarov from upsetting the apple cart in his search to identify the source. Or assume I have something else lined up that is comparable. Good for maybe, say, fifteen years."

Ben rose. "Too much input for me to process. And I'm more than a little annoyed. I'd have to think about if I even want to talk with you about it." *Say, in a week, once I've talked with John Krentz.*

"Well, think about it. Ben, ask yourself what you would rather be for the next thirty years."

Ben looked back at Hardy from the doorway.

"A journalist...or a spy?" Hardy finished.

CHAPTER SEVENTY-EIGHT

Up Here

Mont Tremblanc, Quebec, November 12, 1962

Les pompiers were three deep at the bar, still wearing their hardhats and high boots. Evidently, they had been off duty for a while, given their level of consumption and bonhomie. And it seemed every arriving patron at *Bistro Le P'tit Caribou* was being encouraged to stand the Quebecois firefighters for another round.

Dutifully, Ben waded into their midst and placed money on the bar. The *pompiers* cheered, pounding him on the back. *"Vive L'Americain! Vive L'Americain!"*

Extracting himself from the heavy fumes of LaBatts and stepping through a door into the bistro's restaurant, he spotted a pair of crutches leaning against a far wall, and John Krentz's broad back in a ski sweater at the adjacent table.

"Bon jour, John. May I join you?"

"Ben! By all means, pull up a chair. May I introduce an old friend, Simone Orleans?"

"Enchante, Mademoiselle Orleans." Slim, attractive, elegant. Late thirties?

She nodded, a slight smile.

"Small world, meeting here, Ben."

"Not so small. I had a few clues, one from Hardy that he scarcely intended."

"And how is Hardy?"

"Supremely confident about your welfare, given the situation."

Krentz turned to his companion and spoke briefly in French. "He saved my life a few days ago. Quite a hero."

Ben responded immediately, but in English. "John, I understand French. I'm confident Mme. Orleans understands

English. And I am no hero. I stopped an unpleasant situation and someone died."

Mme. Orleans looked at Ben calmly and exhaled cigarette smoke toward the ceiling in a long, thin waft.

"So, you found me here...how, exactly?"

"You may recall that I conducted your recent background investigation. A half-dozen people I interviewed told me how much you like skiing up here in Mont Tremblanc. For a number of years, annually."

Krentz smiled. "It's a favorite haunt."

"But as you are in no condition to ski, I would imagine this visit has a different purpose." He looked directly at Krentz, and then shifted his gaze to the immobile face of his companion.

Krentz looked around. Through the doorway, the *pompiers* were waving and hooting, ready for another round. As no fresh patrons had arrived, they were trying to recapture Ben's attention.

Ben stood. "Let's get out of here. We can talk more quietly in my hotel room, around the corner."

"With Mme. Orleans in attendance?"

"Of course."

Krentz rose, offered a hand to her, and she took it, rising regally.

Ben gathered the crutches and handed them to Krentz.

On their way out, they clomped through the bar to cheers and calls in French. Krentz and the woman continued on, slowed by his use of the crutches.

Futilely, one of the more inebriated patrons waved his arms, seeking Simone's attention.

"Ici, chéri, ici!"

She ignored them all.

Ben stepped to the bar, plunked down more money, and shouted, *"Vive les pompiers!"*

The firemen toasted and cheered him all the way to the exit.

CHAPTER SEVENTY-NINE

The Price of Admission

Simone sat in one chair, Ben in another. John Krentz stretched his leg out on the bed.

Looking at first to Krentz, Ben slowly turned to Simone. "Actually, a young woman also hinted at your location. She said she expected to visit her mother soon *up there.*"

A infinitesimal flinch, then resumed composure. God, she's as cool as Krentz.

"Your daughter is safe, Svetlana, as I'm certain John came here to tell you."

Her first words to Ben were almost inaudible, in English. "Thank you."

"It was not my doing. Evgeny Nolikin seized the moment during a great time of chaos and they jumped. While I do not know their exact location, I'm confident they are very safe."

Again, softly, "Thank you for reassuring me."

Krentz said, "You didn't come all this way to tell us what we already knew."

"No, I did not. I wanted to meet for myself the woman for whom you've taken extraordinary risks for so long. It is a miracle your relationship was not discovered by the Russians or the Americans."

"Hardy said you'd be asking me questions next week. Are these those questions?"

"Perhaps I'll think of others, but I have a few I'd like answers to now. I have no intention of exposing either of you to anyone. Call it my quest for self-enlightenment."

At that, they both smiled softly. Krentz looked at Svetlana.

She nodded.

"Ask away."

"This is as direct as it gets. Does Evgeny know you are Natasha's father?"

On the bed, Krentz lay still. No reaction, no expression.

Svetlana answered slowly. "Perhaps yes, perhaps no, but I don't think so. Or I think he doesn't want to think so. About Natasha, his feelings are complex. He might suspect he is not her father, but she doesn't. And it is obvious he is devoted to her and she to him. For Evgeny, that may be enough. In matters of intimacy, he is asexual. That is why my father chose him as my protector."

"And who concocted the fiancée and marriage scenario?"

"Again, my father. It was his wish for me that I be shielded from the less attractive aspects of the Soviet hierarchy."

"Such as?"

"Marriage to a member of the organyi, the NKVD or the GRU. It was a common practice for the leadership to marry into one of the organyi as a protection against being spied upon. My father saw a way to avoid that with Evgeny."

Ben turned to Krentz. "Were you directed to subvert either Nolikin or Svetlana in Berlin?"

"Never. We simply fell in love."

"And maintained the secret of it for seventeen years?"

She smiled wistfully and took Krentz's hand. "We have."

"Seeing each other how often?"

Svetlana sighed. "Counting now, forty-three times we have been together since I left Berlin in 1945. In Germany. Moscow. Belgium. France. Never in the United States. And mostly here in Canada, where I have served three separate tours as an interpreter in the embassy in Ottawa."

"Have you ever come close to getting caught? By either side?"

A light, short laugh. "Never. For my part, I am somewhat immune."

"How so?"

"My father has risen to a powerful position, since 1948 a member of the *politburo*. Anyone at that level is greatly feared. Russians go out of their way to avoid insulting, embarrassing, or confronting top leaders. It's unhealthy. A legacy instilled in the Russian character by Joseph Stalin."

Krentz chimed in, "Svetlana, and for that matter, Evgeny

and Natasha, enjoy the protection of her father, who is fond of Evgeny and overjoyed with Natasha, his only grandchild. The privileges of the leadership extend to his immediate family, including unescorted travel outside the USSR and the elimination of holding family members at home to ensure a traveler's return."

"So, you are the least Russian of Russians in that regard."

Svetlana bristled. "I am very Russian. I love my country. I'm fortunate enough to belong to a powerful family and enjoy many privileges. But that doesn't mean I have to succumb to its worst habits, including forced marriages, being trained to be the bait in sex-traps, or being passed around for a regiment's pleasure. I hope to live long enough to see Russia become a better country for everyone and not just for those who would like to conquer the world. It would be an extraordinary accomplishment just to conquer ourselves."

"I meant no offense. What I'm wondering is what would happen to you—and to your father and mother—if you were exposed as having a long relationship with an American intelligence officer?"

"I'm way past that concern. I have set a course that requires my dedication. And John is the rock that I cling to." Her eyes flashed.

"You're losing me a bit here." Ben turned to Krentz.

Krentz spoke directly at Ben. "I am Svetlana's agent. She recruited me."

"To do what?"

"Receive intelligence from her and pass it on."

She's providing intel to us? What possible access can she, an interpreter, have of sufficient value to warrant the risk?

"Since when and to whom?"

"Since 1945, and to whom do you think?"

Hardy. Devious, byzantine Hardison McIntyre. "I've been doing this since 1926..."

Ben's mind raced, processing.

"It was his idea to have you meet Svetlana. For us to have this conversation. For you to understand one essential fact."

"Which is?"

"We have to go on. Find a way for me to be considered loyal and valuable to the Russians. To keep the conspiracy going. Or failing that, acting as Svetlana's conduit to Washington."

"But Kosarov knows it's you—or he's come to that conclusion and is determined to prove it. He is dogged in his efforts and means to unmask you."

"I wouldn't worry about that happening."

"Why not? He knows the keytainer came from Princeton. How can he overlook all the signs that point to you?"

"We don't want him to. For Kosarov, we wanted me to be his grail. To create an obsession to find me."

"By *we*, you mean you and Hardy? Encouraging him? That's suicide."

"Unless…"

Wait…think…encourage him in the wrong direction? "Unless you wanted to divert his attention from someone else!"

Krentz inclined his head toward Svetlana.

"We needed to make sure Kosarov never looked in Lana's direction. So, we aimed him at me. Gradually, but surely, toward me."

"But what if he catches you or figures it out?"

"He is close to retirement. That will happen before he gets to me. Then he will be neutralized. Out of the game."

"So then what?"

"Hardy's planning to retire, too."

"After orchestrating this extraordinary conspiracy for nearly two decades?"

"Think of him as being kicked upstairs. To become, let's say, the chairman of the board. No longer running things day to day."

"Then who does?"

"You. As Hardy's replacement."

"He spoke with me in more vague terms about joining the Forge. I told him I'd think about it after I talked with you. But I didn't get the full picture until just now."

"Well?"

"You've just added another layer. So I'm still thinking about it."

"Hardy said you'd need a 'sweetener' to say yes."

Ben looked at Krentz expectantly.

Krentz took a deep breath. "Svetlana's source is her father."

Twenty seconds passed.

Of course! Hardy was posted to Moscow before Berlin. Then to Moscow again. Had Svetlana acted on her own, then "recruited" her father? Had her father dealt with Hardy and recruited her? I don't know Orlov, but I sure as hell know Hardy. At least the part he wants me to know. Christ!

In a flash, the echo of Hardy's voice came back to him from the day they stood on the banks of the Brandywine above Chadds Ford. *"You can never have too much intelligence. And always assume a fourth ford, even when you think there are only three."*

Krentz spoke solemnly. "In 1942, when Russia became America's ally against the Nazis, Gennedy Orlov and Hardy reached an informal agreement. Hardy was a military aide at the embassy in Moscow. Gennedy shared a comment by Stalin that registered with Hardy. Stalin remarked that sometimes the most valuable assets a country had were its interpreters, not as spies but as those responsible for making sure that communications were clear and precise between allies and adversaries.

"Stalin added that he thought the interpreters from countries with opposing languages should, as he put it, 'be as one.' Drink together. Eat together. Live together. Orlov reminded Stalin of his comments in 1943, before the Tehran Conference. Stalin insisted on putting interpreters together and we were housed in the Canadian embassy—Russians, Americans and the British. In 1945 at Yalta, we had Russian, American, and British interpreters housed and fed in one wing of the Livadia Palace. From that precedent came the Babel Building in Berlin where we all lived and worked. And the rest, you now know."

And fell in love! And became the link between Orlov and FDR through Hardy! Hardy, you fox! Did you match-make? Did Orlov? You saw ahead and seized the moment, creating an operation that has endured nearly twenty years and it may not be over yet! But in any case, one I'll never be able to write about.

"So, Ben, are you in or out?

How do you preserve John Krentz's standing with the Russians? Is it even possible? How do you balance that with getting more gold from Orlov?

Hardy's last comment to him came roaring back, as the old warrior knew it would: *"Ask yourself what you want to be for the next thirty years. A journalist...or a spy?"*

Actually, I don't have to ask. I guess down deep I've always known.

Epilogue

Snapshots

Moscow, December 12, 1962

Responding to the summons by his superior officer, Colonel Dimitri Kosarov arrived promptly at headquarters in the Lubyanka. The moment he entered the third-floor office, two KGB men seized him by each arm and he was searched for weapons. They then stood him in front of a bare wooden desk. The door opened behind the desk and a heavy-set man in his seventies, dressed in civilian clothes, walked in, carrying a briefcase. The two guards stiffened to attention. So did Kosarov.

Member of the Praesidium and Minister of Internal Security, Gennedy Orlov, sat down at the desk, placed a thin file on it, opened it, and leafed through it. He looked up. He spoke in a flat, slow cadence, staring at Kosarov.

"You have betrayed the Motherland."

Stunned, Kosarov nonetheless spoke vehemently. "Preposterous! No officer has been more zealous than I have, and you know it, comrade. I have been in the vanguard of the Revolution since 1917!"

"And a traitor since 1945."

Orlov held up a pair of grainy black-and-white photographs. "What I know is that you have been in the pay of the Americans for nearly two decades."

The first picture was taken from a low angle, as if almost under a cloth hanging over the edge of a table in what appeared to be a smoke-filled tavern. Centered in the frame were two thighs, side by side; on the left, a leg swathed in a Russian uniform; on the right, a leg in US Army khaki. On the thigh of the American rested a packet of money wrapped in rubber bands.

The second photo was taken from across the table and

showed Kosarov sitting at a table full of American and Russian soldiers. Next to him sat a young American lieutenant with his arm around Kosarov's shoulders. The table was littered with bottles, glasses, and overflowing ashtrays. On the wall behind his head was a crudely painted sign that read "Two Joes."

Kosarov sneered. "This is disinformation, A deliberate provocation, comrade. Surely you know me better than this."

Orlov held up a sheet of paper and read from it. "Account Number 45-2361, bank account."

"And what of it? It's certainly not mine."

"What I am certain of, Kosarov, is that a search of your apartment produced this same number, written on a scrap of paper pasted to the back of a drawer."

"It must be a plant."

From the file, Orlov read from a second sheet of paper. "Bank of Bern. Account number 45-2361. Initial deposit of $500. American dollars. Signature. Markov. Your cover name in the NKVD for many postings after the Revolution and revived again for operations in Berlin at that time."

"There is an explanation. I was entrusted the money by the organs of state security and sent to Switzerland to open the account in 1945."

"On whose authority?"

"By a General Machentirov of the NKVD. A Hero of the Soviet Union."

"There is no such person in the NKVD, or for that matter, in the whole of the Soviet Union."

"There must be! It was a secret conspiracy."

"And who has access to this account besides you?"

"I don't have access to the account."

"The instructions at the bank are that only you may withdraw funds from this account."

"I have never done so. Proof that this is a conspiracy."

"The records show you withdrew $10,000 in U.S. $100 bills on October 25th."

"No, no! General Machentirov gave me the money. It was for the American spy Oppor. It is a conspiracy against me, I tell you!"

"The NKVD conspiring against one of its own? In any case, you are again a liar."

Another piece of paper, placed on the desk.

"On your instructions over the past seventeen years, you have deposited over $200,000 in this account. The paperwork confirms it. Yet the current balance is under $100. You have stolen $200,000 from the Soviet people. This is your signature, on a final withdrawal receipt for $50,000 dated a month ago?"

"A forgery! I do not have $50,000. I did not withdraw $50,000. The account is not mine."

"Did you not visit Germany a month ago. For a meeting with an agent in Schopfheim? A town three miles from the Swiss border and sixteen miles from Bern?"

Kosarov nodded.

"And did you not then fly to Portugal from Bern for a so-called visit to a potential agent?"

"The agent missed the meeting. He never showed up." Kosarov's spirits sank. "I then received orders to go to Lisbon."

"From whom?"

"Again, Comrade General Machentirov. The same officer who had sent me to open the account in Bern in 1945."

"Seventeen years later and you recognized him? This general is your invention. He does not exist."

"It was the same man. Older, yes. He still wore a Hero of the Soviet Union medal."

"It is you who is decorating. Inventing lies that simply reinforce your guilt as a thief and a spy."

"But I was ordered to Lisbon immediately by General Machentirov."

"For what alleged purpose?"

"To meet a possible recruit."

"I am sure you will tell me he never showed up. How convenient!"

Kosarov was silent.

Another piece of paper hit the desk.

"Lisbon! Where you purchased a decadent villa for $46,000. Your signature is here on the deed."

"I own no Portuguese villa! It is all a conspiracy. It is all a mistake. I am the victim of imperialist spies. A conspiracy."

"The *Rodina* is the victim here. But no more." Orlov closed the file. "Extract a confession from this cretin." He gave a barely perceptible nod to the guard standing to Kosarov's right, who responded by slamming the butt of his machine pistol into Kosarov's stomach. The guards raised the writhing Kosarov from the floor. Before he could regain his senses or speak, they dragged him from the room.

Standing, Gennedy Orlov gathered the papers into the file and restored it to his briefcase. He rose and the remaining aides snapped to rigid attention. Paying them no mind, he left the room, trailing Kosarov writhing in the arms of his two captors.

The trio halted and wrestled Kosarov through a doorway off the hallway. Orlov walked on.

• • •

On the street, a large Zil limousine sighed up to the curb. The passenger inside swung open the rear door. Entering the Zil limousine, Gennedy Orlov sat comfortably in the plush back seat, the glass partition between the two men and the driver closed.

He spoke to his passenger in Russian. "You heard all from behind the door?"

Hardy McIntyre nodded. Orlov had spirited him into the Lubyanka and placed him in the adjacent room, honoring his request to follow the Kosarov proceedings.

"Any questions? Loose ends?"

"None."

"Can I drop you near the embassy?"

"Not too near. On Novinskiy Bulvar. But make it ten blocks away."

"I don't always drink this early in the day, but I think a toast is in order."

Orlov opened a compartment and produced a bottle of vodka and two glasses.

Orlov raised his glass. "To absent friends." He sipped. "In citadels far away. Another. To the maintenance of our agreement."

Hardy matched the toast. "And to its furtherance."

How long ago did we hammer it out and conclude that we must preserve the balance of power between the two warring behemoths? You said you'd bury us. We said you'd crumble from within. We both said mutually assured destruction was the worst scenario, and pledged to do what we could to see neither side ever reached that option. Came close, perhaps. But no Armageddon. Both patriots to different isms. Both pledged to keep our nations from the precipice. We would share what we had to so both could adjust and keep the other from tipping the balance away from the other. A life on the seesaw.

They sat silently for a few more minutes as the Zil made its way through a sunny Moscow morning.

Orlov leaned forward and tapped on the glass partition. The driver looked into the rearview mirror and observed his hand motion to pull to the curb.

His companion, dressed in a shiny, double-breasted suit, the very image of a Russian *apparatchik*, stepped to the curb. With a slight smile, Orlov leaned out the window and spoke as his companion alighted.

"Convey my warmest regards to Oppor."

A nod.

Watching the Zil disappear down the boulevard's center lane for the transports of the privileged class, Hardy turned and strode briskly toward the American embassy.

Full Disclosure

December 14, 1962, Washington, D.C.

A press conference at the Forge Foundation was a rarity, made even more so by the presence at the podium of its chairman and founder, so there was robust attendance by the Washington press corps.

"Let me begin by welcoming you to the Forge Foundation. As we do our work here, we prefer to maintain a level of privacy as our scholars and research fellows draft position papers and documents on issues of national importance. For those members of the press here today, I do not intend to depart from that practice...with one exception. I want to note the appointment of Benjamin Reimer Oliver as Director of Special Projects and Assistant to the Chairman." He paused. "That would be me."

There was light laughter from the assembled staff, less from the journalists.

"Ben impressed us greatly while here this year as a Visiting Fellow. And we felt it important not to let him get away at the end of his fellowship. As you may know, he has a degree in journalism. But you should not assume he will be a source for you to pursue at the Foundation. He has taken a vow of silence in matters related to our projects. We firmly believe it is the province of our customers, be they a government department or in the private sector, to disseminate the content of the work we provide.

"Now, to other news at hand. I am chagrined, embarrassed, resigned, but ultimately proud to describe the circumstances of my obscure receipt of the Congressional Medal of Honor many years ago. In 1918, I was determined to join the Army and fight the enemy. I was also too young. Sixteen. So, I resorted to what many teenagers do—I added a couple of years to my date of birth. The recruiters didn't check, and I was in. My parents were, to say the least, not amused. But, careless of their feelings as I was, I was thrilled to be headed for battle.

"I couldn't wait for the opportunity, but by the time drill sergeants had done their best and I was ready to ship out, the war was over; over before I could engage the enemy. But not quite. Champing at the bit, my infantry unit was in training exercises every day—training! That's how the Army keeps you busy when there's no fighting. I despaired. There I was, stuck in an enlistment for two years and no war in sight. Heaven forfend! Someone actually thirsting for war. That's what immaturity will do for you.

"Salvation for my quest arrived with a call for volunteers to join the British-American Expedition to relieve and rescue White Russians fleeing the wrath of the Revolution. Winston Churchill said that the expedition's true object was '*to strangle the Bolshevik state at birth.*' Well, you all know how that turned out."

More audience laughter.

"Off we went to an unsuspecting hell. In hindsight, the expedition was ill-equipped and ill-prepared for the Russian terrain, the Russian weather, the Russian food, and above all, the fervor and fanaticism of the Russian military reveling in their Revolution. War correspondents old enough to have covered the disaster—and that's what it was—will share with you the horrors and privations of the expedition's failure. Suffice it to say, it was no picnic. Apparently, no one had thought to study outsiders' efforts to wage war on Russian soil during Russian winters. They forgot to ask Napoleon and Hitler.

"The 7th Red Army pursued, pounded, and pulverized us until it became obvious that we faced annihilation unless we could withdraw. Murmansk was our Dunkirk, and by a miracle, one of our few battlefield successes was to commandeer a train. The tracks led north to Murmansk and the sea, ships at the ready to evacuate. We armored the train. Made several sixty-mile runs to the coast. Returned to the town of Bolshie Ozerki. Bolshie was right! The advancing Bolshevik Army would soon surround it.

"As the last run to Murmansk was loaded to overflowing with troops, women, and children fleeing the artillery shelling of the town, a few of us—me included, that young kid who wanted to go to war—were detailed to hold off the advancing Russian assault, and then, as the train pulled out, we would run and jump on the caboose. A classic Hollywood image.

"It didn't happen. We were within moments of, as the Army describes it, a tactical retreat, 'bugging out'—when the Russian infantry stormed into Bolshie Ozerki. Pinned down, no train to catch, we laid down heavy fire to buy the departing train some time, and the next thing we knew, we woke up being pulled from the rubble. The Red Army's artillery had hit the building we were next to with a massive shelling, and we lay unconscious or dead under the bricks.

"The doomed expedition was over. Most in my unit were killed. The Russians saw me for the seventeen-year-old prisoner of war I was. After six months, they sneered and sent me back to America as a puny example of what they'd defeated. I arrived in poor shape, and the Army whisked me to seclusion. I confessed that I had enlisted under a name made up, but much like parts of my own: Jay Handy.

"I was the sole survivor of my platoon that had fought while the train pulled out. Soldiers onboard had witnessed our fusillade against the advancing infantry, and arriving in Murmansk, reported it up the chain of command. On the strength of their eyewitness accounts, the Army had initiated the paperwork for a posthumous awarding of the Congressional Medal of Honor.

"To great embarrassment, I showed up, obviously not posthumous. In the spontaneous decision to hold off the Red infantry and the chaos of retreat, it was unclear who the others with me had been. The Army simply marked my name alone in the medal application.

"While I was being interviewed by the recommendation board, the State Department sent an observer. By that time, the administration had decided that while they would continue to withhold recognition of the Soviet Union, diplomatic steps should be taken to downplay hostilities, as American businesses were trading with the Russians and some were pressing claims to recover assets seized by the Bolsheviks.

"The Army was adamant about the medal application, as

were some Congressmen. The Wilson administration's solution was to award the medal to Jay Handy and then list it as posthumous. That way, no interviews. No adoration. No offending the Russians. They asked me to concur. The government would hold the medal. The fictitious Jay Handy had no living relatives. The press—I apologize to the journalists present for the actions of the Wilson administration and my required silence—would have no one to interview. The medal was presented by a family friend, the Assistant Secretary of the Navy, FDR. He loved secrets and was delighted to keep one more.

"As recent events have punctuated, well covered by journalists in this room, time does not seem to change the ongoing antagonisms among the world's superpowers. President Roosevelt recognized Russia in 1933—they our ally in World War II, our adversary ever since. In foreign affairs and diplomacy, timing is everything. And at this particular moment, Russian-American relations are at such an ebb that the belated revelation of a medal for a soldier in a long-forgotten adjunct to World War I some forty-two years ago hardly makes a ripple in the Russian pond.

"In the meantime, we celebrate over fifteen years of good works here at the Forge Foundation. When I was fortunate enough to be on the receiving end of a modest windfall after the war and thought it would be well spent in developing a foundation to work on national issues, I could not have foreseen how far we've progressed as a result of attracting so many remarkable talents to the enterprise.

"In closing, I thank you for your forbearance. Were the story not leaked about the Medal of Honor, I would have continued to honor the Wilson administration's request for silence until my quietus, which I pray is still in the distant future. At present, I intend to enjoy some time off in the near future, knowing that the Forge Foundation is in capable hands of the next generation of its leadership. Ben Oliver is but one example. Thank you."

Account Closed

In the back of the room, the Foundation's suave Stuart Endicott, watching the audience file out, turned to Walt Storek. "Well, I think that went well."

Storek replied, "A question, Stuart. After as long as I can remember, I hear Hardy is cancelling his annual January trek to Switzerland. He no longer skis? What gives?"

"It was never a ski trip. It was always a private business trip. He told me that a longstanding business commitment was recently concluded."

James Hardison McIntyre remained, greeting all who came to offer their congratulations. He smiled, demurred, politely fended off further questions, and when the last of them had departed, retired to his office and closed the door.

Pouring a short glass to the brim with a bottle of Russian vodka, a gift from a faraway colleague, he toasted a blank wall. "Spy, lie, die." Then in Russian, he softly added *"Do svidaniya."* Goodbye.

And in classic Russian style, he downed the contents in a single swallow.

Author's Note

Momentous events unfolded in the early 1960s when I served for three years in Army Intelligence. At the conclusion of a lengthy training course at Fort Holabird, wedged in the soot-swathed underbelly of Baltimore, we graduates awaited our first assignments in the field.

One classmate, scion of a genteel Tennessee family, called home to announce his posting to Vietnam, where the once-miniscule Military Assistance Group was growing exponentially each month.

His mother gently inquired, "That's nice, dear. Do they have an Episcopal Church there?"

Having listed preferences for posting to various Army commands abroad and in the U.S., my lot was light years less exotic: the Trenton Field Office. No jungle greensward. No Stuttgart or Berlin. Just civilian clothes in urban America.

As news out of Southeast Asia filtered into America's consciousness, I settled into the routine of conducting background investigations on civilians and military personnel who sought to work on classified projects and in sensitive posts. Scientists. Engineers. Academics. Newly minted lieutenants. Grizzled master sergeants. Colonels. And the occasional general officer.

A rare CTI—better known as a Complaint Type Investigation—was assigned to an experienced agent in the field office. That CTI raised the possibility that an Army NCO was passing classified information to the enemy.

All this transpired as the Cuban Missile Crisis boiled over. When the armed forces went to DEFCON three, we agents had our hands full with urgent demands to stand ready to fulfill pre-specified tasks of physical security for sensitive sites in the Garden State should the country go to war.

Background investigations, security clearances, and even CTIs were put on hold for two tense weeks. And when the risk abated, and we again exhaled normally, I had but a few weeks left to work on my only CTI and a couple of other background investigations. And then, completing my last agent report, I took terminal leave before returning to civilian life. Adios to Army acronyms!

In the ensuing half century, I've pondered the convergence of my lone CTI, the investigative routines, and the freezing interruption of it all by a saber-rattling, superpower confrontation. In doing so, I gathered some threads of what I recollect, some others made of imaginary strands, and with keyboard as loom, wove them together into the web you've just read.

I concede there are some skeins of truth in this fable, but emphasize it's about few, if any, real people, with the exception of a couple of world leaders and a handful of others for whom I have conjured up imaginary conversations and actions given the sheen of verisimilitude by occasional insertion of verbatim quotes. Along the way, I shifted a few dates to make it easier to spin my yarn.

Poss Pragoff
March 2016